Mike Gayle

Turning Forty

HODDER

First published in Great Britain in 2013 by Hodder & Stoughton
An Hachette UK company

This paperback edition first published in 2014

1

A CIP catalogue record for this title is available
from the British Library

A Format Paperback ISBN 978 1 444 78749 8
B Format Paperback ISBN 978 0 340 91855 5

Typeset by Hewer Text UK Ltd, Edinburgh

Printed and bound by Clays Ltd, St Ives plc

Hodder & Stoughton policy is to use papers that are natural,
renewable and recyclable products and made from wood grown
in sustainable forests. The logging and manufacturing processes
are expected to conform to the environmental regulations
of the country of origin.

Hodder & Stoughton Ltd
338 Euston Road
London NW1 3BH

www.hodder.co.uk

'I found a really long grey hair and it kind of flipped me out. It's not my first, but it's the fact that it was so long. I was like, "Oh that's been there. How many others are there, and what does that mean?" It actually brought me to tears slightly.'

Jennifer Aniston

'I liked turning forty. Maybe I had a crisis earlier or something. Maybe I had it in my thirties. One thing that sucks though is that your face kind of goes, and your body's not quite working the same. But you've earned it. You've earned that, things falling apart.'

Brad Pitt

Grateful acknowledgement is made for permission to use
extract from the following copyrighted work:

From *The Velveteen Rabbit* by Margery Williams.
First published in Great Britain in 1922. Published by
Egmont UK Ltd London and used with permission.

In the middle of the journey of our life
I found myself in a dark wood,
for the straight way was lost.

Dante

For everyone who's turning forty –
the only way is up.

Acknowledgements

Thanks to Sue Fletcher, Swati Gamble, and all at Hodder; Ariella Feiner, Simon Trewin and all at United Agents; Phil Gayle, the Sunday Night Pub Club, Blake Woodham, The Board, and above all to C, for everything.

Birmingham

1

Wiping my hand against the steamed-up window of the taxi I press my nose against the cold glass to get a better look at the worn but sturdy façade of my destination: 88 Hampton Street, the three-bed Victorian terrace that my parents have called home for over forty years.

It looks exactly the way I left it following my last visit at Easter: same windows, curtains, and front door and even though I haven't lived here in decades, it still feels like coming home.

The cabbie waves the receipt I've requested (more out of habit than a desire to keep my expense records up to date) under my nose and I hand him a twenty-pound note and unload my bags on to the pavement. A smart young couple I don't recognise carefully navigate their neon coloured state-of-the art pram around me and up the path to the house to the left of my parents' that will for ever be known to me as the O'Reillys'. I watch surreptitiously as they open their front door and manoeuvre the pram inside. I feel envious. A happy couple, a young baby, and a family home: all the boxes of adult life ticked off one after the other. Compared to them I'm a walking cautionary tale.

The cabbie is holding out my change. There was a time when I wouldn't have given the handful of shrapnel he was proffering a second glance. Not any more. I have to make every penny count. I scoop up the change and funnel it deep into the pocket of my jeans. As I head up the icy front path I spot my mum's Capodimonte figurines collection on the windowsill. Despite my current gloomy state of mind the tramp on a bench, the cobbler mending a boot and the Edwardian lady posing with an umbrella actually manage to bring a smile to my face. I've lost count of how many times my siblings and I accidentally broke off the odd limb only to have my dad Evo-stick them back together. Ugly and damaged as they are, it's reassuring to see them again. In a city that feels increasingly alien it's an apt reminder that there are still a few things in my home town that thankfully will never change.

I take a deep breath to bolster my spirits as a sharp gust of October wind sends a shudder through me. Everything's going to change once I open this door. Nothing will ever be the same again. Maybe I should've called to let them know I was coming up after all. I tried a couple of times but didn't get much further than staring at their number on the screen of my phone. For a moment I seriously consider running after the taxi and getting him to drop me back at the station but then the front door opens to reveal my dad, disconcertingly dressed in a thick brown cardigan, jeans and market-stall trainers.

'All right, Dad?'

His face lights up. 'Matthew! What are you doing here? I was hoping you were the postman. Your sister ordered me a new pair of slippers off the internet. I could really do with them coming today. You haven't seen him, have you?'

'No, Dad.'

'Ah, well,' he shrugs, 'maybe later. To what do we owe the pleasure?'

'Just passing through, Pop. Thought I'd swing by and say hello.'

Dad makes a great show of leaning to one side to get a better view of my bags. 'For someone who's just swinging by, you've got a heck of a lot of stuff with you.'

'You know me, Pop. I'm like the Boy Scouts. I like to be prepared.'

He looks back up the path. 'Where's Lauren?'

'Back in London.'

'You didn't bring her with you?'

'She had to work.'

Dad looks disappointed. Despite Lauren's innate poshness they really hit it off on our first visit to the UK. It wasn't just that she was easy on the eye (though Dad never could resist a pretty face) it was that she made such an effort to make Dad feel comfortable. He couldn't stand being too formal and the fact that Lauren mucked in getting dinner ready with the rest of the family increased her standing with him more than a million perfectly selected Christmas and birthday gifts could ever have done.

'You should bring her with you next time,' says Dad forlornly. 'Your mother would love to see more of her.'

I hope this might be an end to his questioning but as I open my mouth to suggest that he might actually let his first-born son inside the house rather than interrogating me on the doorstep like a rogue double-glazing salesman, he sparks up with another.

'Where's the motor?'

'It's gone. I gave it up, Dad.' I mentally picture the pristine basalt black Porsche 911 Turbo that was my pride and joy. It almost brings a tear to my eye. 'I came up by train.'

Dad's disappointment once again becomes apparent. 'That's a shame. It was a lovely little number you had there! So what's that company of yours giving you next then? I bet it's a cracker! I can't believe some of the flash cars they've let you have!'

'They gave me an allowance and I topped it up out of my wages. Thought a nice car would compensate for the fact that I'd part-traded my soul. As for the new motor, there won't be one.'

'How come? Won't you need one? I suppose not given how often you're gallivanting around the world these days. You're barely ever in this country.'

'It's a long story, Pop, I'll fill you in another time. Are you going to let me in or do I have to tell Mum you made me stand out here so all the neighbours can see our business?'

'Your mum's not here,' says Dad, putting his huge hand in mine, 'but come in if you must.' We shake hands awkwardly but it doesn't feel like near enough contact. I give him a one-armed hug and he tolerates it with the grace of someone who, while loathing the awkwardness of physical exchanges, has at least learned to appreciate the sentiment behind them.

Dad insists on carrying my bags inside and then ushers me into the kitchen. He runs the tap and fills the kettle.

'Still not much of a tea drinker?' he asks, setting down the kettle on its stand and flicking the switch.

'I have one now and again,' I reply, 'but I'm more of a coffee man these days. Can't make it through the day without at least half a dozen.'

'Don't touch the stuff myself,' says Dad. 'But I'm pretty sure your mother's got some in for guests.' He begins searching in the nearest cupboard, which even I know is where Mum keeps her baking stuff, canned goods and pasta. Mum still clearly does everything domestic.

'Try the next one along,' I suggest.

Dad snorts that he knows his own 'bloody kitchen' better than I ever will. Once it becomes clear that he's looking in the wrong place he simply mutters, 'Well of course I chose the wrong cupboard, you were distracting me!'

'There you go,' he says, setting down a jar on the counter. 'Will that satisfy you and your fancy London ways?'

The sight of the jar of supermarket own-brand instant coffee causes me to reminisce fondly about the seven-hundred-quid titanium silver Gaggia bean-to-cup coffee machine sitting on the granite counter in my kitchen back in London. 'That'll do nicely, Pop.'

I sit down at the kitchen table and flick through a local free newspaper next to the fruit bowl. 'So how have you been, Pop?'

'Oh, you know me,' he says. 'I'm fine in myself.'

I raise a sceptical eyebrow which is about as much as I'll ever raise to my dad. Four years ago Dad had a heart attack. Things had been dodgy for a while and every time my phone rang I was convinced it would be one of my family calling to let me know the worst, but he pulled through in the end. The drugs seemed to sort out the problem for the interim and eventually he was lined up for a bypass operation, which seemed to have done the trick. To look at him now you'd never guess he'd been through all that but to this day I can't take an unexpected late-night call from a member of my family without a split-second replay of that whole nightmare.

'Anyway,' continues Dad, 'it's your mother who's the one to worry about. I'm always telling her to slow down but she won't listen. Now that your sister's moved closer she's always volunteering us for babysitting duties even though it's a good forty minutes in the car.'

My kid sister, Yvonne, and her family moved to Worcester from Plymouth the previous summer for her paediatrician husband Oliver's job. Since then nearly every conversation with Mum begins with an update on how big my newest niece, Evie, is getting and how, despite being only seven months old, Mum's convinced that she'll be walking soon because 'all Beckfords walk before their first birthday', or an update on Evie's brothers, two-year-old Peter and three-and-a half-year-old Jake.

Dad pulls out an envelope of photos from behind the radio on the kitchen counter and gives me a running commentary as he shuffles through them. As befits my father's skills with a digital camera at least half of them appear to have been taken within a split second of each other, with only the slightest variation between them, but there are a few, like the one in my hands of a just-woken-up Evie smiling at Yvonne, which even I can't help getting lost in. In the end Dad and I become so engrossed in the photos that we don't hear Mum's keys in the front door. So when I look up and see her laden down with shopping bags and she says, 'Matthew! What are you doing home?' I'm taken so much by surprise that without getting my brain into gear I say the first words that spring to my lips, which happen to be the unexpurgated truth. 'It's me and Lauren, Mum, we're getting a divorce.'

2

It was a sunny Saturday morning in April when Lauren and I split up.

I'd been watching workmen from Gregson's Shed and Fencing unloading shed panels from the back of their flatbed van and I remember thinking it significant that although I was watching history in the making I was also watching history in the making alone as once again my wife had chosen to make herself absent by going into work. However, not even this could take the shine off my day as I was finally going to get the one thing I had longed for most of my adult life: a garden shed. Not just any garden shed mind you, but an eight-foot by six-foot overlap softwood apex shed with a single door, three windows, a roof topped with premium quality sand roofing felt and planks treated with a red cedar basecoat, just like the one my dad has in the back garden of the house where I grew up.

Some might think that getting your own shed isn't much of an ambition for a man staring down the wrong end of the barrel at his fortieth birthday and maybe they've got a point. It's not like competing in a marathon, trekking around Mongolia, climbing Mount Kilimanjaro or any of the other goals that automatically pop into the heads of thirtysomethings the moment they realise that forty is just around the corner. But when I turned thirty-nine I had no desire to push my body to its limit, watch the sun rise over Haleakala volcano, or even have a go at skydiving. All I wanted was a shed I could call my own.

Of course it wasn't like I needed to be thirty-nine to own a shed. In fact I knew plenty of people of my generation who have had their shed for years. My best mate Gershwin, for instance, got his nine-foot by eight-foot apex in spruce green with double doors when he was thirty-five (but then again at the time he'd been married with kids since his early twenties). But me, I just didn't feel ready for a shed because the ultimate truth of shed-buying is this: a real man only buys a shed when he has to take stock of his life, has surveyed all that he has achieved and is one hundred (not sixty, seventy-five or even ninety-nine point nine) per cent satisfied with the results.

And it was exactly that shed-worthiness survey I'd undertaken some seven days earlier as I sat in the business lounge at Frankfurt airport waiting for a flight back to Heathrow. Over a complimentary gin and tonic I reviewed the last decade of my life, and boy, was I happy with the results! I had a great job as head of development for a financial software company; owned a huge four-bedroom house in Blackheath that cost me a small fortune in mortgage repayments every month; and in Lauren, my wife of six years, I had not only the longest-standing relationship of my adult life but easily the best-looking partner of anyone I knew. Not bad for your average thirty-nine year old and pretty damn amazing for a comprehensive school kid from inner-city Birmingham. Can I have my shed now? I think I bloody well can!

Now, there are some people out there who think that turning forty is no big deal and that the age-related running of marathons, climbing of mountains and buying of sheds is a mug's game. I make no bones about it: these people are idiots. They have to be, because no one but a certifiable idiot would ever spin such hackneyed untruths as: 'Forty is just another birthday' or worse still: 'You're only as young as you feel.' Idiots of the world listen up: forty is the end of the race, the deadline of deadlines and the point at which excuses are no longer permitted.

Because, let's face it, if at twenty you find yourself messing about in dead-end jobs, backpacking around Asia or still trying to find your 'true self', no one is going to bat an eyelid. Even if you do that kind of thing at thirty, the worst you might get would be an 'Each to his own,' and a quick raise of the eyebrow from your nan because there's still a very tangible feeling that there's time to turn the ship round. Cut to a decade later however, and it's a completely different story. If you haven't got your life sorted at forty, no one, not even your own mum, is going to hand you a medal and say well done. Because the universal truth of getting older is obvious: IF YOU ARE A LOSER AT FORTY YOU WILL BE A LOSER FOR LIFE.

That's why turning forty is such an absolute kick in the crotch. It means you finally have to put your house in order, get your act together and pull your finger out from wherever it's been hiding. It's like when you're a kid and you're pulling faces out of the car window and your dad tells you that if the wind changes you'll stick like that. That's what turning forty is: the point at which the wind changes. The point at which you'll be stuck for good with a complete mess of a life if you don't get all your ducks in a row, and preferably have them tucked away in your shed for safe keeping.

The guys from Gregson's worked hard all afternoon and soon a job that would have taken me an eternity was finished and I was asked to give it the once-over.

I hadn't got a clue what I was supposed to be looking for but I couldn't let them know that and so I gave them my best 'bloke face' (showing neither approval or displeasure) and opened doors, checked windows and jumped on the spot in the corners but honestly, all I wanted to do was get myself a chair, put it inside and spend the rest of the day inhaling that great fresh wood smell.

I allowed my bloke face to break into a grin. 'A job well done, guys.'

'It'll need another coat of preservative straight away and regular coating once a year to keep it in top condition,' said the head workman.

'Goes without saying,' I replied.

'And just keep an eye on the roof felt,' he added. 'It's guaranteed for ten years so if you do have any problems call us and we'll get it sorted.'

As the workmen collected their tools and saw themselves off the premises I remained at the top of the garden drooling over my shed. Now I'd got it I couldn't wait to fill it up with the kind of useless ephemera that used to occupy my dad's: rusting push lawn mowers, pristine Flymos, Black and Decker workmates, the constituent parts of dilapidated rabbit hutches, plastic ice-cream tubs overflowing with screws, nuts and bolts, open jars half filled with turpentine and paintbrushes and, of course, the icing on the cake, multiple kids' bikes all with flat tyres.

A noise from behind me alerted me to the fact that I was no longer alone. I turned to see that Lauren had joined me. As befitting the weather she was dressed in a lightweight jacket and jeans. She looked beautiful and I wanted her to want to come closer and kiss me but she didn't move.

'So is this it?'

I nodded. 'What do you think?'

'It looks nice,' she said unconvincingly (I was well aware of Lauren's true feelings about my shed but at this point it was all water off a duck's back). She drew a deep breath and added quickly, 'Can you spare a minute? I just need a word with you about something.'

'Can it wait?' I kept my eyes firmly on the shed, 'I really want to get the shed organised.'

'Oh, come on Matt, it's just a shed.'

'Not to me, OK?'

She put a hand on my arm.

'But I really need to talk to you.'

'And like I said, now is not a good time.'

'Just a few moments.'

'I'm busy.'

'Matt!'

She was crying now but I still didn't turn round.

'We need to talk, Matt, we need to talk right now! Can't you see it? Can't you see that I don't love you any more?'

I finally allowed my gaze to shift to her tear-streaked face.

'Of course I can. What do you think I am, blind?'

'Then why didn't you say something?'

I looked at my shed, and then back at Lauren and without another word I headed back indoors.

3

Lauren and I met in Australia eight years ago. Our meeting
had followed on from what I can only describe as a period
of extreme transition which had begun when I'd split up
with my live-in girlfriend, Elaine, while living in New York.
Thousands of miles from home, with a thirtieth birthday
looming, I'd packed my bags and bought a one-way ticket
back to the UK.

Safe in the arms of friends and family in Birmingham
I set about trying to turn thirty without losing the plot.
And it worked, up to a point. Although there was a major
complication where I briefly mistook the hazy warmth of
nostalgia for something more, thankfully everything came
good in the end. Fresh to thirtydom, I embarked on a new
chapter of both my professional and personal life in Oz;
and as most of my contemporaries were settling down and
starting families I opted instead to get to the top of my game.
I'd always worked hard but suddenly I upped a gear, always
the first to arrive in the mornings and regularly working late
in the evenings. When it came to weekends I spent more
time in the office than anywhere else. In short I became a

workaholic but as it was the only thing that seemed to give my life meaning I decided that the best thing I could do was just go with it. My increased work ethic did not go unnoticed and not only did I get paid very well, but I also climbed up the career ladder very quickly indeed.

One night a group of colleagues and the strategic business consultants with whom we'd been locked in a conference room for the best part of the day suggested that we all go for a wind-down at a bar near our office. Tempted as I was to say, 'Actually, I think I might stay here and go through these development reports,' I found myself saying, 'Yeah, fine. I could do with a break.' It's a good job I did, because that was the night I met Lauren.

'Rumour has it you're the hardest-working employee at the company,' she said, taking a seat next to mine. Her accent was English, Home Counties to be exact, which wasn't that much of a surprise given the international make-up of companies like Benson-Lawless.

'And you are?' I hadn't meant to sound abrupt. I was genuinely interested. The Benson-Lawless people had been coming into our offices for months for various meetings and consultations and I'd never had a conversation with one of them that wasn't work-related.

'Lauren Murray, strategic analyst for Benson-Lawless.' We shook hands and although her grip was firm her hands were soft. For some reason this took me by surprise.

'Nice to meet you Lauren,' I replied, 'and yes, I can confirm that rumour.' 'You don't think much of us do you?' she asked, scrutinising my face. 'You think consultants are a waste of time.'

'Glorified accountants billing us at a thousand dollars an hour to tell us what we already know in a way that we can't understand? I don't think you're a waste of time, I think you're geniuses. I just wish I could get paid as much for doing so little.'

It was a bit of a gamble, insulting her like that, but whether it was the beer, or the tiredness, throwing caution to the wind seemed to be the order of the day.

'Do you smoke?' she asked, reaching into her bag.

'No, but I'm told I'm good company by those who do.'

Lauren arched her left eyebrow coolly. 'Is that so, Mr Beckford? Well, I think I'll be the judge of that.'

We made our way to the outside terrace where half a dozen other smokers were huddled under a canvas canopy.

'So what brought you to Oz?' she asked, grinning, as she drew deeply on her cigarette, sending a plume of bluish smoke into the air.

'Take a guess.'

'A girl,' she replied. 'You look like the kind of guy that would move continents to woo a lady.'

'Wrong,' I replied. 'It was work, although to be fair a girl was sort of in the mix too but not in the way you're thinking.'

'Was she nice?'

'She was the best.'

'Do you always speak so highly of your exes?'

'Only the good ones.'

'Well, that would rule me out,' she said playfully. 'No ex of mine has ever had a good word to say about me.'

'Maybe you've been going out with the wrong guys. If you'd dated me and we'd split up I'm pretty sure I'd find something good to say. I mean, don't get me wrong, I'd be devastated that it was over, and I'd do everything I could to get you back but I don't see why I wouldn't be able to sing your praises to some pretty girl outside a bar one day.'

'What exactly would you say to this,' she paused and raised that eyebrow again, '*pretty girl* outside a bar?'

'Well, Lauren,' I replied, 'I'd say how you were always great fun to be around and to illustrate the point I'd tell her about that great weekend we had when I took you scuba-diving on the Great Barrier Reef.'

Lauren laughed. 'I was great, wasn't I? None of your friends' girlfriends were interested in diving but I had a go even though it wasn't my usual thing.'

'That's right,' I replied, 'I was so proud of you and all my mates were really impressed.'

'And how about that night we both got crazy drunk and ended up gate-crashing a karaoke party in that Cantonese restaurant? I couldn't get the microphone out of your grip! It was like power ballad after power ballad, all the greats: Benatar, Turner, Tyler! You slayed them all!'

'I was on form that night,' I said as Lauren beamed a killer smile in my direction. Wide, mischievous and steeped in suggestion, it confirmed that a connection had been made.

Cigarette over, we returned inside and I offered to get her another drink but at the bar I got sucked into a conversation with my boss that proved impossible to escape until he'd finished. By the time I managed to break away and get served at the bar Lauren had inevitably been sucked into a conversation of equally epic proportions with her own boss and with two drinks in my hand and an ache in my heart it felt like our moment was over. However at the end of the night as colleagues were finishing off drinks and calling cabs, she came over and said: 'For what it's worth, it was fun being your ex. I hope you'll always speak fondly of me.'

'It's a promise,' I said, 'but how will you speak of me?'

She pulled a goofy face, screwing up her eyes and flaring her nostrils, but she still looked good enough to eat. 'It goes without saying that I'll trash you like all the rest of my no-good exes. If you really were that good, then why did it all come to an end? I guarantee you were to blame.'

'Of course it was my fault,' I replied, 'the ends of relationships are always my fault even when they aren't. But if I'm going to get trashed for being a rubbish boyfriend in the end I think you should give me a shot at a decent beginning. I don't know whether you remember the early days of me and you but they were pretty legendary.'

'You're right,' she said, 'your beginnings were pretty legendary. How could I say no?'

That weekend I took her to a new sushi bar in Kings Cross and twelve hours later, as I watched her leave my quayside apartment building, I knew that I'd finally found someone

I'd love more than work. I proposed to her on our sixth date, she said yes on our seventh, and by our eighth we were making plans for me to sell my apartment, return to the UK, buy a place in London and get married. Our future shone before us like a beacon in the night sky. Everything was going to be OK.

4

Although in the end it took us three years to leave Australia it didn't take too long at all for me to find a new job once we were in the UK. Lauren was ridiculously proud of me when after only a few weeks I landed a contracting position in Milton Keynes, which paid well but bored me senseless. But when a year later I was headhunted by a big-name recruitment firm for a great job that paid crazy money she was absolutely ecstatic. Suddenly we could afford to buy a house instead of rent, and all the dreams that we had back in Oz looked like they were about to come true.

The position they wanted me to fill was similar to the one I had had in Sydney but on an international basis, so instead of spending Monday to Friday overseeing teams across a single country, I would be visiting offices across Europe and Asia. I'd also be working with the sales director to bring in new business from around the globe. As far as my career went it was a very big deal indeed and seemed to be the ultimate pay-off for all the personal sacrifices I'd made over the years. The package they were offering was bigger and better than anything I had ever enjoyed; the perks were lavish; and the

the future prospects ('we'd be looking to make you a director within five years') were everything I'd ever wanted.

From the business-class flights through to the car allowance that I splurged on the first of the two Porsches I ended up leasing, it was obvious to everyone in the industry that I had moved up a level and now that I was finally on my way to a directorship I drove myself harder than ever. Being away from home on weekdays was tough, but Lauren seemed to understand and when we were together we more than made up for it by treating ourselves to the best of everything, from Michelin-starred restaurants to extravagant luxury holidays that made friends green with envy. We were living the high life, or so it seemed, and I was convinced that the days of plenty would never cease.

The first sign that everything was not as it should be came two years into the job when I started getting chronic stomach pains. At first I ignored them, putting it down to indigestion, until one night while away on a four-day trip to Hong Kong I woke up in such agony that I had to ring down to reception and get them to call an ambulance.

Of course the job came with great health insurance and the hospital kept me in overnight but as I was due home the next day they simply made sure I was fit enough to fly home and advised me to see my own GP.

My GP referred me to a specialist who ordered a gastro-intestinal endoscopy, which revealed that I had a peptic ulcer. The consultant asked me lots of questions about diet, work and exercise and concluded that while work stress had not necessarily caused the problem, she didn't doubt that it had been 'a significant factor' in aggravating the situation and suggested that I take a long holiday and perhaps consider a different career path.

In an attempt to show willing I compromised by finishing the course of medication she prescribed and booking a two-week five-star holiday to Antigua with Lauren. However once we got back to the UK it was business as usual.

A year on I was sitting in a sales meeting in Stockholm when I felt a blinding pain behind my left eye of such intensity that I had to leave the room. Twenty minutes and some strong painkillers later it was gone, so once again I dismissed it as 'one of those things', and carried on with my day. When it happened again though, a week later while I was in Oslo on business, and the week after that during a flight to Rome, and then two days later while Lauren and I were out for dinner with friends, Lauren insisted that I get it checked out.

'I'll make an appointment first thing Monday,' I promised, then promptly forgot about it until a few months later in a meeting in Tokyo when a pain so debilitating shot through my head that the airport doctor forbade me from flying and sent me for an emergency CAT scan at a local hospital. Although the scan revealed nothing physically wrong the consultant commented that he had seen similar sets of symptoms many times before in what he called 'chronic workaholics' and attempted to sign me off work for three months.

Fearful that these illnesses meant that perhaps I wasn't

up to the job, after I returned from a long break in the Maldives I casually brought up the subject of health with a few colleagues over drinks in a hotel bar in Beijing where we were pitching for a new maintenance contract with one of the largest banks in southern China. Every single member of the team around the table had a stress-related story of their own, many of which made mine pale into insignificance. For every chronic stomach pain there was someone urinating blood, and for every tale of blinding headaches there was someone who had actually temporarily lost their sight and the ability to feel their legs. It would have been funny, like a twisted version of Monty Python's two Yorkshiremen sketch, had they not been so deadly serious about it. 'Bodies get stressed,' explained my boss a few days later as we sat together in the executive lounge at Beijing airport waiting for the flight back to London, 'but if you want to make the kind of money we do you just grit your teeth and get on with it.'

And so that's exactly what I did: I got on with it, and for a long while I thought it actually worked, but then Lauren told me that she didn't love me any more, and that was pretty much the beginning of the end.

On the Monday after she officially ended our marriage I was up and out of the house for five in the morning to drive to Heathrow to catch the nine fifteen a.m. Qantas flight to Singapore. On my way I thought about the day ahead. I was heading out to pitch to a group of regional banks looking to upgrade their system software across all 158 of their branches. It would be a long, tedious day that would involve us talking shop for the entire flight, arriving late at night jet-lagged, grabbing a couple of hours' sleep if we were lucky before spending the next day taking the company walkabout, sitting in on divisional meetings and eating more meals than our stomachs could bear before reaching the point of our visit: the sales pitch in which I would try and sell them three products that wouldn't do the job in order to talk them into taking the one product that would but cost three times the amount they had budgeted.

Just thinking about this made me feel nauseous though I tried to take comfort in its predictability. But as I pulled up in the long-stay car park at Terminal Three, something weird happened. Out of nowhere my heart began pounding furiously, sweat started pouring off me and I could barely catch a breath. Convinced that I was having a heart attack all I could think was how much I didn't want to die. I was too young. There was too much I hadn't done. It wasn't fair. This couldn't be the way it was all going to end. Fumbling for my phone as I felt my chest getting tighter I frantically dialled Lauren's number.

'You need to come quick,' I said between stifled breaths. 'I don't want to die alone in an airport car park.'

An ambulance arrived in a matter of minutes and before I really knew what was happening I was on my way to Hillingdon Hospital where I was scanned and checked by a number of doctors and nurses before being informed that although there was nothing physically wrong with me there was no doubt that what I had suffered was a somewhat extreme panic attack brought about by work-related stress.

It was a relief, I suppose, to be handed back my life like that. I wasn't dying; I was just overworked and splitting up with Lauren had tipped me over the edge. But even on the way home as she attempted to override the awkwardness between us with talk of holidays that I should take and yoga retreats that I should visit I knew that nothing could ever make me go back to that job. For a few moments back in that car park at Heathrow I'd been convinced I was going die and now that I wasn't there was no way I was ever going to put myself in that situation again. I was done with the life that I had made for myself, or to be more accurate it had made it clear that it was done with me. Either way, the experience was all I needed to prompt me to hand in my notice the following morning and resolve to do absolutely nothing for the best part of half a year.

5

It was Lauren who brought up the small problem of us still living together six months after we'd supposedly separated. I was sitting in front of the TV tucking into a bowl of pasta. She sat down opposite me and almost as if she was in the middle of a conversation with herself said: 'I can't believe how much you don't want to talk about this! Surely you don't want to drag things out any longer?'

If I'd been in the mood for an argument this probably would have been the spark that took hold of the kindling that finally burned the whole house down, but the time for backbiting had long since passed and anyway, she was right. The situation in which I found myself was no good for me, yet I clung to it.

How had six months passed by without one of us moving out? In the end I think it all came down to logistics. Having bought at the top of a bullish market the house had cost a small fortune, the renovations we'd undertaken even more, and while we fully expected to realise a profit at some point in the future I think that we both knew that it wouldn't be soon. Then of course there was the fact that I'd quite clearly been ill. Initially spending day after day in bed after my episode, it had been weeks before I'd even ventured outside, and as hard-hearted as I think Lauren wanted to be not even she could kick a man who was so obviously down. And so she'd waited, and knowing what she was up to I'd waited too: real life would come round all too soon. It didn't need my help.

'You know we need to talk about this, and I don't understand why, every time I bring it up, you run a million miles. We're supposed to be separated, Matt, we both agreed that it's over. And yes it's sad, and heartbreaking, but we've cried our tears and now we need to move on.' Raw emotion worked its way into her voice. 'Just give me one good reason why tonight shouldn't be the night that we finally cut the cord.'

'One reason?' Lauren glared at me, daring me to start off all the turning-forty stuff again. But that was the real reason I was hanging on. If I could just get past my birthday on 31 March, then I was sure I'd be OK.

'I mean a proper grown-up reason, not a made-up half-reason that you've conjured up for the sole purpose of dragging this situation out even longer.'

'Well in that case I haven't got one.' I picked up my plate and took it to the kitchen table in the hope that I had bought myself some extra time. Less than a minute later she was standing in the doorway.

'Is it that you want me to be the one to go?' she asked.

My food was suddenly as unappealing as it was cold. I'd overcooked it a bit and the pasta had gone all rubbery.

Lauren sat down opposite me and looked around our kitchen-diner as though seeing it for the first time. 'Do you remember when we first viewed this place?'

Even though she was simply trying to lull me into a false sense of security I decided to play along. 'How could I forget? You got me here under false pretences!'

Lauren smiled and I half expected her to go all soft focus like they do on TV just before a cheesy flashback. 'It was awful of me to swap the house details round like that! You walked in expecting to see a hallway out of *Elle Decoration* and got something more akin to a junk shop. The expression on your face was priceless!'

'Still,' I replied, 'if you hadn't done then we wouldn't be here would we?' The irony was unintentional but now it was out there it was impossible to escape. 'I mean that in a nice way,' I said, backtracking.

'But it's true whichever way you look at it, isn't it?' she said, lifting her gaze to meet mine. 'We're in a mess and we don't seem to be able to find our way out . . .' Her voice trailed off. 'You must know we can't go on like this.'

'Now's not a good time for me.'

'Is there ever a good time to end a marriage? Don't you get it, Matt? We've done the hard bit already, all we need to do now is push on through.' Lauren's use of business-speak cliché didn't go unnoticed by either of us.

She apologised straight away. 'I forgot where I was for a moment.'

'Really, it's fine. I get it and to be fair you're not wrong. We've been treading water for too long.'

'We've been fighting just to stand still.'

'So what do we do?'

'For better or worse we make a change. I've been offered first refusal on a work colleague's flat and I'm going to take it.'

I couldn't believe this was happening. She'd sorted something out knowing full well that I was broke. My entire life savings, the money I made from the sale of my apartment in Oz, the cash from all the stocks and shares I'd owned and every last penny I had saved was tied up in the house. And what little I had in the bank had been eaten up by my share of the mortgage and paying off the huge loan we'd taken out to do up the house. Right now I couldn't have been any less liquid if I had been carved out of solid granite.

'But you know I can't afford to keep this place on by myself!'

'Which is why I told you not to quit your job. The doctor said he'd sign you off sick for three months. But no, you've got to be a drama queen and quit! If you'd hung on a bit longer you would have had more options.'

'You know I hung on for as long as I could!'

'All I know is that everything's been on my shoulders for over six months. Well, it stops now. One way or another, Matt, one of us is leaving next week.'

*   *   *

For the next few days I walked around in a total daze. I couldn't believe how unlucky I'd been. Just over five months left before I turned forty, Lauren had made a terrible situation even worse. From the day she told me she no longer loved me I'd been resigned to turning forty without a wife, but now thanks to her I was facing the prospect of waking up on the big day without a roof over my head. I'd be screwed for life! The next stop would be a park bench with a can of Special Brew and me yelling obscenities at passing strangers.

After spending what remained of the week with my head in the sand on the day of Lauren's deadline I went for a run to try and clear my thoughts. I must have overdone it a bit because when I came to a halt my chest tightened and my head began to spin. Fearing I was about to have another panic attack I pulled out my earphones and sat down on the wall outside the house to get my breath as one of Bryan Adams' greatest hits spilled into the world.

Inside the house I called out Lauren's name even though I was pretty sure she wouldn't be back from work yet. Upstairs, I shed my running gear on the floor of the bathroom ready to shower. Passing by the mirrored wall cabinet above the sink I caught a glimpse of myself and stopped. Did I look like a man in his late thirties? The flecks of grey in my stubble and by my temples seemed to answer that question, but I ran once or twice a week and although I'd had to let my gym membership slide since I gave up work I still felt pretty fit.

But did I look like I was about to turn forty, like a man who was statistically over halfway through the only life he was ever going to live? I shuddered at the thought and from that point on did my best to stop thinking.

After I showered I made myself a cheese and ham sandwich and plonked myself in front of the TV where I remained until I heard Lauren's key in the front door.

'Are you hungry?' I called. She was still wearing her black winter overcoat and boots. Her hair was tied away from her face, and with her tightly pursed lips she looked every inch the business professional.

'I ate earlier but thanks anyway.'

'How about a drink? I bought a bottle of that Shiraz you like. You know the one—'

'Have you thought any more about what we spoke about?' she said, talking over me.

I set down my sandwich.

'You're right,' I said, 'one of us should move out and I think it should be me.'

She looked relieved. I don't think she'd ever dared imagine that getting me to move out would be this easy after all this time.

'That's really good of you.'

'It's not like I have much choice.'

'Well no . . . but even so . . . it's appreciated.' She looked down guiltily. 'Have you any idea where you're going to go?'

'To Birmingham.'

Lauren looked horrified, probably because I'd always insisted that past the age of twenty-one moving back in with your parents is a guaranteed route to insanity.

'Are you sure that's the right thing to do? Couldn't you just find a place here in London for a while and then start putting your CV out there? You'd walk into a job in no time and when the house sells you could move on.'

I'd done my thinking and I wasn't about to be swayed by anyone. 'I've told you a million times, Lauren, I'm never going back to that kind of work. It nearly broke me. I can't do it again even if it will save me from having to spend the last days of my thirties living with my parents. I want my next job to be different. Something fulfilling. Something that doesn't deaden my soul. So while I work out exactly what that might be I'm going to go home, see my folks, catch up with some old mates and . . . turn forty with as much dignity as I can muster. And maybe, by the time I've dealt with the big four-oh, the house will be sold, and you and I can finally . . . well, it's like you said, isn't? We've done the hard bit, we just need to push on through.'

She seemed to accept my speech at face value, which was a relief, because had I told her my real reason for going home she'd think that I was completely insane. In truth I was heading back to my home town because I was pinning all hopes for a brighter future on an old on/off girlfriend who I first kissed at a school disco when I was seventeen.

6

I would never have spoken to Ginny Pascoe if it hadn't been for fellow student and lanky half-brained narcissist Dave Harriett pushing his tongue down the throat of Amanda Dixon (dressed that night in the garb of the day: black top, short denim skirt, thick black woollen tights, black ankle-length Doc Martens boots and cheap silver jewellery) thereby breaking my heart and completely crushing my dreams.

The sixth-form Christmas disco was the social event of the school year and the date I had been planning for since laying eyes on Amanda on day one of the new term. While the majority of my fellow students had come up through the ranks of Kings Heath Comprehensive to do their A levels, Amanda was only there because she had failed to attain the correct grades to stay on at the nearby grammar school sixth form and so was, in every sense, slumming it.

During the course of that first term I made it my mission to make Amanda mine. I made her laugh, made her compilation tapes and talked to her like she was a human being instead of the most beautiful girl in the school. And even though we never made it past this superficial level of intimacy I took comfort from the fact that whenever she saw me in the common room or in the corridor she would stop and chat as though we were good friends.

Having laid all this groundwork, the sixth-form Christmas disco, with its unparalleled opportunities for a slow dance in the darkened surroundings of the main school hall, was the obvious place to make my move. What I hadn't factored into my plans, however, were the fickle desires of girls like Amanda Dixon.

Reasoning that it was pointless to stay at the disco a moment longer but barely able to stop tormenting myself with the sight that was currently offending my eyes, I mumbled in the direction of my friends Gershwin, Pete and Elliot that I was leaving. Even though there was still an hour before the night was over none of them tried to dissuade me. Wishing myself home to get on with my mourning in the relative privacy of the bedroom that I shared with my brothers, I zipped up my jacket and headed out across the vast, empty expanse of the playground towards the exit. Then I spotted a lone female figure sitting on a bench facing the main school entrance.

'Pascoe!'

The figure looked up, momentarily unsure where the noise had come from. I walked over to her and she took off her headphones.

'You scared the life out of me!'

'Sorry. Didn't mean to. It's just that I saw you sitting there and . . .'

'And what?'

And what indeed? It wasn't like Ginny Pascoe and I were friends or anything (at least not then). She was just a girl. One of many, neither over-cool nor over-pretty and given that I had eyes for no one but Amanda Dixon, to all intents and purposes Ginny had been invisible to me.

'I just thought I'd see what you were up to,' I replied, dousing my words in liquid nonchalance. I stared at her. She seemed different. For starters she was prettier and had that same air of confidence that all girls my age appeared to have been handed over the long summer break – along with proper breasts and womanly hips – that marked them out as being so much more complicated than us boys could ever be.

I asked her what she'd been listening to.

'You won't have heard of them.'

'Try me.'

'The Pinfolds.'

'Never heard of them.'

'Any good?'

'They're the best,' she said.

I looked back at the school building. Through the partially drawn blackout curtains in the main hall I could make out the strobe effect lighting put on to accompany the opening drumbeats of 'Blue Monday'. With a world-weary sigh that came from bitter experience I shook my head in embarrassment as half-a-dozen people who should know better failed to resist the temptation to do the Robot.

'What are you doing out here anyway?'

Ginny checked to see if the coast was clear before producing a two-litre bottle of Coke from inside her coat. 'It's not mine,' she said, offering me a swig, 'it's my friend Katrina's and somehow I've ended up babysitting it.'

Desperate to maintain my cool I accepted the bottle she proffered and took an overzealous gulp, spraying the contents of my mouth over my jeans.

'What's in there?' I spluttered. 'Whiskey?'

Ginny grinned. 'Jack D.'

'You could've warned me.'

'And miss out on that? You must be kidding.'

I wiped my mouth. I wasn't about to be outdone by this girl. I put the bottle back up to my lips, took another swig and swallowed, blinking back tears as thousands of tongues of fire licked up my throat.

'How rubbish was tonight?' I croaked, handing the bottle back to Ginny.

'On a scale of one to ten?' she mused. 'I'd give it full marks for crapness. The teachers really killed the mood: did you see Mr Woodman dancing to Kylie earlier? What was he thinking? The food was disgusting, and the music! Don't get me started on the music!' She took a sip from the Coke bottle and handed it back to me. 'This place is such a let-down! I knew I should have gone to sixth-form college instead of staying in this crap-hole breathing the same air as bitches like Kate Barrett.'

Intrigued by her attack on Kate Barrett (easily one of the most popular girls in sixth-form), I sat down on the bench next to her.

'Don't you like Kate?'

'Hate her,' snapped Ginny.

'Why?'

'Do I look like I need a reason?'

Earlier I'd seen Kate outside the school secretary's office with her lips attached to the face of sixth-form Lothario Nathan Spence. I hadn't thought much about it at the time other than briefly wondering what it might be like to be Nathan Spence's fingertips but now I could see its significance. At least if you happened to be one of the many girls who fancied him.

I looked up at the night sky. 'I can't wait until I'm out of this dump.'

'You're in for a long wait. We've only just finished the first term.'

'Don't care. This place is for kids. University is where it's at.'

'What do you want to do?'

'Computer Science.'

'Where?'

'Up north somewhere, maybe Leeds or Salford. I don't really care as long as it's away from here.'

'And then what?'

I shrugged. 'I haven't got that far. I wouldn't mind working in computer games, you know, for someone like Atari, creating the next *Space Invaders* or *Commando*. Someone's got to do it and I don't see why it shouldn't be me.'

Ginny laughed. 'I like your confidence. You'll go far.'

'So what about you, Miss Clever Clogs? What does the future hold for you?'

'Fine Art at Sussex,' she replied between sips from the bottle, 'although I'll have to do some sort of foundation course I guess. And once I get my degree I'm going to move to London and be a painter.'

'Is that right? Will you do wallpapering as well or will it be strictly gloss and emulsion?'

'It'll be gobby wannabe computer game-makers if I have my way,' replied Ginny. 'Which shade of phlegmatic green do you think would suit you best?'

Considering her use of the word 'phlegmatic' I needed a good retort if I wasn't to look like a fool but for the life of me I couldn't think of anything snappy enough so I just said, 'You're funny,' and tried to make it sound suitably sardonic. But it actually came out more like a compliment.

In the space of an hour I learned more about Ginny than I had during the entire time we'd been at school. I discovered which bands she liked to listen to; which films she loved to watch; and which local pubs she'd been to where she'd actually been served and after all of this I was left with the impression that she was a whole lot smarter and funnier than any girl not on my radar ought to be. Did this new information mean that I should try and kiss her? I was pretty sure it did, but just as I was about to make my move an unexpected burst of music interrupted me and we both looked over to the hall from where dozens of our fellow students were beginning to emerge.

'Looks like the nightmare is over,' said Ginny, rising to her feet.

'I think I might be drunk,' I replied, sounding quite pleased with myself.

'I think I am too,' she said, grabbing hold of me. The friends she had been waiting for would be leaving the disco any minute and I had to do something. Just as I was about to take action she planted a kiss full on my lips and in a few moments we were kissing so intensely that I could still taste her mouth (a heady concoction of illicit alcohol, cigarettes and spearmint chewing gum) long after we had parted.

And that night a precedent was set: from here on in we were each other's consolation prize, each other's back-up plan, the original friends with benefits long before being a friend with benefits was even a thing. And although it was hardly the most romantic of beginnings our developing friendship enabled us to continue this arrangement through our A levels, our degrees and beyond. But somewhere around our mid-twenties life happened, and jobs happened, and the opportunities for friendship, let alone our temporary couplings, seemed to all but disappear until eventually I forgot about the people who used to mean the world to me and instead concentrated on the people who were right by my side.

Consigning that part of my life to the shoebox of my youth along with much else that, while enjoyable, was inherently bad for me, as I approached thirty I tried to focus my energies on activities that were the complete opposite. Good food, healthy relationships, things that would improve my life. But then as I've already remarked, at the grand old age of twenty-nine I split up with my American girlfriend and found myself briefly back in Birmingham. And that 'hazy warmth of nostalgia' I mentioned earlier and which I mistook for something more than it was, was of course the one, the only, Ginny Pascoe.

The last time I saw Ginny in the flesh had been at my own wedding. She'd been single at the time but seemed really happy in herself and when she'd kissed me on the cheek that day and wished me well I saw a look in her eye as if to say: 'It's OK that this is the end of our story. I think we've both got what we needed.' It was oddly life-affirming, like attending the funeral of an old man who everyone knew had lived a full and love-filled life.

But if all that was true, why after six years without a single word between us had I returned home from a run unable to think about anything or anyone other than Ginny? I've tried long and hard to come up with a theory. I've considered everything from the possibility that my personality's gone haywire perhaps due to an undiagnosed mini-stroke on the day of my fake heart attack right through to the idea that I am just too damn lazy to find someone new to fall in love with. The conclusion I've come to however is this: the night that Ginny and I first kissed remains one of the happiest of my life. And facing the four-oh as I am without a wife, job, or indeed a home, right now I'd give anything, absolutely anything, to be that happy again.

7

'So it's been like this for what? Days? Weeks?'

I look down at the floor like a wayward schoolboy who's been caught up to no good. My mum sounds angry and disappointed at the same time, which I'll admit wasn't the response I had been hoping for. No one on this earth can make me feel guilty quite like she does.

'More like months,' I confess.

'So when we had that get-together at Edward's in the summer and you said Lauren was working you were what, lying?'

I feel myself growing smaller as I nod. Soon I'll be invisible to the naked eye.

'I thought it was for the best.'

'So where have you been living all this time?'

'In the house.'

'And where has she been living?'

A raised eyebrow says it all.

'You carried on living together?'

There's hope in her voice and although a lifetime admirer of my mother's propensity for hopeless optimism, I find this only makes things harder. 'There's no chance of us getting back together, Mum,' I say, dashing her hopes. 'We carried on living together because it was easier, that's all, but even the easy stuff gets difficult after a while. That's why I'm here now.'

'But you always seemed so happy together.'

People always say this when a couple splits up even though it's not what they mean. What they actually mean is that when they think of you they don't think of a couple who hate each other, which isn't exactly the same thing. Lauren and I never hated each other. That's not what happened here, and frankly I sort of wish it was. No, what happened to Lauren and me was far more insidious: somewhere between her working all the time and me working all the time we fell out of love, but only one of us was prepared to say it.

I look at Mum. She has tears in her eyes. 'You're right, Mum, we did seem happy together but it just wasn't enough.'

'You weren't messing around with somebody else, were you?'

'No of course not,' I reply, sounding scandalised even though Mum is not the first person to have asked this question and I doubt she'll be the last. Everyone I tell about the split seems to believe that I'm to blame for my marriage falling apart as though it would be too far-fetched to even consider laying the blame at Lauren's door. To be fair, if I'd heard from me that my marriage was over I'd probably blame me too.

I look over at Dad to see whether there's any chance he might step in and reel Mum in a bit but he's too busy staring at the tiled floor hoping that this situation will blow over without his involvement to acknowledge my need for assistance. 'We split up because it just wasn't working any more. It was working, then it stopped working and by the time we got round to taking a proper look at it, it was broken beyond all repair.'

'But I don't understand, why didn't you tell us when it happened? Why did you have to leave it until now?'

'So you could have done what, exactly? Whipped out a magic wand and made it all better? She wanted out, Mum, OK? She got sick and tired of putting up with my crap day in and day out so you'll forgive me if I didn't feel like broadcasting the news to the entire world!'

Even before the words have left my lips I hate myself. How hard is it to let Mum say what's on her mind without making her feel like she doesn't count for anything? I'm dealing with a lot of stuff but now she is too. I've dropped my life and its problems in her lap and she's responded in the only way she knows: by sifting through all the information she can find in the hope that a solution might lie somewhere within. It was pointless having a go at Mum for being herself and having given vent to my exasperation all I'd succeeded in doing was making us both feel worse.

She turns her back and starts tidying away our mugs even though they're still half full. Dad throws me a look that says: 'You made the mess, now clean it up,' and so I follow my mum to the sink. 'I shouldn't have spoken to you like that, I'm sorry. It won't happen again.'

She wipes her eyes and looks up at me. 'You've obviously been in the wars and I should've given you time to adjust. I won't keep on at you, I promise. I just worry, that's all. All your dad and I ever wanted was for all of you to be happy and when things like this happen it feels like we've failed.'

She gives me a hug and I hug her back to let her know that I have accepted the terms of our truce but I know that I'll feel guilty for days to come. This will lead to me offering to run numerous errands for Mum which in turn will mean us spending more 'quality' time together which will (despite our newly signed accord) inevitably end in one or other of us losing our temper and saying something we'll regret. Once again I consider getting the train back to London and begging Lauren to let me sleep in my shed until we've sold the house. Then I think about how cold it was the night before last and how nothing puts a potential buyer off a house like finding a homeless man in a garden shed recovering from frostbite.

'How long are you actually here for?' Mum asks.

'I'm not sure,' I reply. 'A while I suppose.'

'What about your job?'

It's time to drop my second bombshell.

'I quit.'

This time even Dad looks up at me.

'You quit?' he says. 'To do what?'

I shrug and my parents exchange looks of bewilderment. In their world people don't just give up their jobs to do nothing.

Dad eyes me as though I am mentally ill, on drugs or possibly both.

'Will they take you back?'

'It doesn't matter, Dad. I'm not going back.'

'But it was a good job!'

'I know it was,' I reply, 'but it wasn't making me happy.'

Neither of my parents is the kind of person who spends a great deal of time thinking about happiness. They are very much in the 'keep your head down, get on with it' camp and to be fair that has seen them through all kinds of troubles in their lives. Maybe if this had been a different time I would've been like that too. But I was born in an age in which happiness is supposed to matter even if you're not 100 per cent sure what exactly happiness is and have to make yourself unhappy trying to find out.

There's a further exchange of worried glances but neither says a word. I can tell they both have a million questions but are afraid to ask in case I go off on one again. Finally Mum says: 'You must be tired after all that travelling. Why don't I show you up to your room and then you can come and have a bite to eat?'

I don't argue, even though I'm well aware of the location of the guest bedroom that used to belong to me and my brothers. I allow Mum to lead the way upstairs and follow with my bags.

'You've decorated,' I say.

'I just gave it a little spruce.'

When Lauren and I had last stayed here, the room had been little more than a freshly painted magnolia box but now the walls are adorned with floral patterned wallpaper, swags of decorative material hang round the windows, pictures of my nephews and nieces have been artfully displayed on every free surface and there's a large Constable print of a countryside scene in an ornate gold frame on the chimney breast. The room looks like one HRH Queen Elizabeth might have chosen had she been evicted from Buckingham Palace, stripped of her fortune and forced to live in a terraced house in south Birmingham.

'Well, I'll leave you to it,' says Mum even though I can see she's got something more to say. Given the circumstances I decide the least I can do is give her an in: 'I am OK, Mum, I'll be fine.'

'I know you will,' she says but the abject sorrow in her eyes says otherwise.

8

I'm woken the following morning by a sharp knock on my bedroom door. I open my eyes to see Mum standing over me wearing her outdoor coat.

'I'm checking to see if you're awake yet.'

I look at my watch. It's just after ten. Given the bombshells I dropped yesterday plus the fact that she gets up at six in the morning every day it's hardly pushing the boat out to suggest that she's been lurking at the door waiting for me to emerge for some time.

I sit up in bed. 'What's on your mind, Mum?'

'I'm nipping to the shops and I wondered what you'd like for your tea tonight.'

'Tea?'

She nods. 'Yes, it's either lamb chops or pork chops because I've just heard on the radio they're on special at the supermarket. Which is it to be?

It would be futile to point out that I haven't got a clue what I want for breakfast let alone tea, so I hope to bring the conversation to a close by saying, 'Pork,' very firmly.

Mum pulls a face. That is clearly the wrong answer.

'Are you sure? I've never heard you say they're your favourite. Did Lauren cook them a lot?'

'No,' I sigh. 'Not really. I tell you what, though, get the lamb chops. They sound nice now you mention it.'

'I'll get both,' she says, clearly pleased with this decision. 'I can always put one lot in the freezer can't I? What are your plans for the day?'

'I might take a walk,' I say, 'you know, clear my head a bit. It's a shame we haven't got a dog. That's the kind of walk I could really do with right now.'

Mum nods as though she understands the whole walking-a-dog-that-we-don't-own thing, which she clearly doesn't. I can see the cogs whirring. Why's he talking about dogs? We haven't got a dog. Is he saying he wants a dog? We haven't got room for a dog!

'Do you need some money? There's a twenty-pound note on the mantelpiece behind the clock. You must be getting a bit short with you not working.'

My heart melts. This is typical of my mum. Just when you're at your most exasperated, having been woken up early and interrogated about evening meals, she'll make a gesture so full of love and compassion that you feel terrible for all the horrible things you've been thinking. My little old mum giving me – who used to think nothing of spending a hundred pounds on a bottle of wine in a nice restaurant – money from her pension: it's heartbreaking.

'I'm all right for cash at the minute, Mum, but thanks anyway.'

As she leaves the room I head for the shower and set the controls to a few degrees below scalding in the hope that the intensity will clear the fog currently clogging up my head. Grabbing a bottle of suitably masculine-sounding shampoo that has been my brand of choice for years I give it a big squeeze and am disappointed to see that nothing is coming out. I exchange it for a bottle on the lower shelf that I know to be my mum's (Dad has never used shampoo in his life, preferring a bar of soap 'It's exactly the same stuff but three times cheaper!') and feel depressed. My mum's shampoo is a generic supermarket brand a million miles from the fancy-monikered, floral-smelling gunk that Lauren uses and I'm struck by the thought that I may never live with a woman who buys fancy shampoos again.

Ready for the day ahead, I'm about to head downstairs when I think about Ginny. She's the reason I'm here, the reason I'm enduring the indignities of living with my parents, and yet aside from getting on the train at Euston I haven't actually done anything to further my plan. Should I simply call her out of the blue? Or perhaps I should drop in on her at home or engineer an 'accidental' meeting in the street? In the end I decide that the only thing I can do is the one thing everyone in the world has already done bar me: join Facebook.

As someone who worked in the IT industry and regularly spent huge swathes of my life staring at one screen or another I'd always found the idea of Facebook entirely unappealing. With barely enough time in the real world why would I want to waste time I didn't have in a virtual one social networking with people who under normal circumstances I would have lost contact with? Did I really need to keep in touch with sixty-odd people I had only ever met once and would never meet again? And even if I did why would I need to see their holiday photos or receive notifications whenever they visited the pub? But as I open up my laptop, join my parents' next-door neighbour's unsecured Wi-Fi network and set about searching for signs of Ginny, it occurs to me that as a tool for hunting down old on/off girlfriends it is unparalleled.

I spend a couple of minutes trawling through a dozen or so Ginny Pascoes from Bristol to North Carolina but when I find the right one I know it's her straight away. She looks just the way I remember and just as beautiful. Gazing at her photo I can't help but wonder how I will look to her after all this time. I always imagine myself looking cool and debonair but in reality I fear it may be more off-duty geography teacher.

I try to find out more information about her life (where she's living, what she's doing and most importantly whether she's single) but her privacy settings are set pretty high so that the only thing I learn is that she's still living in Birmingham.

Frustrated, I consider sending her a friend request but somehow it doesn't feel right and so instead since I'm here I look up a number of former school mates whose privacy settings are low to non-existent just to see how their lives are treating them in comparison to my own. I discover the following: Emma Francis (then the girl most likely to be a vet) is living in Bromsgrove, has two kids with a third on the way; Joseph Maloney (then the boy most likely to die at the hands of the police during a shoot-out) is back from a tour of duty in Afghanistan, living in Bristol, and likes Metallica and playing Xbox; Neema Patel (then the girl most likely to become a GP) is a part-time optician in Glasgow with two teenage daughters, and describes her relationship status as 'complicated'; and Gary Turrell (then the boy most likely to turn his obsession with Dungeons and Dragons into a career) is now living in Indonesia, teaching scuba-diving and (if his profile picture was to be believed) sporting the kind of six-pack only ever seen on the cover of *Men's Health*. So this is what turning forty is all about, I conclude as I close my laptop: kids, war, scuba-diving, complicated relationships, excessive body building and a whole lot of shattered dreams.

Desperate to keep my spirits up I follow through with my idea about taking a dogless walk up to Kings Heath park but even after several laps I've still got energy to spend so I carry on towards the environs of Moseley, a better-off cousin to Kings Heath popular with university lecturers, medics, renting graduates and (judging by the flash cars) the occasional highly paid executive. Maybe if I'd opted to live in Birmingham while earning the kind of money that I'd been earning in London I would've lived here too – a nice five-bed residence tucked away from the high street but not so far that I couldn't stagger home from a night out at the King's Arms.

Reaching the high street I take a walk along St Mary's Row and reminisce about some of the shops and cafes that were here when I was seventeen: the hippy place that sold tie-dyed T-shirts and silver jewellery that Ginny loved; the tiny café that would turn a blind eye to us bringing in sausage rolls from the bakery next door; the chain pub that served the cheapest beer for miles but played the world's worst music.

Crossing over the road I pass Boots, a curry house I don't recognise and a couple of cafés before I come to a halt outside an upmarket charity shop which appears to fancy itself as a cut above the rest. Not for this emporium dog-eared copies of Catherine Cookson novels, semi-naked Barbie dolls and dead men's clothing. Instead, judging from its tasteful window display it's all literary novels with unbroken spines, pre-owned must-have classic albums in vinyl and arthouse DVDs. It's like a cooler version of the Exchange shops in Notting Hill run for the purpose of aiding humanitarian works. Intrigued, I dodge past the pristine vintage pistachio Lambretta parked outside and enter the shop.

The first thing I notice is that they're playing The House of Love's debut album. The moment I hear 'Christine', I'm transported back to a scene of my youth: me, Gershwin and the rest of the gang hanging out at Ginny's listening to music and pontificating about life. I haven't heard this album in years, and it immediately puts a smile on my face, a fact that doesn't go unnoticed by the guy behind the till. He looks familiar but I just can't place him.

Despite grey hair and lived-in craggy features, there's something eternally youthful about him. He's easily ten years my senior, but he looks effortlessly cool. Not for him the male fashion menopause that has afflicted most of my generation. He is exactly the kind of man I want to be ten years from now, a pinnacle of maturity and style rather than some combat-trousered off-duty dad lookalike in sagging T-shirt and comfortable footwear.

'Cracking band weren't they?' he says in a soft Brummie accent.

'The absolute best,' I reply. 'I saw them a few times. They were a great band live.'

'We were probably at the same gigs. Dunno what they're up to now. I had a guy in this morning trying to talk down the price we were charging. I told him to sod right off and then put it straight on!'

I laugh politely and try desperately to think of something else to say because I don't want this conversation to end. I've just realised who he is. He's Gerry Hammond, lead singer of The Pinfolds, and this is easily the best thing that has happened to me for ages.

The Pinfolds were Birmingham's answer to The Smiths. Ginny got me into them after we became friends and as teenagers we saw them countless times before they got famous and moved to London, and even after that at least half a dozen times between the release of their debut album, *Newhall Lovers*, and their final tour some three years later.

On behalf of my seventeen-year-old self I want to say something to Gerry but my mind has gone blank. We do the awkward smile thing to signal the end of the conversation and then I start browsing the paperbacks behind me while conjuring up reasons why one of my all-time heroes is working in a charity shop.

After much deliberation I pick up a copy of *The Return of The Native* for £1.99 and Leonard Cohen's *Songs of Love and Hate* on CD for £2.49 by which time I have concluded that Gerry is one of those pop stars who like to give something back. This, I decide, is very much in keeping with The Pinfolds' left-wing ethos as I remembered them and only serves to make him even cooler.

'Hardy and Cohen at the same time,' he says, chuckling as he puts my purchases through the till. 'You'll be a barrel of laughs tonight in the pub!'

Retorts (cool or otherwise) elude me so I just laugh and nod. He hands me the bag with my purchases in adding: 'Come back soon. We've always got tons of new stock coming in.'

That night I spend half the evening watching old Pinfolds videos that fans have uploaded to YouTube. It's great hearing songs like 'Charmed and Delighted' and 'Union Street Nightmares' again but disappointing to see how few times they've been viewed (in the low thousands as opposed to the millions that Smiths videos have) and it makes me wonder whether I might have exaggerated their success. Obviously to me at the age of seventeen they had been this huge band, local heroes living the dream. Was it possible that their place in the pantheon of pop wasn't quite as secure as it was in my head? Closing the lid of my laptop I find myself thinking about Ginny again as though my unconscious is trying to make a connection between her and The Pinfolds. Have I exaggerated what we used to be to each other? When I see her will she take one look at me and wonder who I am? If I really am going to make contact with her then I'll need to get a bit more background information on her and who better to get it from than Gershwin Palmer, my oldest mate, and my eyes and ears on the streets of Birmingham. If anyone will know what Ginny's up to he will and so I reach for my phone and type out the following text: *Split up with the missus and back in Brum. Fancy a pint?*

9

It's just after nine and Gershwin and I are nursing our pints in the crowded rear bar of an Irish pub in Moseley. I've told him my news and rather than asking me why it's taken six months to tell him about me and Lauren, which would be fair enough, he says: 'Mate, I'm really gutted for you. No one knows better than me how tough divorce can be.'

It was hard to believe it had been five years since Gershwin and his wife Zoe had split up, especially as they'd been together since their late teens. Of course they'd had their ups and downs and had once even separated for a short while, but after fifteen years together I'd been convinced they were in it for life. No one was more surprised than me when Gershwin called and told me it was over. They'd been rowing all the time and eventually Zoe asked him to move out; a few months later she met someone else. The thing that really broke my heart about it was that even after the divorce was finalised it was obvious he still loved her.

'So what's your plan?' asks Gershwin. 'Sell the house and move on?'

'Pretty much, although it doesn't help that I quit my job too.'

'I thought you loved it.'

'So did I. Turns out I was wrong. Truth is I just couldn't do it any more. I've been in this business nearly twenty years and I'm burned out.'

'But you're not going to come back here, are you?'

'Of course not,' I say. 'I'm just here to lick my wounds and move on.'

'Good,' says Gershwin, relieved.

His reaction is confusing. I decide to ignore it but he immediately corrects himself. 'I don't mean it like that, of course, I mean . . . you know it's good that you're not just going to sit around here. You don't want to come back to this place. It'll suck the life out of you.'

It isn't like Gershwin to criticise his home town like this. In fact there have been times when he's almost come to blows with people who have had a go at the city in his presence. Something feels wrong but I have no idea what it is.

'Are you OK?'

'I've been better,' he replies in a voice so steeped in Brummy lugubriousness that it would put even Ozzy Osborne at his most melancholy to shame.

'Work stuff?' Gershwin was deputy programme director for a new government regional health initiative that was always taking him off around the country. Maybe his job was getting him down as much as mine had been.

'There's rumours floating around about redundancies and cuts,' he says. 'It doesn't bode well.'

'I'm sorry to hear that. You'll be safe though won't you? I mean, you're pretty senior.'

Gershwin shrugs. 'It's impossible to tell.'

I look around the pub. The Patrick Kavanagh, with its open fire, worn oak floorboards and comfortable ratio of under thirties to over which meant that people like Gershwin and me could have a pint without feeling like we're in a disco or conversely a retirement home is as good a drinking venue as any, and under normal circumstances I wouldn't be fussed; but it isn't The King's Arms, the place that used to be our home from home.

'It changed hands and went downhill,' says Gershwin when I question him about the pub that had over the years acted as the unofficial clubhouse for Kings Heath Comprehensive alumni. 'The new people did a big refurbishment and started doing fancy food so it lost every drop of atmosphere that all the years of neglect and indifference had given it.'

'Sooner or later change kills everything, mate,' I say. 'It's the way of the world.'

For some reason the conversation falls flat after this. Gershwin sips his pint and I sip mine and occasionally one of us nods as if to say, 'Wow, look at this we're having a drink together.' It's good to see him though. His hair is all but gone now, shaved right close to the scalp with only minuscule stubs of silvery grey to show that he'd ever had any at all. But the mischievous grin that was perched on the schoolboy I first met on my first day at Kings Heath Comprehensive is still just about there.

I want to ask about Ginny, if he's seen much of her and what she's up to, but it seems a bit too obvious now that he knows about Lauren. Gershwin, as well as being aware of the 'complicated' nature of my relationship with Ginny, is also an expert in how my mind works. If I even mention her he'll assume I've come back to start things up again and as a fully fledged thirty-nine-year-old man it feels a bit school playground to be that obvious.

I get another couple of pints in and decide on a different tack.

'Heard from any of the old crowd?' I say, referring to Pete, Bev, Katrina and, of course, Ginny.

'I'm terrible about that kind of thing,' he says. 'Haven't heard from anyone in ages. I have got one piece of big news that'll blow your mind a bit: Ginny got married.'

'Ginny? Married? When?'

'Back in the summer, apparently.'

'Did she tell you that?'

'Haven't seen her in ages. I can't even remember where I heard it first. You know what it's like. You go out, you have a few and you bump into an old mate and they tell you a bunch of stuff and you only remember when you wake up the following morning.'

'So who is it she's married to? Do we know him?'

Gershwin shakes his head. 'I think it might be some guy she works with.'

I don't know what to say. All this time I've been so focused on the changes in my own life I haven't given any thought to the changes that might be happening in hers. She's married. Ginny's married. And now the only hope that's been keeping me going these past few weeks is gone.

'You look a bit stunned, mate.'

'That's because I am,' I say. 'You might as well know this given it's not going to happen but I don't know . . . I had this big plan to look her up again and . . . you know . . .' I laugh. 'It's ridiculous, look at me, I'm not even divorced yet and already I'm looking for another happy ever after. Is that stupid?'

'Of course not,' says Gershwin, 'You two have a lot of history. But it's probably for the best she's not single. You know how complicated stuff got whenever you guys got together.'

'Do you think I should go and see her and wish her well and all that? I mean, we are still friends.'

Gershwin looks disapproving. 'Bad idea, mate. Think about it: she didn't invite you to the wedding. I doubt that she wants you turning up on her doorstep. Believe me, you're best off steering clear.'

A night at the pub with Gershwin traditionally only ends when the bar staff are stacking chairs around us as the two of us hatch plans to go on to somewhere else but tonight on the dot of ten Gershwin drains his glass and announces that he's got to be up early in the morning for a meeting in Bristol.

'I know, I know,' he says, 'no one's more gutted about it than me. But you know how it is with work, mate. Next time I promise we'll do it properly: pub, curry, the works.'

Standing outside the pub with our breath rising up into the cold night air we prepare to part ways: me towards Kings Heath and Gershwin towards his garden flat in Church Road.

'So I'll see you soon, fella,' says Gershwin, giving me the kind of hug men of my generation no longer feel the need to douse in irony. At forty it's an achievement to have any mates at all, let alone ones you've known over half a lifetime, and though the Book of Bloke says you must take everything for granted, when it comes to mates this is a step too far.

'Absolutely,' I reply, 'it's been good to see you. I know it's not for a while yet but have you given any thought to your fortieth? We should book something in now. You know how much planning these things take.'

'I'm giving the whole thing a miss,' he says. 'I mean, what's the point? All that forced jollity, to celebrate a birthday that I'm not even vaguely interested in. Forget it.'

'This is your fortieth, mate! The big one! You can't just let it pass you by. Just tell me who you want to be there and I'll sort everything.'

'It's not going to happen,' he says firmly.

'OK, then why don't we do the curry and beer thing like you said?'

Gershwin shakes his head, unmoved. 'Cheers mate, but honestly I'm fine giving the whole thing a miss.'

'So when it happens you're just going to stay in?'

Gershwin nods and it seems as if there is no more to say. We do the man hug again and then he stands back and looks at me like he's got something on his mind. 'Listen,' he says, 'I'm sorry about Ginny. I know she meant a lot to you. I shouldn't have . . . well, you know . . . I should've been a bit more sensitive about it.'

'Nah, it's fine, mate, honest. I'm just glad that I knew before I made a bigger fool of myself than I already have. I mean, it's not like we're seventeen any more, is it?'

10

The morning is all but over as I come downstairs and slope into my parents' kitchen. Scratching the back of my head I yawn and glance at the clock next to the back door: it's half past eleven. A year ago at this time of day I would either have been at work for four hours, or more likely than not on my way to a pitch meeting in an identikit office somewhere around the globe and now I'm only just getting up having spent yet another night in my parents' spare room. Verily, my life is falling apart and there's not a damn thing I can do about it.

I suspect that my lethargy is in no small part due to Gershwin's news about Ginny. Without her in the picture I am effectively a man without a mission. Why didn't I come back to Birmingham when Lauren and I first split up? Maybe things would've been different if I had. Who am I kidding? Who's to say that it would've made the slightest difference? What? Am I that much of a catch that Ginny would have chosen me over some guy who she was actually planning to marry? And anyway, who in their right mind convinces themselves they're in love with a woman they haven't seen or spoken to in six years? This whole exercise was pure pie in the sky, a desperate attempt to make life right before time runs out and I get stuck in Loserville for good. I need to face facts: Ginny isn't going to fly in to the rescue; I'm probably going to end up living with my parents long after I turn forty; and I may never see another woman naked in the flesh ever again. And the sooner I accept this state of affairs the easier it's going to be for me in the long run.

Still frowning at my own idiocy, I turn round to see my mum looking for all the world like a woman on a mission.

'Who's rattled your cage? You look like you're about to punch somebody.'

'I'm fine, Mum, honest. I was just thinking, that's all.'

'How was last night?'

'OK.'

'You didn't drink too much, did you?'

I look to see if she's joking and the absence of a smile tells me all I need to know.

'What's that supposed to mean?'

Mum scowls to indicate it's a completely legitimate question. 'Your father used to frown like that whenever he had a hangover.'

'I had three pints and a pack and a half of salt and vinegar crisps. Shall I call Alcoholics Anonymous or do you want to do the honours?'

Her face immediately becomes outraged. 'I asked you if you wanted seconds at teatime and you said you were full and then you go off stuffing your face with junk food. Well from now on I won't bother listening to you!'

I hope we've come to the end of the conversation and to test the waters I edge towards the cupboard and take out the cornflakes. Big mistake.

'What are you doing?'

'Getting breakfast.'

'Not while I'm still talking to you, you're not. Your dad and I are thinking that you might like to come with us to see your sister and the children. What do you say?'

'I'm not sure.'

'Your sister's been hoping you'd pop over ever since she heard that you were back and the boys are desperate to see their favourite uncle.'

'I'd be no fun in the mood I'm in right now. Tell her I'll be over to see her some other time. I promise.'

'What will you do with the day instead? Go back to bed? This is no way for a man of your age to be spending his life. Is that what your father and I sent you to university for? To waste your life dossing? At the very least you should be outside, getting some fresh air!'

'I was out late. I've got a lot on my mind. I don't want any fresh air, I just want to get some rest.'

My mum can barely control her indignation. 'Rest? What do *you* want rest for? You haven't even got a job to make you tired in the first place! Don't you think I wanted a rest when I was working all hours as a nurse and then coming home to look after a house, a husband and four children? I would've loved to have had a rest, believe you me!'

Over the eighteen or so years that I was resident at 88 Hampton Street I had heard this speech in all its forms and the result is always the same: her point gets made and I accept defeat.

'You win, OK?' I say, desperate for the emotional blackmail to stop. 'I'll come!'

'Good,' she says firmly. 'I've made you a fried breakfast – it's plated up and in the microwave – your father and I are just nipping up the high street to get some bits to take with us. When we come back we'll go, so be ready.'

As my mother leaves the kitchen virtually strutting like an on-his-game Muhammad Ali victoriously exiting a boxing ring following a knockout, I abandon my cereal and move over to the microwave. How little time has it taken her to move on from her softly, softly approach and start kicking me up the backside? Three days. To be fair, I'm sure that if I had a thirty-nine-year-old son who had invited himself to stay indefinitely and looked like he was about to make sleeping late and eating me out of house and home part of his daily pattern, I too would have taken off the kid gloves pretty sharpish.

Relieved to finally be left alone I stare vacantly at the microwave watching my food rotate. It's a moment of pure bliss. I have no thoughts at all. My mind is completely empty.

Then my phone rings.

I check the screen. It's Gershwin. I cross my fingers and hope he's calling to let me know he's changed his mind about his birthday. Right now I could do with a party, or indeed any excuse for a good time.

'All right, mate?'

'Not so bad.'

'How's Bristol?'

'Wet. How's Brum?'

'Cold.'

There's a long silence; even without him being physically present I can feel his tension. I guess he's not calling about his birthday. Gershwin's never been one to just check in without a reason and so I draw the only conclusion that makes sense: he's dying of cancer. That's why he seemed so quiet, left the pub early, and isn't bothered about his fortieth. He's only got a week left to live and he wants me to promise that I'll keep an eye out for his kid.

'Listen mate, about last night. I just wanted to say sorry again about, you know, Ginny.'

He's called to talk about Ginny? This makes no sense at all. Why's he bringing her up when he knows that all I want to do is forget about her? 'You've got nothing to apologise for, mate. It's not like I want to shoot the messenger.'

'Yeah, well . . . cheers. Anyway listen, I could do with having a proper chat with you about something. Not right now, but soon.'

'Not a problem,' I reply. 'When are you thinking?'

'I'll give you a shout, OK?'

'And that's it? That's all you wanted to talk about?'

'Why? What else is there?'

I breathe a sigh of relief. He's not dying, he's just being weird. 'I was hoping you'd changed your mind about your birthday.'

'Nah, mate, my mind's made up on that one. Anyway, I'd better go. But listen, let's talk soon.'

Determined to eat my breakfast before it goes cold I grab the ketchup from the fridge and a slice of white bread from the bread bin but as I reach for the margarine my phone rings again. Assuming it's Gershwin I place the phone to my ear without checking. Only when I hear my estranged wife's voice do I realise my mistake.

'Lauren, how are you?' I splutter, as I begin churning over potential reasons for her call. Had the house sold? Was she missing me? Was she about to sue me for alimony?

'Work's busy but nothing unusual there. How are you coping at your parents'?'

'As well as can be expected.'

'You're doing great,' she says. 'I'm not sure I could do much more than a weekend at mine, so you're doing well to have managed this far.' A braver man would have chosen this moment to point out that technically I'm only here because of her but I say nothing. 'It's about the house,' she continues, 'I've just received the last of the estate agents' valuations and the news isn't good. They've all valued it at quite a lot less than we'd hoped and to top it all there are at least half a dozen comparable properties up for sale within throwing distance of ours. On the plus side, they're all pretty sure they can get a sale but I think we're talking months rather than weeks.'

'So I'm stuck here indefinitely?'

'Well, let's not panic. We need to get the ball rolling. I've made the decision to put the house on with Millward and Lewis. I've got the contract here so I'll sign it now and have it to you by first post. If you sign it and send it back straight away with a bit of luck we could be taking viewings by the end of the week.'

I feel my blood start to boil as I imagine an endless queue of monied young professional Londoners traipsing through my home, commenting about the 'finish' of my bloody kitchen and how they're going to knock all the downstairs rooms together to make one huge 'entertaining space'.

'So, you'll get the contract back to me asap?'

'Of course.'

'Oh, and they also need us to fill out the fixtures and fittings list. I've ticked what I think should stay and if you're in agreement just sign your name at the bottom.'

'What sort of things?'

'All the usual suspects: curtains, carpets, light fittings and the like.'

'What about the shed?' The question had come out of nowhere but the more I thought about it the more I could see that it was never that far away.

'I've ticked that it's staying. That was right, wasn't it? Sheds aren't really the sorts of things people take with them.'

I picture my beloved shed and all of the things I never got to do inside it.

'Whatever.' It's like my licence to be a fully fledged adult has been revoked. 'I mean, what use has a guy like me got for a shed?'

Days left to turning forty: 163

71

11

It's hard not to be impressed by my sister's huge glass-fronted barn conversion. Surrounded on all sides by open countryside, it couldn't have been more different from the house we grew up in and my heart swells with pride at how well my kid sister has done for herself.

As we pull up on the gravel drive the front door opens and out stream my sister and her family to greet us. Once we're out of the car Dad starts fussing around my nephews while Mum makes a beeline for my brother-in-law, plucking baby Evie out of his arms and leaving me alone with Yvonne.

She hugs me tightly. 'It's good to see you, Matt.'

'You too,' I reply. 'This is some place you've got here. It's practically a castle.'

'I still can't believe how lucky we are. The garden's so huge that Oli's just bought himself one of those sit-on mowers. Whenever he's on it he's got a huge grin fixed to his face like a big kid. Dad's a fan too.'

'I think they're fans of everything you do at the moment. They haven't stopped talking about the kids or your house.'

She laughs and studies my face as though analysing me. 'You sound a bit jealous. Afraid your place as number one child is being usurped?'

'Me? Never. They'll always love me more than you, Ed and Tony because I was their first! You guys were just an afterthought.'

Yvonne raises a mischievous eyebrow. 'So is that why they're always talking about moving out here?'

'They're just saying that,' I scoff. 'They wouldn't dream of moving in a million years. Remember when we tried to book them a cruise for their wedding anniversary and they turned us down because 'there's no place like home'? That's Mum and Dad all over. A bomb couldn't get them out of that house.'

Yvonne laughs and shakes her head and for a moment she's the spitting image of the photo of Mum as a young woman that hangs in the front room. 'I hate it when you're right.'

'I know,' I reply, 'but you'll get used to it one day.'

I look over at my nephews, who are eyeing me carefully while playing with my dad. This is their warm-up game. They do it every time they see me even though we all know that in ten minutes' time we'll be racing around the house and battling each other with light sabres.

They're much bigger than I remember and their features have changed too. Fat faces getting thinner, thin faces getting broader and more elements of our side of the family coming out. How is it possible that human beings can change so much in such a short space of time? How is it possible for them to have changed so much and me not to have changed at all?

'Mum says you've been in the wars,' says Yvonne, looping her arm through mine as we walk towards the house.

'Just a bit.'

'I'm sorry to hear that things didn't work out for you and Lauren. I had no idea you were having problems.'

'Neither did I until it was too late. I'll live though. Down but not out and all that.'

'And the word on the street is that you've given up your job as well? You're not having some kind of breakdown, are you?'

'There's no such thing. Didn't they teach you anything at shrink school?'

As well as being the smartest in our family Yvonne is also a trained child psychologist. She slaps my arm playfully. 'They taught me enough to recognise when someone's being evasive.'

'No,' I say, 'I'm not having a breakdown, or a mid-life crisis or any of that malarky. I've just run out of steam, that's all. With a bit of TLC I'll be back up and running before you know it.'

Once we're inside the boys warm to me in no time. I start by catching up on their news and getting them to tell me stuff about what they've learned at pre-school and then once they start to lose interest in talking I move on to some gentle chasing around the living room with me being a monster determined to eat them before finally they hand me a light sabre and we move on to all-out war. It's fun doing the uncle thing. I feel like I finally have a role I can play well. The downside is that seeing the boys makes me feel a little out of sorts because I know I would have made a terrific father.

Like most couples Lauren and I had talked in a general fashion about starting a family. We'd talked about the ratio of boys to girls that we'd want (one of each) and what names we'd choose (Connie and Samuel) and speculated about our own parenting skills (we were sure we'd be great). But we never set ourselves a deadline and maybe that made sense. With Lauren being seven years younger than me there was plenty of time for us to be casual about our imaginary family's future.

Nevertheless, forty seemed like the perfect age to become a dad. Yes, there was the perennial argument about starting early so that you'd still be able to run about and play football with your kids but I'd already missed that boat and anyway, there's more to life than football. At forty, I reasoned, I would've seen enough of life to be fully committed to the fatherhood thing; I'd be in a better position to push for a more strategic role at work that wouldn't involve so much travelling; and above all I'd feel mentally equipped to take on the job of a lifetime because that's how seriously I took the idea of being a dad. I wasn't going to do it lightly. My dad had been the best dad ever and with him as a role model I was going to give it my all.

Life would've been so different if everything had gone to plan. Maybe Lauren would be pregnant and looking forward to the autumn birth of our first child. How weird would that have been, to have a gorgeous little boy or girl? And how different would my life have ended up? Everyone says how hard it is saying goodbye to the child-free life but no one ever mentions how tough it is to say goodbye to the things you never had.

Looking around Yvonne and Oliver's house filled with photos of their life together hung on every wall of their home; listening to them tell stories of family holidays they had taken and hearing their plans for the future; watching the kids crawling in and out of their laps, asking for and on occasions demanding their attention and seeing the looks of love and frustration in their eyes as they gave in to their constant requests was like seeing family life incarnate. The sum total of two lives combined in order to make something new. Even my parents, who aren't exactly the greatest social observers, felt it; I could see it in their eyes. There was a joy there, a real sense of pleasure at seeing my sister's family in action in the present, while simultaneously recalling those cherished moments from their own family life. Over lunch I lost count of how many times something my nieces or nephews said or did reminded my parents of a story from our shared past back in the days when they themselves were parents of young children. And I could see that whenever they looked at me their eyes were filled not with disappointment – my parents' appetite for grandkids had been more than sated by my siblings' kids – but rather sadness that I was missing out on something that they felt should have been mine by rights.

After a late lunch, Yvonne suggests that we go for a walk, so all of us apart from my mum, who wants to stay with Evie, put on our coats and head out to the fields behind the house. The boys look like miniature Michelin men in their overstuffed shiny winter jackets and they grab the biggest sticks they can find and begin battling each other so that Oliver and Yvonne constantly have to monitor them to ensure they don't poke out each other's eyes. Dad and I are left to our own devices and for the most part we walk in silence and take in the scenery. As we come to a stile my dad stops and looks out across the field.

'It's beautiful out here, isn't it?'

'Stunning,' I reply. 'Yvonne and Oliver have done well getting a place like this.'

'They've worked hard enough to make it happen. Yvonne was telling me there are some nights Oliver doesn't get home until gone ten.' He stops and points to a huge black bird sitting in a tree in the middle of the field. 'Is that a rook or a crow?'

'I've got no idea, Dad. Biology was never one of my strong suits.'

He nods but I know he's not listening. 'I reckon it's a rook.'

'What's the difference between a rook and a crow anyway? They look pretty similar to me.'

Dad just shrugs. 'Your mum wants me to check in with you, you know, make sure you're all right and all that,' he says.

'I'm fine, Dad.'

'She's worried about you.'

'I know and there's no need.'

'That's what I said. I told her you're a grown man and you've got to find your own way.'

'And what did she say to that?'

'You know your mother. When she's got a bee in her bonnet she doesn't listen to any opinion but her own. Can I tell her that you're OK?'

'It'd be more fun if you didn't.'

'True, but she's a worrier, your mother. Always has been, always will be. Nothing's going to change that. So shall I tell her you've got a plan?'

'A plan?'

'To sort yourself out.'

For the first time in this conversation I realise that he isn't articulating Mum's worries, but his own. My mum would never ask if I had a plan when she'd be far happier to give me the benefit of her own. It scares me to think that Dad's this concerned because my dad doesn't tend to worry about anything. He pretty much takes everything in his stride. If the man who'd sooner stand and watch than get involved has felt the need to speak to me it can only mean that my life (from the outside at least) is looking a lot worse than I thought.

I look over at the rook or whatever it is. It pecks the ground a few times before taking to the air. 'Yes, tell her I've got a plan. Tell her everything's in order.'

My dad nods but I can see that he's not convinced.

For the next few days not a great deal happens. I eat, sleep, catch a cold and watch a lot of needlessly gory US police procedurals with my parents but without Ginny to think about, life has no focus. Just as I'm feeling at my lowest however I get some post forwarded by Lauren, and although most of it is useless junk mail there's one that brightens my day immensely.

'You look like you've won the lottery,' says Mum, as she passes me in the hallway. 'Good news?'

'Great news. It's a cheque for five hundred and eighty-six pounds. Apparently I overpaid on my tax last year and this is the amount plus interest.'

My mum peers at the cheque. 'You should spend it,' she says, 'before they tell you it was a mistake and try and take it back off you!'

I hand her the cheque. 'You take it and we'll call it rent money.'

'I'll do no such thing!' she says, affronted. 'I don't want your money, thank you very much.' She shoves the cheque back in my hand. 'If you want to make me happy, burn those tracksuit bottoms you've been living in these past few days, go into town, buy yourself some new clothes and smarten yourself up. You're nearly forty, Matthew, and you need to start dressing like it!'

12

Heading towards the architectural wonder that is Selfridges in the Bullring, admiring its bulging bug-like compound-eye exterior, I marvel once again how much the city I love has changed. All the landmarks I once used to get my bearings have been moved, revamped or bulldozed. The old rundown grade-two listed Moor Street Station has been renovated to look like the location for a cosy BBC Sunday night Agatha Christie adaptation, the Rotunda has been transformed from a tatty office block to a designer apartment building, and the old fruit and veg market down where Don Christie's record shop used to be is now a huge space-age shopping centre. Is it too much of a stretch of the imagination to suggest that people, like cities, are in need of an overhaul from time to time if they are going to keep pace with the modern age? Could a sartorial revamp be the first step in turning me from a tired rundown thirtysomething into a gleaming example of twenty-first-century manliness?

Despite my mother's input, clothes have in fact been on my mind for some time. Now that I am turning forty there are some items of clothing in my wardrobe that I will no longer be able to pull off. Take for example my T-shirt collection. I have jokey ones (e.g. a drawing of a huge thumb gesturing to the left of me with the words: Who's this jerk? above it), I have designer ones with fashionable logos on the front that make me feel like a walking advert and I have a few cool ones with abstract images that used to look quite good underneath a suit jacket, not to mention the obligatory band T-shirts from my twenties that I haven't the heart to throw away.

There's nothing intrinsically wrong with these. In fact I'm sure that at least one of my brothers might leap at the chance to own a few of them. But this is the end of the road for me because one of the rules of turning forty is that the logoed T-shirt is the T-shirt of youth. It says: Look at me being needlessly casual, look at what the words and images on my clothing say about me. And while that might be fine if you're twenty-one with a body as lithe as a snake's, when you're forty and daily fighting the effects of decades of beer and bad eating habits, drawing attention to the fact with an image on your T-shirt is a sign to all the world that you don't own a floor-length mirror. No, from forty onwards if you're over-warm and wish to get some air to your lower arms it's either a shirt with the sleeves rolled up or a plain T-shirt (preferably in black, grey, or white although blue is just about acceptable).

And that's just the beginning.

Don't get me started on jeans (can't do too baggy or too tight or too Marks and Spencer), shirts (no bright colours or daft 'fashion' collars, footwear (no trainers for non-exercising purposes), headwear (that's a definite no to the baseball cap) and as for trousers the whole leg width thing gives me a headache just thinking about it.

As I wander into Selfridges debating whether to head straight up the escalators to the Paul Smith concession or stay on the first floor dominated by casual clothing for the needlessly young, out of the corner of my eye I spot Gerry Hammond from The Pinfolds again; but he's not alone. This time he's got a gorgeous girl on his arm who – dressed in a black tailored jacket over a Led Zeppelin T-shirt teamed with an incredibly short frayed denim skirt – looks like a young Anita Pallenberg.

The girl stops to look at the T-shirts on the table in front of me and I stare at Gerry. He's wearing a black leather jacket, white jeans and expensive-looking shoes. He seems to have got this growing older but staying cool thing down to a fine art. I want to ask his advice not just about clothes but about life too.

I nod in his direction in the hope that he might remember me from the shop but there's no recognition on his face and he simply carries on browsing. Lingering ironically next to a table of T-shirts that I know I'm never going to buy (I can't really see me pulling off any item of clothing that declares to the world: I am your homeboy), I watch him for a good few minutes before realising that I'm in danger of stalking him and so I make my way upstairs to continue shopping.

*   *   *

Sitting empty-handed on the bus some hours later feeling somewhat dispirited (there had been an OK jumper in Paul Smith but it would have wiped out my little bonus in one swipe of my credit card) I plan to cheer myself up with a trip to the cinema but my phone rings and from the screen I see that it's my mother. My gut instinct tells me to ignore it. But plain old-fashioned guilt makes me answer the call.

'Matthew, it's your mother here,' she says as though there was any doubt in my mind. 'Your father and I went to the Teals' for lunch and ever since we've got home he's been going on about how good Mrs Teal's ham sandwiches were so I was just wondering if you wouldn't mind picking me up a few slices from the supermarket.'

'Can't it wait?' I reply. 'Dad's not going to eat a ham sandwich now, it's teatime.'

'I'm sorry if it's putting you out to get your dad some ham but tough luck, young man, you're getting it!'

Even at the best of times there's little point in arguing with my mum but on the top deck of the bus packed with people on their way home from work I have little choice but to agree to her demands as a list that was supposed to begin and end with ham grows to include corned beef, Cheddar cheese and sausage rolls.

My reluctance to pick up the odds and ends that my mum wants is less to do with laziness than a desire not to bump into anyone I know. Given my current circumstances I have little or nothing to crow about and the thought of having to listen to others' success stories depresses me greatly. As it was, I'd already had to make a quick exit from the HSBC on the high street to avoid Darren Hemmings (then, the boy most likely to make a career as a football coach; now, head of customer liaison at HSBC); and had to leap behind a Jamie Oliver book display in WHSmith to avoid talking to Faye 'wild child' Wiederman (then, the girl most likely to lift up her shirt and show you her bra for no reason; now, harassed mother of four) all because I didn't want to tell anyone about the current state of my life. Given the sheer volume of people supermarkets attract every day, entering the Kings Heath branch of Sainsbury's would be tantamount to walking into an oversubscribed school reunion.

True to form I've barely stepped into the shop when from behind me I hear a voice boom: 'Boffin!' just as two huge hands come down on the backs of my shoulders. I turn round to see a tall bloke in a fur-trimmed parka laughing hysterically. I recognise him straight away.

'Jason Cleveland!' I say, my voice chock-full of fake bonhomie. 'How are you, mate?'

Jason Cleveland was the supercool kid of my secondary school. He was the guy who wore the best clothes, got invited to the best parties and dated the best girls. Being what Cleveland labelled a 'boffin' meant that I hadn't had much to do with him. And having witnessed first-hand his ability to destroy anyone who made the mistake of crossing his path wearing the wrong trainers or brand of designer clothing I was mightily relieved. The sickening thing about Jason is that he pretty much looked exactly the same as he had done in school. He was still ridiculously tall, and still ridiculously good-looking and judging from his multi-coloured Day-Glo trainers still had a thing for designer footwear.

'I knew it was you the second I saw you walking in!' he says. 'How are you, mate?'

'Couldn't be better. You?'

'Excellent. Just come from work. I'm shattered.'

'So what are you doing back in town?' he asks. 'Aren't you supposed to be something flash in the Smoke? Something to do with banks wasn't it?

'I work in IT.'

'That's it. How's that treating you?'

'Couldn't be better, mate.'

'I knew you'd do well, Boff! You were always good at that sort of thing. Not that I haven't done well myself, like.'

I rack my brains.

'That's right . . .' I begin, 'you work in . . .'

He pulls out his wallet, removes a card and thrusts it into my hand: Cleveland Double Glazing.

'Best business ever, mate, I am rolling in it! You should see my new Beemer, fully kitted out, all the works, it'll blow your mind! In fact why don't we go for a spin now? We could have a few beers afterwards and a proper catch up.'

'I'd love to, mate,' I say, 'but I've got something on tonight. Maybe another time?'

'Another time it is!' he says, and I hope that he's going to leave it there but of course he demands my mobile number and I have no choice but to give it. 'I'll text you in the week, Boff!' he says as a parting shot, 'I'll sort out something legendary for us to do.'

I leave Jason buying lottery tickets from the kiosk, pick up a basket and head inside the supermarket where it takes me all of five seconds to spot Andrea Bell (then, girl most likely to tattoo her boyfriend's name on her arm using a compass and a bottle of Quink; now, partner to a long-haired rocker type currently weighing loose peppers). Heading towards the chilled meats fridges I spot Toby Emmanuel from the year above me at school (then, boy most likely to become a professional actor; now, it appears, a manager in Sainsbury's) talking to a woman unpacking a box containing packets of cheese. After giving him a wide berth and picking up the ham I set my sights on the corned beef but then I see the older sister of Ruth Burrows (then, girl most likely to get pregnant before her seventeenth birthday, now, the mother of a twenty-four-year-old son) and I'm so desperate to avoid her that I walk straight into a woman pushing a trolley coming the other way.

I apologise without even registering my target. 'My fault entirely,' I say and it's only when she doesn't move that I raise my head and see Ginny.

13

Ginny doesn't say a word and neither do I. All we do is stand and stare at each other as though waiting for something to happen. It's only after several seconds of this that it occurs to me that just as I am expecting her new husband to appear from the tinned goods aisle at any moment she's probably waiting for Lauren to do the same. In the end, with neither of our spouses apparent, it's Ginny who speaks first.

'Matt.'

'Ginny.'

'How weird to see you in here of all places. That's why I didn't say anything at first. I kept thinking, who's this guy who really looks like Matt? What are you doing here?'

'My folks are in the market for sandwich-making material and yours truly was nominated to get it,' I say, noticing how great she looks. Older, yes, but no less attractive. I try and get a look at her wedding ring but of course she's wearing gloves.

'How long have you been back?'

'About a week. I was going to call but you know how it is. You have to do the rounds with all the family and then everything else gets tagged on later.'

'Of course. How long has it been anyway? Five? Six years?'

'Six,' I reply a little too quickly. It sounds as if I've been marking off the days on the walls of my prison cell.

Ginny winces. 'Where did the time go? It feels like five minutes.'

'I think when you get to our age everything feels like five minutes ago until you get the calendar out.'

Laughing, Ginny narrows her eyes as though sizing me up. 'Have you been working out? You're looking pretty buff for a computer nerd.'

'I wish,' I reply instinctively sucking in my stomach. 'I run but that's about it. What about you, though? You're looking good.'

'For a forty-year-old! Can you believe we're forty?'

'First off, some of us are still thirty-nine, thank you very much, and second, I'm pretty sure there are thirty-year-olds who would kill to look like you!'

Ginny rolls her eyes. 'I bet you say that to all the middle-aged women you meet! I forgot your birthday isn't until the end of March. Have you got any plans or are you in denial?'

'I'm keeping my head in the sand just a little longer.'

'Message received. So how's work? Are you still doing the software thing?'

I'd like to say that I seriously considered telling her the truth, in the middle of Sainsbury's, but I didn't. Not for a second.

'Yes, still doing the software thing.'

'And it's going well?'

'Brilliantly.'

'And how's married life treating you?'

'Couldn't be better.'

'And Lauren's well?'

'Very well indeed, in fact she's—' I stop suddenly and meet Ginny's gaze directly. It's pointless not telling her the truth. Sometimes you just have to tell it like it is. 'Lauren and I have split up.'

'*What?*'

'That's why I'm back,' I say in an effort to come clean. 'I need somewhere to crash while Lauren tries to sell the house.'

'So you're back at your mum and dad's again?'

'For the time being. Oh, and I've jacked in my job too. I quit the software thing about six months ago and have done nothing since but sit on my arse and watch TV. I mean, there's no point in having a mid-life crisis without going all the way, is there?'

'I'm so sorry to hear about you and Lauren. I can't really believe it. I know I didn't know you guys as a couple all that well but you both seemed really happy.'

'We were, but things change, don't they?'

'All the time,' says Ginny, more to herself than anything. 'Sometimes I just wish they'd bloody stop for a while so I could get my bearings.' She hugs me and kisses me lightly on the cheek. 'Welcome home.'

I keep waiting for her to mention the fact that she's married but she doesn't say a word about it. Instead in an attempt to make the conversation a little less intense she starts telling me how she doesn't normally go shopping straight from work but had to today because she's had a manic week and completely run out of food and then she stops as she realises that people are getting annoyed at us blocking the aisle.

'We should get out of the way,' says Ginny. 'How's this for an idea? Why don't you carry on with your shopping and then meet me out in the car park when you're done – it's a bright yellow Beetle, you can't miss it – and come back to mine for something to eat.' She gestures to her shopping trolley. 'I have food now so I can offer you something more substantial than Cup-a-Soup and toast!'

Ginny is referring to the first time I went to visit her during her first year at university. She was so broke that packet soup and toast was all she could afford to feed me the whole weekend. It was one of the best weekends of my entire life.

'Thanks,' I reply, 'but I'd better get back.'

'Are you sure? It wouldn't be a bother. Come on, Matt, I haven't seen you in ages. We've got six years' worth of catching up to do.'

I really don't want to go. The last thing I need right now is to spend the evening making polite conversation while Ginny and her new husband sit across the table from me looking adoringly into each other's eyes. I might be a lot of things, but I am nobody's third wheel.

'Honestly, Gin, I'd love to but I can't. Maybe some other time.'

'Of course,' she says, but she looks hurt. 'Some other time, definitely.' There's an awkward silence. We both want to get as far away from each other as possible but don't seem to know how. 'I suppose I'd better get off then. It was nice to see you, Matt.'

'You too,' I reply. 'And I'll definitely be in touch.'

I watch for a moment as she joins a queue at the tills and then make my way towards the tinned goods aisle, narrowly missing bumping into Toby Emmanuel coming the other way. Although he's deep in conversation with one of the shop's shelf-stackers our eyes meet and I see a flicker of recognition but he doesn't say anything. To be honest, even if he had I'm not sure that I wouldn't have told him my entire life story and asked him to spread the word to everyone we know with the express aim of making myself feel worse. I've just hurt an old friend for no reason other than ego.

By the time I emerge with a carrier bag full of food designed to appear between two slices of bread, I have beaten myself up to such an extent that all I want to do is go home and go to bed so when I see Ginny coming back into the store I'm half tempted to keep walking.

'Ginny. What's up? You looked troubled.'

'It's typical. All I want to do is go home and I can't because I've lost my car keys somewhere between here and the tills.'

'Are they black and attached to a wooden heart key fob?'

'How did you—'

'They're hanging out of the bottom of your trolley,' I kneel down and pluck them out for her.

'Matt, you're a life saver!'

'No, I think you'll find I'm a misery. I'm sorry about turning down your offer to feed me.'

'It's fine, you've obviously still got a lot on your mind.'

'That's just it. I haven't.' Ginny smiles. 'OK, maybe I have a bit but it was really rude of me to say no like that. So if losing your keys hasn't put you in too much of a bad mood I'd like to take you up on your offer if it still stands.'

'I can't think of anything that would cheer me up more. Come on.'

As we approach Ginny's car it occurs to me that my parents are expecting me home.

'You carry on,' I say, getting out my phone. 'I'll be with you in a sec.' I wait until Ginny is well out of earshot before dialling my parents' number.

'Hi, Mum, it's me. I'm just calling to let you know I won't be back for tea.'

'What do you mean you won't be back for tea? Where are you going?'

'I've bumped into an old mate and she's offered to make me dinner so I'll see you later.'

'But what about all that food you were getting?'

'I've got it.'

'So you're bringing it home then?'

'Do you need it right now?'

'Well no, it's for tea tomorrow.'

'Then I'll bring it back with me later tonight.'

'Why don't you just bring it now? I don't want your dad eating ham that's been sat out all night.'

'It's fine, Mum, honest. Ginny's got a fridge.'

'Oh, it's Ginny you're seeing? That's lovely. How is she?'

'She's fine, Mum.'

'She's not still single is she? The single life can be hard for a woman, you know.'

'No, Mum, she's married.'

'How lovely! Have they started a family yet?'

I look over at Ginny and wave so she knows I'm still coming. Little does she know that I'm discussing intimate details of her life with my mother. I have to end this conversation.

'No, Mum, not yet. Listen—'

'What's she waiting for? She's the same age as you isn't she? I bet she's one of those career women like Lauren. It's never a recipe for happiness. I was reading an article in a magazine at the dentist about these career women. They're all full of regret, you know.'

'Really, Mum I—'

'One especially, an Irish woman I think she was although now that I think about it she could have been Welsh, lived in a huge house in London which she shared with two cats. It was decorated lovely though. The curtains especially were—'

'I've got to go,' I say finally.

'Oh,' she says, sounding disappointed. I feel terrible.

'Listen Mum, it's not you, it's just that I've got to go. I promise we'll have a proper chat soon.'

Mum seems to accept my apology in the spirit that it was given but this doesn't stop her reminding me twice more to put my dad's ham in the fridge before I end the call.

Returning the phone to my pocket I look over at Ginny in her car and she waves. I wave back and as I walk over to her I think to myself that even if she is married, I'm still grateful to have her back in my life.

14

We reach her house without me having to say much. Ginny seems happy to chat away and the only response required from me is those 'Mmm, mmm,' I'm-a-really-good-listener-noises at the appropriate junctures in the conversation. Of course it's not like I don't want to talk to Ginny, I think I'm actually desperate to, but not right now when I know so little about her situation. And although I learn about changes to the high street (there's a fancy new French café on Poplar Road) and how she spent Christmas (with friends in Nottingham) the one thing I don't glean any information about is her husband, so I let my imagination go to town. I imagine he's called Hugo, works at an art college and specialises in multimedia disciplines (whatever that is). At the weekend he plays football and squash and is currently in training for the London marathon. In addition to this he plays the saxophone, is younger than me, and permanently smells of cinnamon. Make no mistake, Hugo is a right tosser.

I help Ginny unload the shopping from the back of the car and walk up the front path towards her house. It's strange being back here after all these years because during my last extended stay in Birmingham I had actually lived here with Ginny, first as her lodger and then as substantially more than that. We had had a lot of fun times in this house, watching TV, eating takeaway, playing daft games, making each other laugh. Those days now felt like a lifetime ago. The pasts of two altogether different people.

'You've decorated?' I say as we enter the house. The walls in the hallway used to be a pale cream but are now a sophisticated shade of grey.

'You sound surprised.'

'No . . . well yes . . . you know what I mean. It's just that, you know, it's weird when you expect one thing and get another.'

Ginny laughs. 'You've never been good with change, have you?'

We head along the hallway and even though I haven't heard anything to warrant this thought I'm convinced that Ginny's Mr Perfect will be in the kitchen. I brace myself for the impact but the only thing that comes my way when I open the door is an overweight tabby cat.

'Is that Larry or Sanders?' Although I'd never been much of a cat man I'd always had a soft spot for Ginny's when I'd lived here.

'Neither,' she replies, kneeling down to fuss the cat. 'Larry got sick about five years ago and I had to have him put down. Then a month later the same thing happened with Sanders. This one's name is Hank. I got him as a kitten from a rescue centre.' She kisses the top of his head, 'You're my boy, aren't you, Hank?' and right on cue Hank purrs loudly.

Still unsure which moment she will choose to unleash 'Hugo' I enter the kitchen, which has changed too. It's all swanky-looking white gloss units in a not altogether dissimilar style to my own back in London, set against a dark-grey porcelain tiled floor. I set down the shopping on the pale wood counter and she begins to pack it away. For the first time I look at her hand and notice the absence of a wedding ring.

'Do you want a cup of tea?' I ask, even though I haven't the faintest clue about how her kitchen is arranged.

'That would be lovely,' she replies, laughing. 'Be my guest.'

It's clearly a challenge, but one that I feel I am up for and even though I have to open every cupboard to find the mugs and tea bags and every drawer to find the teaspoons, the tea gets made and although it's a small victory it makes me feel great.

'It really is good to see you,' I tell her, as we sip our tea.

'You too. It's been too long. When was the last time?'

'My wedding.'

'Wow. A lot of water under the bridge since then, eh?'

'At least an ocean's worth.'

I decide to ask the question I'd been dying to all evening.

'I heard on the grapevine that you've finally taken the plunge.'

'What do you mean?'

'You know, got married. It's just, I didn't like to ask because – like me – you're not wearing a ring.'

Ginny stands up and pours herself another cup of tea. 'Well I don't know who you're getting your information from, Matt, but they're wrong. I'm not married.'

'Oh,' I say, trying not to sound too pleased. 'I must have got the wrong end of the stick. No one on the scene at all then?'

Ginny laughs. 'Not unless you count Hank.' She fetches a pouch of cat food from a cupboard and forks some into Hank's bowl. I sense that she's not particularly comfortable with the conversation and so I change the subject quickly and tell her about my parents and their plan to move to the country.

'Do you think they're serious?'

'Leave the house where they raised four kids, the site of all our family Christmasses and countless birthdays? No way. That place holds way too many memories.'

'Maybe they want to make some new ones. Not everyone wants to live in the past.'

As a kid it had just been Ginny and her mum and apart from a brief stint living with her nan the house in which we were now sitting had been the only home she had known up to the age of nineteen when she left to go to university in Brighton. Eight years on, having established a career as an art teacher, Ginny returned to Birmingham to look after her mum who was seriously ill. Her mum died within six months of her return, making Ginny at the age of twenty-seven the owner of her own home, and having lived there ever since it now looked like she too was thinking about moving on.

'You're really considering moving?'

'To tell you the truth I think anywhere would be fine if it meant I was making a change and moving on. No one knows more than I do about the importance of keeping hold of memories but it's like I said earlier, you can't always live in the past because if you do you might just find yourself stuck there for ever.'

Before I can get to work considering the deeper implications of her statement she asks if I'm hungry and I tell her that I could eat a horse.

'What sort of thing do you like?'

'I'll take whatever's going.'

'Prawn curry it is then,' she says, 'I got the recipe from a friend of Mum's a few years back. Apparently when she was younger it was what she always asked for when she went to see her so I like to cook it whenever people come over.' She flicks on the radio and the air fills with a song that 'the kids' no doubt think is cool but which makes me think: 'This is how Magic FM listeners are made,' and then she starts grabbing pots and pans and opening cupboards and begins cooking in earnest.

Instructed by Ginny I open a bottle of wine and pour two glasses, leaving hers at the side of the chaos happening at the cooker. It's nice watching her cook and it reminds me of all the amazing meals Lauren used to make. Lauren loves cooking and one of her favourite things is to spend Saturday mornings hunting out ingredients for a recipe from whichever cookbook is in vogue and her Saturday evenings putting the meal together for friends. Not for the first time since moving out of the house I find myself missing Lauren.

'Are you OK?' calls Ginny over the sound of sizzling prawns. 'You seem a bit quiet all of a sudden.'

'I'm fine. I was just a little lost in thought, that's all.' I make a lunge for the first topic that springs to mind. 'Have you heard much from any of the old gang recently? Gershwin seems to have been as bad as me when it comes to keeping up with them.'

'So you've seen Gershwin?'

'Yeah, of course, I saw him the other night for a couple of beers in Pat Kav's. Have you seen much of him?'

'Not lately. How did he seem?'

'Honestly? A bit off. I think something must be going on with him and Zoe. You know how he is normally the life and soul and all that.'

'And you think it's down to Zoe?'

'Well, I'm guessing. He wasn't exactly forthcoming with the details. He wasn't the slightest bit interested in making plans for his fortieth.'

'Maybe it's for the best if he's not feeling up to it.'

Her comment seems a touch pragmatic but I can see her point and I consider texting him on the spot to suggest that we do a joint birthday get-together for the two of us at some point, but then Ginny asks me a question.

'So come on,' she says, 'given your well documented tendency to freak out around big birthdays how are you feeling now the big-four-oh's coming your way? You're not going to lose it this time, are you?'

'Me?' I grin. 'Never. It'll be fine. A walk in the park. How was it for you?'

'Well, the music in the restaurant we went to was too loud, the waiters were too snooty for my liking and I had the worst cold I've had in years but I would have had to be dead not to have had a good time while surrounded by my friends and hopped up to the eyeballs on Benylin and apple mojitos.'

'And how's forty for you now?'

'If you're looking for a positive "Thirty is the new forty" type spin on it you've come to the wrong person,' says Ginny. 'I hate it. I really hate it. I'm tired all the time. I wake up shattered. I go to bed shattered and in between sometimes it's all I can do to resist the temptation to curl up next to the radiator behind my desk when I'm lecturing and take a nap. The worst of it all is that I haven't even got the excuse of having young kids keeping me awake. I'm just tired.'

'Maybe you've got some kind of vitamin deficiency,' I suggest.

Ginny isn't convinced. 'Then again maybe it's because I've said goodbye to my thirties once and for all. I don't feel like I should be forty yet. I don't think it's fair.'

'I know what you mean. Last summer Lauren and I were sitting on the terrace of some bar on the South Bank and the wine was flowing and I looked around the table at all of these great friends of ours and I thought to myself, maybe turning forty won't be so bad . . . the next morning I started to get out of bed to take a shower and my back went. And when I say it went, it wasn't an "I've just pulled a muscle" kind of pain, it was a proper full-on sitcom moment, frozen to the spot, completely terrified that I'd done some kind of permanent damage to myself. It took me three months and eight visits to a chiropractor to recover properly.'

'We're all literally falling apart, aren't we?' says Ginny.

'Just a bit.'

'We need something to keep us together.'

Right on cue the radio that's been on in the background throughout our meal plays 'Don't You Forget About Me'. Ginny looks over at me, wide-eyed and grinning with excitement. This song was our anthem during our sixth-form years, and the soundtrack to not only every great party but needless to say to the one film that we agreed was the best film ever made and the only film that we knew all the words to: *The Breakfast Club*.

Ginny grabs my hands and drags me into the middle of the kitchen and then we turn up the volume and start dancing and singing along. As we move around the kitchen, yelling our 'la, la, la, las' into the air and laughing like idiots all I can think about is how good it feels to be in the presence of someone who has known me for a lifetime.

Like we haven't missed a beat.

Like we're picking up right where we left off.

Like we've been dancing to the same song since for ever.

15

Twenty-three years! How is it even possible that the familiar rhythm of conversation Ginny and I have shared all evening and which had kept the two of us going through the years as underage drinkers, university students, fresh-faced graduates and beyond . . . had been going on for more than twenty-three years? Whether it was the biggest cliché in the book or not it really did seem like it was five minutes since we were seventeen with the world at our feet. Now we were back together and (from what I could gather) neither of us was in possession of the kinds of lives that we'd guessed we'd end up with, we were still as unsure and unsteady about the future as we'd ever been. Wasn't life supposed to get easier as time went on? Wasn't there supposed to be a point set in the future where you would finally understand how this whole 'life' thing worked? How is it that people who can still remember what it was like to have nothing to do and have all day to do it can suddenly find themselves turning forty?

'So,' Ginny says, opening our second bottle of wine of the evening, pouring two glasses and returning to her position on the sofa next to me. 'We haven't done more than skirt around it all evening, but how are you doing, Matt? Divorce is a huge thing and you're acting like it's no big deal but I know you, everything's a big deal, so why don't you tell me how you're really feeling?'

I consider for a millisecond fobbing her off with a glib response, something along the lines of 'Am I being charged for this session, Dr Pascoe?' but I know she'll only accuse me of deflecting, which is annoying because she would be right. The only option here is to man up and tell the truth.

'I feel battered. Bruised if you like. With parents like mine you don't get married thinking that it won't last for ever.'

'So it was Lauren's decision to end things?'

'Well she was the one to bring it up, but I know for a fact that I played my part in that passive-aggressive way I do so well. May I refer you to my two-week relationship with Ruth Morrell when I was nineteen and my month-long fling with Nicky Rowlands when I was twenty-one.'

Ginny laughs. 'I remember them well. You forced both of those poor women to break up with you by being a total and utter git. You're like the very definition of the toxic male.'

'I was doing them a favour. You know as well as I do that the dumper always feels better than the dumpee. I should be thanked, not vilified. It's like those cautionary tales parents tell their children about the bogeyman to keep them safe. In the annals of crap boyfriendom there's a whole chapter about me and my kind. Be warned.'

'But that's not who you are, Matt, and you know it.'

'Maybe it would be easier if I was. The worst thing is that I knew exactly what was happening – we were growing apart – but I just couldn't seem to pull us back together again. Nothing, not the holidays we took, the restaurants we ate in or the money we spent on the house made any difference. What we needed was love like we had at the start, but that kind of love just wasn't there.'

Ginny looks at me intently. 'You still miss her, don't you?'

I nod even though I've barely admitted this to myself. 'Is that wrong?'

Ginny shakes her head. 'It's not wrong but it is hard.'

We talk more about the break-up and I don't know whether it's the wine or the fact we're so at ease with each other but I tell her things I haven't told anyone else. Stuff about how I thought Lauren might be having an affair (she wasn't) and how I nearly had an affair (with a woman I met while on a work trip in Munich and although I liked her a lot just couldn't follow through with it) and stuff about my fear of facing forty divorced and alone. It feels like therapy.

I pick up my wine and take a long gulp in an effort to subdue my self-consciousness. 'Anyway, enough about me, what about you? OK, so you're not hitched, but is there anyone else on the scene? Don't tell me you've been married to your job for the last six years.'

'Oh, Matt, where to begin? It's tough out there.'

'Great! Way to cheer up the about-to-be-divorced guy!'

Ginny laughs. 'Oh, you know what I mean. Funnily enough, I actually met a guy at your wedding who I saw for a little while.'

'That's the first I've heard about it. Who was it?'

'Don't worry, no one of your acquaintance.'

This is getting weird. 'You mean someone from Lauren's side?'

'Look, if you must know it was the DJ.'

'You got off with our wedding DJ?'

'It was a whole thing. I went up to ask for "Dancing Queen" and the next thing I know he's put on the twelve-inch of "Fool's Gold" and we're snogging behind the amplifier for the next nine minutes and fifty-three seconds.'

'Classy.'

'I know. We saw each other for a couple of months but I ended it when for the third weekend in a row he'd got me lugging his decks and lights in and out of numerous function rooms up and down the country. I realised that I'd become a sort of poor man's roadie. He needed an apprentice, not a girlfriend.'

I can't help laughing. 'You know how to pick them, don't you?'

'That's the understatement of the decade. After him there was Mr Serious Artist who borrowed six hundred quid off me and used it to part-fund his research trip to Goa and never came back, then there was Mr Sweet But Too Young, an NQT who bought me flowers, wrote me poetry and cried when I told him it was over; and after him there was Mr Safe

Pair of Hands who was attracted to me because he thought I was arty and edgy but got bored the moment he discovered that I buy my pants from M&S just like everyone else.'

Ginny has me laughing so hard by the end of this sorry tale that I can barely breathe. I attempt to take a sip of wine but it goes down the wrong way and I have a coughing fit so severe that Ginny is forced to come to my aid.

'But seriously,' I say, pausing to take a sip of wine now that I've got my breath back, 'It's criminal that someone like you should still be single. Haven't there been any real contenders in the last six years?'

'There was one.'

'What happened?'

'We wanted different things.'

'Like what?'

'It doesn't matter.'

'How long were you together?'

'About a year.'

'So it was serious?'

'Enough for me to say yes when he proposed.'

'You were engaged? What happened?'

'It's a long story, but it's like I said, we both wanted different things and neither of us was prepared to compromise.'

'And do you miss him?'

'Every second of every day.' Ginny wipes her eyes. I hadn't noticed her tears until now. I wish we'd never ventured into this terrain.

'Look at us, we're a right mess. What we need is to bring

the mood back up. You used to go out with a wedding DJ – what would he play right now to liven up the room?'

Ginny drains the last of her wine and stands up suddenly. 'I've got just the thing,' she declares and leaves the room only to return a few minutes later clutching a paint-splattered portable stereo, a framed photo and what looks like a cassette tape.

'What's going on here then?'

'Prepare to journey back through the mists of time,' says Ginny, tossing the cassette into my lap. I pick it up and read the label. Written in biro in my own barely legible scrawl are the words: *Party Toons!!!!* I recognise it immediately.

'I can't believe you've still got this!'

'Funnily enough neither can I. I only came across it recently when I was redecorating the spare room. It was in a plastic bag with a whole bunch of other stuff from my student days. It really put a smile on my face.'

I was eighteen when I put together this tape for one of Ginny's legendary house parties and it was wheeled out at every opportunity thereafter. I can remember the care I'd taken over it, selecting the tracks, balancing the commercial with the obscure and attempting to show off the depth of my musical knowledge gleaned from years of reading the *NME*. I try to remember exactly what I'd put on there: Public Enemy, New Order, The Wonderstuff, James Brown, Madonna, Bowie and if I'm not mistaken, a bit of Elvis too.

I gesture to the portable stereo. 'Does that thing work then?'

'Listen mate, this was state of the art when I got it and it's lasted way longer than the last iPod I bought I'll have you know.'

I throw the tape to her and she pops it into the machine, bends down, plugs it in and presses play. It's Elvis singing 'Kentucky Rain'.

'I haven't heard this in years! Do you remember how we used to sing this on our way home from the King's Arms? Your neighbours must have loved us.'

'I'm sure they didn't mind that much. We were young.'

'And stupid.'

'And tone deaf.'

She hands me the framed photo. 'Remember this?'

It's a picture of the old gang: me, Ginny, Gershwin, Pete, Bev, Katrina and Elliot taken at school on the day we got our A level results. We all look so young, so innocent of what the world had in store for us which was no bad thing given that Elliot was taken from us so soon afterwards.

'Where did you find this?'

'In the same bag as the tape. I had it blown up at a shop on the high street. Can you believe this is us? We look like babies and yet we felt so grown up, like we knew it all.' Ginny laughs. 'We didn't know anything.'

'I wouldn't go that far. There are some things I'm pretty sure we knew even then.'

'Like what?'

I take the photo from her hands and set it carefully down on the coffee table in front of us and as 'Kentucky Rain' fades out I lean across and kiss her. And for the first time since leaving London I finally feel like I'm home.

16

It's just after eleven the following morning and I'm curled up in bed next to Ginny. We've been awake for a while and after chatting about nothing in particular have now entered some way into what I believe will be a protracted period of comfortable silence.

'What are you thinking?'

As I look at her lying in the crook of my arm I'm desperate to absorb everything I see: her sleepy eyes, bed hair, make-up-free face. She looks completely and utterly beautiful.

'Are you really asking me this? Or are you just winding me up?'

Ginny laughs and rolls on to her side until her naked thigh is pressed right up against my own. 'You'll never know now will you? So just spill the beans and tell me what you're trying to hide.'

'Nothing.'

Ginny gives me her hardest stare which, if truth be told, verges on the adorable. 'You're lying, Beckford. And do you know how I know you're lying? I know because I can see it in your eyes. You do a bit of a squinty thing when you're lying. You always have done and you're doing it now.'

'I do not do any kind of "squinty" thing,' I reply scowling even though I know it's true, 'and I reject the allegation that I do.'

'Fine,' says Ginny, staring right into my eyes in a manner so playful that I want to rewind time so that I can kiss her for the first time in a decade all over again. 'If you're not lying why don't you just tell me what it was you were thinking and we can move on to talking about something else?'

'You don't really want to know what I'm thinking do you?' I tell her. 'Asking blokes what they're thinking is just one of those questions women ask men when they're in an awkward situation and don't know what else to say.'

'Hmm,' says Ginny. 'Is that what you think this is? An awkward situation?'

I refuse to take the bait. 'Now I know for sure you're just trying to wind me up.'

'For the last time, I'm not trying to wind you up, that's just an added bonus. I want to know what you were thinking when I asked the question and I want to know now!'

She's not going to let this go.

'Fine,' I say, 'the truth is: I was thinking about a beach.'

'A beach?'

'Ned's Beach on Lord Howe Island to be exact. I went there for a long weekend with a couple of mates back when I was in Oz. Honestly Ginny, it's got to be one of the most beautiful places on earth. The sea's gin-and-tonic clear, you can hand-feed the kingfish that live there, the whole place is just amazing. You'd love it.'

'It sounds fantastic. What made you think of that?'

'No reason.'

Ginny laughs. 'There you are with the lies again, Beckford. You're as bad as some of the kids I teach. Come on, spill the beans.'

'Nothing . . . it's stupid . . . can we just drop it?'

Ginny sits up, pulling the duvet around her, her face determined. 'No we can't just drop it, actually. I want to know.'

'Are you really going to have an argument with me about this? What's wrong with you?'

'What's wrong with you more like? Why won't you tell me? I mean, is it really that big a deal?' She reaches down to the floor, picks up her top and pulls it on over her head.

I look at her, bewildered. 'What are you doing?'

'What does it look like I'm doing? Getting dressed.'

'And you're doing this because I won't tell you what I'm thinking.'

'No,' she says, 'I'm doing this because I'm sick and tired of the way men always have to keep every tiny thing bottled up. This was a mistake, and I'd like it if you'd leave.'

'Fine, you want to know why I was thinking about that beach? Well here goes: I was thinking about how much I'd like to go there with you one day.'

Ginny stops dressing and looks at me. 'Really?'

'Yes, really.'

'So why didn't you just say that?'

'Because it would have been weird.'

Ginny shakes her head. 'No it wouldn't.' She takes my hand in hers. 'Where else would you like to show me?'

'New York. You've never been, have you?'

'Never.'

'You'd love it. It's got parks, museums, culture, the lot. And I'd love to show you China too. The Great Wall at Mutianyu, the Forbidden City, the Jiuzhaigou Valley nature reserve, the list is—'

'Let's do it.'

I look at Ginny blankly. 'Do what?'

'Go travelling. You want to show me these places, and believe me I want to see them. We should do it, Matt. I'm absolutely serious. What's really stopping us? I'm not massively in love with my job and you haven't got one, neither of us has got kids or ties keeping us here and, let's face it, we could both do with a break. We should do it. Take a grown-up gap year and see the world.'

'You're insane,' I say. 'It's just not going to happen.'

'Why not? Give me one good reason why we shouldn't book a round-the-world ticket right now? Just think of the adventures we'd have—'

'Are you joking? I can think of half a dozen without trying!'

'Like?'

'The fact that I'm broke.'

'Problem solved: I'll loan you the money.'

'And if we're really talking about problems, what about all this?'

'All what?'

113

'You, me, and last night . . . well, we haven't really discussed it have we?'

'What's to discuss?'

'The fact that I'm still married.'

'And?'

'The fact that until last night I hadn't seen you in six years.'

'And?'

'What's wrong with you? Are you doing this to wind me up? There don't need to be any more "ands", those are enough!'

'I'm not sure they are,' says Ginny. 'You want to do this but you're just scared to admit it. If you can look me in the eyes and tell me that those two things are genuinely stopping you from going travelling with me I promise you I won't mention it again.'

'And you won't be weird about it either?'

'Not even slightly.'

'Let's do this.' I sit up and position myself so that I can look into Ginny's eyes. 'I, Matthew Beckford, do solemnly declare that . . .' I stop. It's like something out of a film. I can't get the words out. I try again. 'I, Matthew Beckford, do solemnly declare that . . .' I stop again. This is ridiculous. I can't really be considering this, can I? I know I had this big plan to get back together with Ginny but even at my most deluded I never thought it would happen. Thinking about Ginny was just a way to get myself out of a rut and give me something to focus on. I didn't really love her. How could I after all this time apart? We're not the same people we were back when we were seventeen, not even close! How could anything we started up now be other than a major disaster? I steel myself for one last try.

'I can't do it.'

'I know.'

'So what does that mean?'

Ginny laughs. 'I think it means that you need to kiss me right now.'

Like two giddy teenagers in love Ginny and I spend the rest of the morning reeling off names of yet more places we'd like to see, ordering *Rough Guide* travel books off the internet and drawing up an itinerary. It's like a dream. I can hardly believe it. Yesterday I had nothing positive on my horizon and today I'm looking forward to going round the world with a woman who up until yesterday I thought was married. But even though it feels wild and unpredictable, at the same time it feels real. Solid even. After all, Ginny and I are standing on the foundations of two decades' worth of friendship.

Later that morning we get dressed and go for breakfast at a café on York Road buying a couple of newspapers on the way. Ginny has a veggie burger thing and I have the full English breakfast and a pot of tea and all we do is talk about the trip, leaving our papers on the table unread beside us. When we finish our meal I find myself looking around at the other couples in the café, most of who appear to be a good decade younger than us. How many of them have known the person they slept with last night for over half a lifetime? How many of them could claim to really know the person sitting opposite them right now as well as I know Ginny?

Meal over, we take a stroll along the high street, neither of us wanting this time to end, but once we've had our fill of window-shopping a decision needs to be made.

'We could always go back to yours,' I say, yawning.

'Bad idea. I have a ton of work to catch up on and I won't get any of it done with you there to distract me.'

'I'll be on my best behaviour, I promise.'

Ginny shakes her head.

I know she's right. Why would I waste time sleeping when I could be awake with her instead? 'Well, I want to see you tomorrow then. We'll do lunch or something.'

'It's a date.'

On the corner we kiss like a couple of teenagers and say our goodbyes.

'I'll text you,' she says and gives me a final kiss.

I begin walking away but then I turn round and run after her, catching up with her outside a tiny second-hand record shop. 'This is real isn't it?' I ask her over the booming bass of a dub reggae track coming through the open door. 'It's not just in my head, is it?'

Ginny shakes her head and I feel reassured. 'It's not just in yours, Matt, it's in mine too.'

*   *   *

Three things occur to me as I root around in my pockets for the keys to my parents' house. First, I am still wearing last night's clothes (making me the very definition of a dirty stopout) second, that I couldn't care less about this and third that I left my parents' sandwich stuff in Ginny's kitchen. Still, not even misplaced shopping can dampen my spirits. I feel like doing cartwheels down the street and high-fiving complete strangers. I feel good. So good in fact that I want to call up Gershwin (the only person in the world who will appreciate the magnitude of my news) and tell him (without going into detail of course) all about my reunion with Ginny. I don't, because if I have noticed anything about men of my generation of late (myself included) it's that while we're quite happy to spout forth about the demise of a relationship, when it comes to new relationships we are (without exception) hopelessly coy about the subject of sex as though it's some kind of Edwardian 'bad form' once you get past the age of thirty-five. Still, after a year that has seen all kinds of trouble come my way, I sort of miss being able to brag about my success. And it isn't just that Ginny and I spent the whole night making each other laugh with stupid jokes, or that we spent as much time in bed as we did out of it, or even our mad jaunt around the world; no, what really makes it so amazing is that I can 100 per cent picture this thing going all the way. I'm talking a joint mortgage, kids and maybe (once I'd got my decree absolute) marriage too. All that matters is that finally there's light at the end of the tunnel and I'm convinced that this time at least it's not a train coming the other way.

Mum calls out to me as I close the front door behind me. I find her in the kitchen wearing her sternest of faces. I know exactly what she's going to say.

'I know, I know,' I tell her, 'you're right, I should've called.'

'So why didn't you? Would it have killed you to give me or your father a ring? You could've been lying dead in a ditch!'

I think about pointing out that a) I had been nowhere near a ditch and b) I was off to Ginny's for dinner but I stop myself on the grounds that this wasn't the point she is making. The point is that I have been inconsiderate and given my massively good mood I have no qualms in admitting that I am in the wrong.

I apologise. 'You're absolutely right. I have no excuse and I promise it won't happen again.'

She eyes me warily. I normally don't give in this easily 'And where have you been all this time?'

'At Gershwin's.' Now is not the time to start oversharing with my parents about my private life. 'I bumped into him when I was with Ginny and we all went out and didn't get back until early this morning . . . and so we crashed at Gershwin's.'

Mum shakes her head in bemusement. What I have just said makes no sense to her whatsoever.

'I don't know what's wrong with you,' she says. 'A man your age shouldn't be out all hours. You're not twenty-one any more!'

There's a certain irony in Mum of all people reminding me of this fact but I hold up my ha·ds in submission. 'Absolutely right. No more late nights for ·ie unless I call first.' I give her a kiss on the cheek because that's how good I'm feeling right now. 'Consider me suitably chastised.'

Sensing there's something wrong but not quite sure what it might be Mum reluctantly disappears into the garden. My phone buzzes. It's a text from Ginny: *Hey you, just wanted to thank you for a lovely night and a cracking afternoon xxx G.* And I reply: *Had a great time too. Can't wait to see you again. M x.* I think that might be it but as I'm heading upstairs my phone buzzes once more. *I know you've probably got a lot going on in your head right now but I want to give you written proof that I mean what I say and so here goes: THIS IS REAL. And don't you forget it. G xxx.*

17

'Okey-dokey,' says our travel expert, Jean, with an overdramatic flourish, 'that's the last of the boring paperwork out of the way. Now all you need to do is tell me how you'll be paying today and we'll be done.'

I look nervously at Ginny. There are no words to describe how great this past week has been. I've spent pretty much every night at Ginny's and I'm completely convinced by what we have together but even so I still can't quite believe that I'm about to buy a ticket that will see me visiting India, Vietnam, Thailand, Bali, China, Australia, New Zealand, Fiji and the USA with Ginny. Doing something this reckless when I am this happy feels like I am giving my luck one shove too far.

'Can we have a minute?' I say to Jean as Ginny reaches in her purse for her credit card.

'Not a problem,' says Jean, though her face says otherwise, and as I rise from the chair positioned in front of her desk Ginny laughs and shakes her head apologetically as though I am to be pitied rather than admonished.

'You're freaking out again, aren't you?' says Ginny, joining me in a far corner of the shop next to the window showing all the best flight deals.

'No . . . I'm not,' I reply too quickly. 'OK, yeah I am just a bit but you've got to remember this is a big deal, Gin, a really big deal. These tickets are non-refundable. Which means you're going to have to follow through with everything we've planned from giving up the job you've done for the last twelve years to renting out your house for at least a year—'

'And having the time of my life travelling around the world with a gorgeous but highly neurotic guy I've known half my life.' Ginny laughs and kisses me. 'I've thought it through, Matt, and if it was up to me we'd be going next week rather the end of next term. Since we started making these plans I've felt more alive, more excited, more everything and it's all because of you! I know you think we should be sensible: take things slowly and see how they go. And before my last birthday I would've agreed with you . . . but not now. If I've learned anything since turning forty it's that life's too short for the sensible option. Sometimes you have to just go with your gut and see where it takes you. So what do you say?'

'You had me at "gorgeous", ' I reply. Breaking out into a grin I grab her by the hand and head back to Jean's desk.

Jean looks up from her computer screen. 'All decided?'

'All decided indeed.' On cue Ginny hands over her credit card. A flurry of jabs at the card machine's key pad and the job is done. Ginny (on my behalf as well as her own) has just committed the best part of two thousand pounds that she can ill afford to go on a trip with a man who was never even a proper boyfriend.

Jean hands Ginny the printed receipts and informs her that our tickets will be emailed two weeks before we're due to fly. We thank her, stand up and leave. Straight away my mind starts churning over the full impact of what I've done and more importantly what I'll need to do now. I'll have to find a way of telling my parents that won't make me sound insane, and of course I've got to find a way to explain to Lauren that she'll have to sort out the whole house sale thing on her own and maybe even that I've found someone new. It's all going to be pretty hard to do but as Ginny and I head back to the Bullring car park a huge grin spreads across my face. I'm happy. I'm doing this crazy, reckless, financially irresponsible thing and nothing, not divorce, unemployment or even turning forty is going to stop me seeing it through.

That evening we go to a Moroccan restaurant in Moseley and our only topic of conversation is the trip. Of all the plans I have ever made this one feels like it's going to pay the greatest dividends, to clarify part two of the story of my life. Everything I need to know will be somewhere out there waiting for me to stumble across it. Ginny feels exactly the same. This trip is going to be the making of us.

As usual I stay over at Ginny's that night but in the morning I go back to Mum and Dad's because Ginny's got to pack for a five-day field trip to Barcelona with some of her sixth-form students.

'It'll go faster than you think,' she says as we stand on her doorstep, 'and I've promised myself that next weekend I'm not going to do a single shred of work. It'll just be you, me and whatever you want to do.'

'Sounds like a great plan.' We kiss one last time and then I leave.

I decide to try phoning Gershwin. I'd called and left a message earlier in the week and he still hasn't got back to me and even though he's busy at work I can't help but think there's something more to it. I pull out my phone and try his number but after several rings it goes through to voicemail and so I leave yet another message: 'Mate, it's me. Just checking in. Have news for you so ring or text soon and we'll go for a pint.'

At home my parents are in the garden where Dad is weeding his vegetable patch and Mum is hanging out the washing. This could be the moment that I tell them my plans and as I open my mouth my dad stops digging and looks at me.

'Were your ears burning?'

I look at Dad, confused. 'Why should they be?'

'Your mum and I were just commenting how nice it's been having you home. We were thinking you might like to come to your sister's again next weekend.'

'I'm sorry I can't, Dad,' I reply, 'I've got plans for next weekend but I'm definitely free the weekend after.'

Mum is clearly annoyed at my unwillingness to get into line. 'You're very busy for a man with no job.'

Dad rolls his eyes and nods his head towards the house. 'I'd make your escape now son, if you know what's good for you.'

Taking my dad's cue I head up for a shower but as I'm rummaging in my drawers for clean underwear my phone buzzes with a message from Ginny: *Miss you already! Try not to be too miserable without me!*. I reply straight away: *Have a great time! Will try and keep it together until you get back!* and then I don't hear from her again until Monday evening: *Arrived safely. Hostel is awful but students don't seem to have noticed as they are too busy trying to get off with each other. Miss you, G x.* Late on Tuesday night I get another text: *Am in bar with students watching live music. Think after our world trip we should move to Barcelona and open a bed and breakfast. What do you think? Night, night G x PS Will text again in morning!*

Ginny doesn't text me the following morning or indeed that night. When her text silence continues throughout Thursday morning I begin to imagine that she's had some kind of accident but when I ring it goes straight through to voicemail. In the end I leave three voicemails, send three texts and even leave a message at the youth hostel with my phone number in case she's somehow lost it. But it's only on Friday morning, having barely slept, that I get a message. The contents take me completely by surprise: *I'm so sorry, Matt, but I can't follow through with our plans any more. Please don't think too terribly of me. It's been the most difficult decision of my life to make. Please promise me you'll take the trip anyway. You deserve to be happy. Take care, Ginny x.*

As I return my phone to the bedside table I close my eyes trying to block out all of the self-directed anger I feel. I feel stupid. Stupid and embarrassed. How did I not see this coming? How did I ever think that this thing with Ginny would work? It's not like I hadn't anticipated a car-crash ending from the moment we first kissed or hadn't appreciated that the odds of the crash happening sooner rather than later had doubled the moment we started making plans to go travelling. I mean, who does that? Who gets together with a 'not quite ex' that they haven't seen in six years and the very next day starts making plans to spend a year travelling around the world with them? A year ago I would never have entertained this kind of recklessness and yet here I am making decisions that even a six-year-old would think twice about.

I need a drink.

I get dressed and go and find one.

'Nice weather we're having isn't it?'

I glance up from my fourth pint of the afternoon at the crumpled old bloke sitting opposite and grinning inanely. He's wearing a stained black suit jacket over a bright green zip-up cardigan. In front of him is a half-drunk pint of mild and a bedraggled newspaper that like him has seen better days. He could be me thirty years from now. Turning seventy, now's there's a thought.

'Brilliant,' I reply. It's been chucking it down all day as we're well aware. 'Easily the best day of the year!'

'Good one.' The old bloke chuckles so hard that he hacks up something dreadful from his lungs, which he spits into a handkerchief.

The pub I'm in is the kind of cool, down-with-the-kids drinking establishment that features arty-looking second-hand chairs and posters for various drum 'n' bass club nights, but back in the day it had held a special place in my heart for being where Ginny and I, along with the rest of our friends, had spent many hours watching long-forgotten local bands with ridiculous names in its upstairs function room. I purposely chose it as my destination because I feel like torturing myself and what better way than to select a venue where one New Year's Eve some twenty years ago you and the woman who's just broken your heart spent a good portion of the night groping each other near the upstairs gents' toilets?

And as much as I'd like to blame my behaviour on my separation, or quitting my job, or even turning forty, the real problem here is all the time I have wasted. Time that I'm never going to get back. Whenever I look back on my life all I see is fragments: stints working here, relationships happening there, never a whole picture, and certainly never a picture like that of my own father. By the time Dad was forty he had three kids, a wife to whom he'd been married for ten years and a job that he'd had since turning twenty-one. What did I have to show by comparison? A half-decent career that I'd abandoned just as I was about to reap the rewards of years of hard work, a failed marriage, a big house in London that I can't afford to live in and a long, long line of failed relationships: it isn't exactly the stuff carved on to headstones.

'Got a lot on your mind have ya?'

It's the crumpled old bloke again. I raise my glass towards him and nod.

'Woman trouble?'

'Of a kind.'

'They're not worth it.'

'Do you think?'

'I know. Take it from me, big man. You're better off on your own.'

For a moment I seriously considered that my unwanted companion wasn't just some random alcoholic, but a wise old guru sent to show me the true way. Then he coughs again and pulls out his filthy handkerchief and that convinces me that he's not. He catches me looking at him as he spits into his handkerchief again. 'Catarrh,' he explains.

'You should see a doctor about that. It can turn nasty.'

'Doctors? I've got all the medicine I need right here!' He gestures to his pint.

It's time for me to go. 'Good to talk to you,' I say to the crumpled old bloke and then I hand him a fiver and tell him to have a drink on me.

His face lights up. 'You're a good man. A good man indeed.'

'You're right,' I say, as it dawns on me that I've drunk just about enough to think turning up at Ginny's school is a good idea, 'I just wish a few more people knew it.'

18

I'm sitting on a bench opposite the main entrance to Ginny's school. There are kids dotted about playing football and chasing each other around the playground but to them I am invisible: just a bloke on a bench. I don't have to wait too long before I spot Ginny, dressed smartly in a long black woollen coat and dark trousers and carrying a heavy leather bag. She exits the building and begins walking over to the car park. I don't have a clue what I'm going to say to her. Her text clearly indicates that her mind's made up and it isn't as though I have been half expecting her to change her mind. I mean, I've just stopped living with my wife, Ginny's recently come out of what seems to be a pretty intense relationship and our solution was to book ourselves round-the-world tickets and make out like we're teenagers on a gap year? It was never going to work, yet here I am, determined to change her mind. Maybe this is why people have jobs: having too much time on your hands is a guaranteed way to get yourself into trouble.

I call out her name and she looks over at me.

'How long have you been waiting?'

'Not long.'

'Have you been drinking?'

'Not excessively.'

Ginny shakes her head. My presence here is making her sad. 'I wish you hadn't come.'

'I haven't come to shout. I just want to talk.'

'There's nothing to say, Matt.'

'Ten minutes,' I say, 'that's all I ask.'

She briefly glances over at her car as though imagining herself escaping and then sets her bag on the ground and sits down on the bench. It's only as I sit down too that I realise this is the same bench on which we first kissed all those years ago.

I wonder if Ginny's even aware of this bench's place in our joint history.

'How was your day?'

'Long,' she says. 'We only got back from the trip just after lunch but since then I've witnessed a student teacher being reduced to tears by a fellow member of staff, two fights in the playground and a couple of policemen escorting three year-eleven boys off the premises. It'd be quieter in Beirut.'

'So you wouldn't recommend teaching?'

'Who to? You?'

I nod even though the thought has only just occurred to me. 'I need to find myself a new career and they're always saying how fulfilling teaching is.'

'Who are "they"?' She sighs and rubs her eyes. 'Don't do it. The hours are too long, the job satisfaction virtually nil and the remuneration pitiful. Take it from me, you'd hate it. I know I do.'

We watch a couple of pupils walk by kicking a football between them. With different haircuts, fatter ties and yet still carrying the same Gola sports bags (do those things never go out of fashion?) they could've been Gershwin and me back in our school days.

I decide to get to the point. 'So are we going to talk about this or what?'

'What is there to say? I feel awful about it, Matt. You must know that I didn't make this decision lightly.'

'But I don't understand why you reached it at all. What's happened to change your mind?'

'It doesn't matter what happened. My mind's made up and it's not going to change.'

'But was it me? Something I said or did? I just need to know.'

Ginny places her hand on my arm and I sense that her steely resolve is finally melting. 'It wasn't you. These past few days have been some of the best I've ever had.'

'Well that's how I feel too,' I say, 'so what's changed your mind? I know I don't have the best track record. I know I've let you down in the past but this . . . this would've been different.'

Ginny stands up. 'I've got to go.'

'So that's it?' I stand up too. 'That's all you've got to say?'

'Yes.'

'And nothing I can say will make a difference?' I'd promise her the world and everything in it even though it isn't mine to give. 'Look, Ginny, please, I'm begging you, let's just try and work it out.'

Ginny picks up her bags and starts walking towards the car park.

I'm rooted to the spot, my head spinning, then a thought occurs to my addled brain and suddenly it all makes sense.

'You've gone back to your ex, haven't you?'

Ginny stops dead in her tracks and before she's even opened her mouth I know it's true. I can see it in her eyes, in her face, in her body language. She begins to cry. 'He's changed his mind, promised you whatever it was that you wanted and now you've gone back to him.'

'I never meant to hurt you like this.'

'This was our bench,' I say.

Ginny looks confused. 'What?'

'Nothing,' I reply, and then I stand up and walk away.

There are none of the usual signs of life when I reach home and I find out why from a note for me in my mum's handwriting on the kitchen counter:

Have gone to Yvonne's. Shouldn't be back too late. Help yourself to whatever you want from the fridge. Love, Mum.

It feels odd being in the house on my own. I never liked it when I was kid and I'm still not that keen now. I always remember this house being full of life. With just me, it feels cold and empty and I find myself wishing that my parents had already returned so that I could hear something other than my own thoughts.

I should have known that ex of hers was going to pop up out of nowhere and wreck everything because that's what exes do best. They give the impression they're out of the picture just long enough for you to think you're safe and then in a puff of smoke, they reappear claiming a change of damascene proportions.

It had even happened to me a couple of times in Oz. Jenna, a colleague from work who I'd started seeing a few months after I moved to Sydney, got back with her ex-boyfriend six weeks into our relationship because he was allegedly 'filled with regret' over their break-up which he'd instituted and then a year later my fledgling relationship with Thalia, a single mum who I met at a party in Melbourne, was scuppered by the return of an ex-husband determined to 'clean up his act'.

And this, I suppose, is one of the intrinsic problems of dating when you're my age: too many people over thirty-five have baggage, and the fact that they choose to carry it rather than, say, putting it in a locker and forgetting about it should tell you everything you need to know. They carry the baggage because the baggage still has value. It was true of Jenna, it was true of Thalia and it's true for Ginny and her ex too. My guess is that the 'something' that happened to her in Barcelona was a call from her ex-fiancé that convinced her he had changed. Faced with the choice of the couple of shabby carrier bags she had with me or the embossed leather storage trunk she had with the guy she'd planned to marry and who would give her the family she longed for, I hadn't stood a chance.

As I go upstairs for a shower I pass my room and spot the papers Lauren sent me to sign lying on the bedside table. She'd already texted me three times but I just couldn't bring myself to look at them. Reaching for a pen I sign the papers one after the other, tuck them inside the stamped addressed envelope that she'd enclosed and seal it up. It feels good to have ticked this one thing off. Almost the beginning of a new era: one where I no longer hang on desperately to the past. This nice idea is proved wrong in a matter of minutes when my phone vibrates and I practically leap on it, hoping that it might be a message from Ginny. But it isn't. It's just another text from Lauren asking about the papers. I tell her they're in the post and then switch off my phone.

For the next few days I pretty much go to seed. I don't go out, I field a number of texts from Jason Cleveland asking me when I'm free for a drink, I barely leave my room and I don't speak to anyone other than my parents. Just as I'm beginning to wonder if what remains of my thirties is going to seep away down the plughole of my existence I get a text from an old workmate telling me that he's going to be up in Birmingham for the weekend and did I fancy joining him and some friends for a night out. Unlike Jason Cleveland's proposed night out (which I know will be as horrible as it is beery) this is exactly what I need right now, something fun and out of the ordinary to look forward to, so I text back straight away and get the details.

As the date gets closer, I'm feeling more optimistic. I emerge from my room, even take myself out for a run and on the day he's coming up I resolve that this night out will mark the end of me thinking about Ginny. This will be the weekend when I rid her from my head and heart for good. I'll go out with my old mate, maybe meet someone new and that will be it. I will have officially moved on from my past.

In preparation I take myself up to the high street for a haircut (same as always: short all over) and to Superdrug to replenish my toiletries. I narrowly manage to avoid an encounter in WHSmith with Alice O'Conner (then, the girl most likely to get her elder brother Gary to punch your lights out for no good reason; now, harassed mother of three).

Feeling that the high street is no longer a safe place for me I head home past Peacocks and am stopped in my tracks by a group of three glamorous teenage girls – all lipstick and shopping bags – coming out of the shop. One of them is Gershwin's daughter, Charlotte.

I've known Charlotte since she was a baby so it's hard to think of her as anything else but seeing her, oblivious of the leers of a passing group of teenage boys, it's clear that she is anything but. She doesn't look older than her biological age or anything – she looks and dresses like a fourteen-year-old girl – no, the shocking thing is that she looks like the kind of fourteen-year-old girl for whom any teenage boy would willingly lay down his life if she asked him. It isn't just her curls of dark brown hair, her flawless skin, or her cooler-than-thou sense of style. It's the fact that it is all contained in one perfectly formed single entity. On Gershwin's behalf I want to protect this beautiful girl with her whole life in front of her by locating a sufficiently hefty stick with which to fend off the youths who would inevitably swarm around her if left unattended.

'You do know that I'm going to have to have a word with your dad about locking you up, don't you?' I joke as I throw menacing glances in the boys' direction. 'Either that, or lock up every single boy between the ages of thirteen and eighteen.'

'You're so embarrassing,' she says, throwing her arms round me. 'When did you get back from London?'

'I've actually been here a while but I've been a bit busy.' I look down at the vast array of shopping bags clutched in her hands. 'You're flush, aren't you? What's the occasion? I haven't missed another one of your birthdays, have I?'

She laughs and shakes her head. 'No, not this time. Dad gave me some money and told me to spend it how I wanted.'

That didn't sound like the Gershwin I knew. 'Your dad gave you money just like that? I bet you nagged him to death for it.'

'Didn't have to this time. He's so happy that I reckon he would've given me a Chanel handbag if I'd asked for one.'

'Really? Last time I saw your dad he was a right misery.'

'That was because he'd fallen out with his girlfriend,' she says matter-of-factly. 'Thankfully they're back together now so everything's sorted.'

This didn't make any sense. 'Since when did your dad have a girlfriend?'

'He's had one for ages. Before the split they were even living together.'

'Are you sure?'

'Of course I am!'

'This is weird. I saw your dad only a little while ago and he never said a word about any girlfriend.'

Charlotte shrugs. 'Maybe he was too down to talk about it. You know what Dad's like – it's impossible to get anything out of him when he's in a mood.'

'So who is she, this woman? Is she nice?'

'Maybe this is something you need to talk to Dad about,' says Charlotte. 'I don't want to cause any trouble.'

'Of course you don't. And I can't imagine any reason there would be.'

'It's Ginny,' she says. 'I thought you knew. I thought everyone knew.'

19

'I can't believe he didn't tell you,' says Zoe. She pushes the tin of biscuits on the table in my direction. 'You wait till I see him, I'll give him a right earful . . . treating you like that and dropping Charlotte in it too! What was he thinking?'

Having accepted Charlotte's offer to 'come back to mine and talk to Mum' I'm now sitting at Gershwin's ex-wife's kitchen table having just had confirmation of everything that my goddaughter had told me. Ginny's mysterious ex, the one she told me she missed 'every single day', is none other than my best friend.

'I mean . . . how did it even happen?' I refuse Zoe's offer of biscuits and concentrate on the mug of tea in my hands. I'd never have put Ginny and Gershwin together in a million years. 'Did they always fancy each other?'

Zoe pulls her chair up closer to the table. 'The first I heard of it was about a year ago when Charlotte told me that he and Ginny took her to the theatre to see a play that one of Ginny's friends was in. Charlotte said that the whole time they were there her dad kept acting really odd and making comments about how he and Ginny were just good friends.

The first thing that Charlotte said the minute she walked through the front door was: 'I think Dad's seeing Ginny.'

'So when did he tell you what was going on?'

'It must have been a week or two later. He dropped off Charlotte after a weekend at his and just came out with it. I'd long since stopped caring what he got up to but as it happened I'd always really liked Ginny – she's a lovely girl – and so I was pleased that at least Charlotte would be able to get on with her. But I told him at the time: "Look, I'm glad you're moving on and everything but have you spoken to Matt about it?" because, you know, I knew you and Ginny had history.'

'And what did he say to that?'

Zoe shrugs and rolls her eyes. 'You know what he's like. He was all, yeah, yeah, yeah . . . Matt's married, he's fine about it so I just assumed that he'd get round to telling you in his own time.'

'And this was when exactly?'

'About ten months ago although I'm guessing they'd been together a while if he was bothering to tell me.'

'And they lived together?'

'At Gershwin's place. I don't think it was official, mind you, but she was always round there whenever I picked up Charlotte and I did notice a few items that Gershwin hadn't had a hand in buying if you know what I mean.'

'And what about their engagement?'

'Well, that's where it gets tricky because he didn't talk to me directly about it. From what I can gather from Charlotte, around the beginning of August he started asking how she felt about the idea of him getting married again and dropping hints that he was about to propose to Ginny. Then a few weeks later it was all over.'

'But you don't know why.'

Zoe pulls a face as if to say: 'Beats me,' and leans back in her chair. 'Maybe she came to her senses. But Charlotte will vouch for this: he was a right misery from the moment they broke up. If he wasn't yelling at Charlotte over the smallest thing he was trying to pick a fight with me. He was gutted when they split and he didn't care who knew it.'

'And now they're back together?'

'About a week ago he took Charlotte for dinner and when they turned up at the restaurant Ginny was there and they were all over each other.'

The words 'all over each other' flash up in my head like one of those roadside signs warning you that you're going over thirty. How could she possibly have gone from wanting to go travelling with me to being 'all over' my best friend? I want to ask Zoe more but Charlotte bursts in with a typical rush of teenage energy, wearing the outfit that she's just bought.

'What do you think?'

'Where are you off to?'

'A party at my friend's house.'

'Well in that case I think it's great.' She twirls in the middle of the kitchen in a sparkly silver dress, black leggings and silver plimsolls: the very definition of a party outfit. 'You'll definitely have all the boys after you looking like that.'

'Yuck,' she replies, but she's grinning with so much pride that all I can see are teeth.

'Matt and I are still talking,' says Zoe, 'so as lovely as you are would you mind taking your little fashion parade elsewhere?'

'I'm going to go and show Jimmy,' she says, heading through the back door into the garden to show Zoe's partner.

'I should probably go.'

'You don't have to. Jimmy's fine with you being here.'

'It's not that,' I reply, even though it is a bit weird seeing her doing the domestic thing with this nice enough guy who isn't Gershwin. 'It's getting late and I feel like I've taken up enough of your time already.'

'It's no trouble,' she says, 'I know how much of a shock this must be even if you and Ginny haven't been together in a long time.'

Now is not the time to tell her about my more recent interactions with Ginny. 'I just wish he'd told me.'

'And Ginny didn't mention it either?' Zoe looks thoroughly exasperated on my behalf. 'That pair are both as bad as each other.'

I pour the remains of my tea down the sink and wash out the mug and Zoe comes across and briefly touches my arm. 'I'm so sorry that it didn't work out for you and Lauren. I know it's awful right now but I'm living proof that you can get through it.'

'Thanks,' I reply, 'I really mean that.'

'We only know each other through Gershwin,' she says, drying my mug on a tea towel. 'But I've always felt that you were my friend too. Do you remember when you volunteered for babysitting duties with Charlotte when I was doing day shifts at the childrens' hospital?'

'How could I forget being left in charge of an actual three-year-old?'

'Ah, but you loved it didn't you?'

'Every second.' I think back to the afternoon we spent listening to Michael Jackson records while bouncing on her parents' bed. 'They were good times, the best. I just wish I'd known that back then . . . I would've made more of an effort to savour them.'

Heading home I field texts about arrangements for the night ahead, feeling like I've just been in a head-on-collision with a truck. I go over everything I've learned this afternoon and combine it with the little that I already know:

1. Less than a year ago Ginny and Gershwin went from being friends to being lovers.

2. They both chose to keep their relationship a secret from me.

3. At some point Gershwin proposed to Ginny.

4. Three months ago they split up.

5. And now they're back together.

Setting aside the fact that my recent affair with Ginny puts me slap bang in the middle of points 4 and 5, I'm aware that some people might say that my reaction is quite unreasonable. After all, they might argue, it's been a decade since you and Ginny (albeit briefly) last (sort of) dated. They might add that when Ginny and Gershwin were busy finding each other I was living the high life in London with my wife of six years and that until my arrival in Birmingham neither Ginny nor Gershwin had been aware my marriage had been over for six months. Fortunately for me I DO NOT GIVE A CRAP WHAT THESE PEOPLE THINK ABOUT ANYTHING. I do not care what they think about British foreign policy; the films of Ridley Scott; global warming; or who should win *The X-Factor* and I certainly don't care what they think about me being angry with Gershwin and Ginny because here's the thing: Gershwin is my best mate and that means something. That means we never bad-mouth each other, we always watch each other's back and we never – absolutely never – sleep with each other's exes. The very thought of dating one of Gershwin's exes makes me shudder, even the ones like Amanda Campbell who looked like a miniature version of Beatrice Dalle or Tessa Wyatt who had legs to die for; and let's not forget Zoe, who is pretty much the definition of a yummy mummy.

So if I had to describe my overall feelings the closest expression I can come up with is rage – pure rage. I want to punch something. I want to kick something. I want to smash something into a thousand tiny shards. But more than anything, I want it not to be true, because if it isn't true then I won't have to face up to the fact that despite everything I still want to be back in Ginny's arms.

20

'I thought you were going out?'

I'm at home watching TV with my parents, having texted Paul that I wouldn't be out tonight. Tempting as it is to drown my problems I'm not in the right mood to be around anyone. I want to forget everything that's going on.

Dragging my eyes away from the TV I look over at Mum and shake my head. 'Change of plan.'

'What change of plan? Isn't your friend coming up tonight?'

'Yeah, he is.'

'So why aren't you going?'

'I'm not in the right mood, Mum, that's the change of plan.'

'But he's coming up from London!' She makes it sound like he's travelling up from the North Pole by dog sled. 'Won't he be disappointed?'

'He'll be fine, Mum.'

'And you're not going because you're not in the "right mood"?' You can't leave him high and dry like that! What's he going to do with himself?'

I feel every last remaining drop of strength draining from me.

'He's got other friends, Mum, he won't even notice that I'm not there.'

'Still,' she says, 'it doesn't feel right leaving him in the lurch like that. If it was me I wouldn't invite you out again!'

My phone rings. Without looking I have a good enough idea who's calling and so I let it ring until it stops. The screen says: *Missed call: Gershwin*. It vibrates again to let me know that I have yet another voicemail (my third of the evening so far).

'Aren't you going to answer that?'

'It's a text,' I lie. 'I'm going to make a brew. Do you want one?'

Mum nods while Dad simply raises his empty mug without taking his eyes off the TV.

I swill out the mugs and put the kettle on to boil and as I open a new pack of chocolate digestives the doorbell rings, which sets me on edge. My parents don't believe in capital punishment but if there's one crime for which they would back its reintroduction it would be people ringing their doorbell after dark. I'm with them on this one.

'Who's ringing the doorbell at this time?' calls Dad.

'Ignore it!' commands Mum. 'They'll soon give up.'

'Matthew!' calls Dad. 'Go and see who it is, will you, son?'

'I think we should leave it,' I yell, knowing who it's likely to be.

The doorbell rings again and this is all it takes to get Dad out of his chair and into the hallway. Hiding behind the kitchen door that looks directly out on to the front porch I listen hard and sure enough hear Gershwin's voice: 'Sorry to have disturbed you, Mr Beckford. Is there any chance that I could speak to Matt?

'Of course!' Dad yells in my direction: 'Matthew! It's your friend Gershwin come to see you!'

Gershwin is ushered into the living room by Dad. He's wearing a plain T-shirt, jeans and a jacket: the official smart/casual uniform of men of my generation. Our eyes meet, he gives me a shrug, I swear under my breath and follow him into the living room.

'Look who it is!' says Mum, greeting Gershwin like he's long-lost family. 'How are you, son? Long time no see.'

I'm used to my parents being over familiar with my friends. Back when we were teenagers they barely acknowledged my friends' existence. They'd get a quick nod in the hallway on arrival and a 'shouldn't you be getting home by now?' at the end of the day. But for some reason since we all passed the age of twenty-one it's as if my parents can't get enough of them. It's as if the intervening years had turned them all from dossers and layabouts to fully functioning members of the community, which in many ways is true.

Once Gershwin is settled Mum's questioning onslaught begins: How is that lovely daughter? How is work? Where is he living these days? How is he coping with life after the divorce? Does Charlotte get on well with his ex-wife's new partner? Does he get on with his ex-wife's new partner? How are his parents? What does he think of Matthew's situation?

And so on and so on until his eyes glaze over. It takes twenty minutes before Gershwin can even begin hinting that he hasn't got a great deal of time and a further five before Mum cottons on.

'Look at me taking up all your time! I suppose you two will be wanting to get off for a night on the town!'

'Something like that,' says Gershwin.

'Well don't be a stranger, will you? You're always welcome here.'

Released from my mother's conversational grip Gershwin says his goodbyes and follows me out of the room. In an instant we shift from being old mates with an audience to would-be enemies lurking in a poorly lit hallway. I look at the face of my old friend and wonder what's going on in his mind. Had Ginny told him about her and me or was he simply here because he felt bad about being the world's worst best mate?

'Listen Matt—'

'We're not doing this here!' I spit, surprised by my own vehemence. I walk over to the shoe rack, shove my feet into my trainers and take a deep breath before calling out to my parents through the door: 'Just heading out for a minute . . . won't be long!'

'Don't forget your keys!'

I pick them up off the stairs, open the front door and step outside into the crisp night air.

We walk down the front path in silence. I have no idea where we're going but I want to put as much distance as possible between my parents' house and wherever we decide to have our slanging match.

'It feels like Bonfire Night,' says Gershwin when we're halfway down the road. 'There's that smell in the air and you get that chill like—'

'Listen, let's not do small talk, OK? Just get on with whatever it is that you've got to say.'

Gershwin shrugs resignedly as though I've disappointed him by choosing not to pretend that everything is actually all right. Presumably real men are supposed to employ world statesmanship when they have a problem with one another rather than bare-knuckle-brawling naked aggression. What can I say? Even though Gershwin's got a much bigger frame than me, I'm in a bare-knuckle-brawling type mood.

'Fine,' he says, 'we'll do it your way. But I never meant you to find out like this.'

'You obviously never meant me to find out at all. You even tried to keep me from contacting her by telling me that she was married!'

Gershwin looks simultaneously hurt and guilty. 'OK, but it was a complicated situation, Matt. Ginny and I had split up and suddenly you were back and single and asking after her. I just panicked! I promise I was going to tell you about us. In fact that's why I called you that day and said that we needed to speak.'

'But we never did, did we?'

'Because I didn't know how to say it, did I? You were still dealing with the fall-out from Lauren and the last thing you needed was me dumping this on you. So when Charlotte told me what had happened I was mortified. I couldn't be more sorry you had to hear it that way.'

'But not the rest of it?'

Gershwin throws me a look of pure defiance. 'It's not like we went out of our way for this to happen.'

I feel myself getting angry. 'I don't even know what "this" is!'

'I'm in a relationship with Ginny,' he says. 'I have been for over a year.'

So there it is, straight from the source. My best mate and my 'sort of' ex-girlfriend are together and judging by the fact that he's been on the back foot the whole time we've been talking I'm guessing Ginny hasn't told him about me and her.

'Look, I know you and Ginny have history,' continues Gershwin, 'but you were married, and happily – at least so I thought at the time – and Ginny was single and so was I and . . . well, we just sort of fell together.'

'Fell together?' I want to punch his lights out.

Gershwin shrugs uncomfortably. 'Look,' he says, 'let's forget it.'

'No,' I reply, 'I won't just "forget it"! You're meant to be my best mate! I'd never have pulled a stunt like this with you, never in a million years.'

'Well maybe that's because you've never known what being lonely is like,' says Gershwin, unflinching in his gaze. 'So when you do – and believe me now your marriage is over that time will come – why don't we have this conversation again and see if you still want to be the one pointing the finger. We're not kids any more, Matt, you can't claim first dibs on Ginny just because you got to know her before me. We're adults and it's about time you realised that.'

21

It's just past midday on the day after my encounter with Gershwin and I'm grinning like an idiot as I read the following text from Jason Cleveland: *Boffin! R U better now? When r we going to have that drink then!!!! Text me. Laters, J.* Why am I grinning? Why shouldn't I? Finally after all those lies I have an ironclad excuse never to have to see or deal with him again: I, Matt Beckford, am going back to London.

I made the decision last night after playing my big talk with Gershwin over in my head for the millionth time. He can have Ginny. I don't give a toss about either of them any more. Whichever way they spin it (and I'm pretty sure the spin machine's going into overdrive right now) I know the truth: Ginny and Gershwin have betrayed me and nothing is going to change that.

I tuck my packed bags inside the wardrobe away from prying eyes as I haven't told Mum or Dad yet. My plan is to wait until after lunch when I hope my mum's ability to get mad at me will be reduced by her bread roll and soup intake. Nothing winds Mum up quite so much as people making spur-of-the-moment decisions. It just isn't her way.

The logistics of everything she does from the weekly shop through to the calling of grandchildren have been planned to the smallest degree. 'I don't understand,' said Mum one summer when I told her that Lauren and I were going on holiday in three days but had yet to book a flight, hotel or even choose a country, 'how can you think that living like this is fun?' 'I never said it was,' I replied, 'it's just what we do. We're Generation Last-Minute.' This went down like a lead balloon with my mother who is not even vaguely up on media-speak, and for months afterwards whenever we spoke on the phone and I mentioned something she didn't understand her comment was always: 'Oh, so is that what Generation Last-Minute is up to now?'

I type out my reply to Jason: *Would love to meet up mate, but am off back to London. Some other time, maybe!* and then I head downstairs and try to work out where exactly I am going to go. I'm pretty sure that Lauren will let me stay with her for a night or two but after that I'll be on my own. My best bet is to contact a few old workmates and see if any of them will put me up but I know I'll be pushing my luck given that I've barely exchanged so much as an email with any of them since I handed in my notice. My friend Fraser is the most likely candidate: he's single, owns a one-bedroom flat in Docklands and owes me a big favour as it was me who hired him for his last job.

As I enter the kitchen I type out a text to Fraser suggesting that we should meet up for a drink but before I finish the doorbell rings.

'Can you get that?' calls Mum, who is standing on a stool searching through the cupboard above the oven. 'Your father seems to have gone AWOL and I'm trying to find the flan dish your sister bought me last Christmas.'

I pull a face as if to say that I'm busy but my mother pulls one in return indicating that although her question may have been presented as a request it was actually a command and if I know what's good for me I'll follow it quickly. Being bossed around by my mum (either verbally or non-verbally) will definitely not be one of the things I will miss about home.

I open the door, expecting it to be someone I don't know trying to sell me something I don't need. I have a 'not-interested' look plastered across my face to go along with the 'not-today' speech I'm ready to deliver, so when I see Ginny staring back at me it takes the wind out of my sails.

'We need to talk.'

'I don't want to.'

'Fine,' she says, 'I'll talk and you listen.'

'I don't want to listen either.'

'So what do you want?'

'World peace, to be a stone and a half lighter . . . oh, and for people to stop treating me like I'm a mug.'

'Matt, I—'

'I know,' I talk over her. I want to be angry with her but don't seem to have the required levels of energy to do so. 'Just give me a minute and I'll get my coat.'

*   *   *

'Gershwin told me what happened last night.'

We're in the Fighting Cocks surrounded by hungover twentysomethings doing the Sunday lunch thing with their mates. The smell of roast chicken and garlic hangs heavy in the air but Ginny and I just have a pint of lager each and a packet of crisps.

'If I'd known what had happened I would have come to see you earlier,' continues Ginny, and she looks genuinely remorseful which isn't great because it makes me want to kiss her.

'And what would you have said? That you're sorry? Sorry for sleeping with me? Getting back together with Gershwin? Or being with him in the first place?'

'I never meant any of this to happen.'

'So you say,' I reply. 'And yet through all the time we were together you never once thought it might be a good idea to tell me that you'd been engaged to my best mate?'

'We were over. I didn't think it mattered.'

'And yet it mattered enough not to tell me. I still don't get it. Why him of all people? You're not telling me you've always had a thing for him, are you?

'Oh Matt!'

'Don't "oh, Matt" me! You're engaged to him! I don't even know how you got together!'

'Does it matter?'

'You know it does!'

I say the last part loudly enough to catch the attention of

the couple at the next table. The woman looks pointedly in my direction.

'Look,' says Ginny, 'this isn't going to get us anywhere.'

'So why are we here then?'

'Because I need to ask you a favour.'

I can't believe what I'm hearing. 'A favour? Can you even hear yourself, Gin? After the time we spent together, after all those plans we made only to have you ditch me without a second thought, now you want a favour! What's wrong with you?'

'You're right,' says Ginny, trying not to get upset. 'You feel like I led you on and you're probably right. But hand on heart, Matt, I was so happy that day I bumped into you, and when you told me you were separated I couldn't believe we'd suddenly got this second chance. Matt, you have to believe me – when we made those plans, I was absolutely committed to them.'

'So what changed?'

'Gershwin. He called me in Barcelona. He wanted me to know he'd had a change of heart.'

'About what?'

'Starting a family.'

Everything slots into place. That was why they'd split up. Gershwin had always insisted that if he ever settled down again kids wouldn't be on the agenda. And now Ginny had changed his mind.

'It's what I've wanted for the longest time,' she continues, 'and now it's what he wants too. And it changes everything, Matt.'

'I could give you kids if that's what you really want.'

Ginny shakes her head and places her hand on mine. 'Oh, Matt, you don't really want kids with me! You should have kids with someone you want to be with permanently, not someone you're with because you've run out of options. I'm your back-up plan, and you've always been mine. But I don't need my back-up plan any more. Right now I need a friend to do me a favour which will mean I'll owe them for ever.'

'So we're back to that?'

Ginny nods and I stop breathing until what she's got to say is out in the open. 'I need for you not to tell Gershwin about us. I need you not to say a word about us being together.'

'And what do I get in return?'

'To choose to do the right thing even though you don't have to.'

It's after three by the time I reach home. Heading straight upstairs to my room I remind myself that I'm supposed to be leaving and I collect together my bags, bring them downstairs and prepare to break the news to my parents. They're sitting in the living room on the sofa, gas fire blazing, Mum watching an old black-and-white John Wayne film and Dad dozing beside her. It's like a flashback to the best Sundays of my youth: my family and I crammed into the living room enjoying an afternoon slump in front of the TV. It's a picture of absolute contentment, the way a home ought to be, and I want to be part of it just that little bit longer.

'We've already eaten, if that's what you're after,' says Mum.

'I'm OK.' I sit down next to her. 'I ate while I was out.'

'Are you sure?' She glances over at me as John Wayne mounts his horse and heads out after the bad guys. 'You look like you've got something on your mind.'

'I'm good,' I reply and fully resolved to abandon all plans to return to London I go out into the hallway, pick up my bags and dump them back in my room. Once I'm done I rejoin my parents in the living-room for a good old-fashioned Beckford family sleepy Sunday afternoon.

With my Birmingham friends out of bounds, my activities in the days that follow are reduced to ferrying my mum wherever she wants to go by day (thereby allowing my dad to increase his quota of afternoon naps) studiously avoiding the build-up to Christmas, watching DVDs on my laptop in my bedroom, killing time on the internet and occasionally venturing out to the cinema at night. It is barely an existence but when on the following Friday night I check the cinema listings to find that there's nothing on at the cinema that I want to see and then discover that I have seen every DVD in my possession at least half a dozen times, I realise that I have no options left and do something I never expected to do. I text Jason Cleveland: *Hi, mate, Boffin here, spoke too soon about leaving for London. How do you fancy a pint?*

Days until I turn forty: 120

22

As I enter Bar Babylon soundtracked by the kind of disposable autotuned nightmare that passes for music these days and scan the punters inside – crowds of young tattooed men in designer clothing and young women in barely there dresses – my heart doesn't so much fall as plummet, and when it reaches the ground it doesn't so much land as explode, sending tiny pieces of cardiac tissue and blood splattering into the air like a miniature fountain. This is going to be the longest night of my life.

Pushing deeper into the already crowded bar past guys flexing their tribal tattoo-covered biceps and girls flaunting their overstuffed cleavages, I search for my drinking companion and when I finally discover him on the other side of the bar I am taken aback to see he's not alone. He is flanked on either side by two guys who even though I haven't seen for twenty years I recognise immediately from my school days: former Jason Cleveland clones Aaron Baker and Nick D'Souza. My stomach tightens. Without knowing, it appears that I've just walked into the middle of a school reunion with the three people I liked least out of a potential cast of a hundred and twenty.

I greet the men one after the other, paying particular attention to the newcomers. Much to my disappointment Aaron, who had been the school's star rugby player, looks like he's carved in flesh-covered granite and Nick (who was always lean like a middleweight boxer) could have easily passed for a man ten years younger were it not for his completely grey hair. As it is he looks stupidly refined, as if he's just walked out of an advert for men's antiperspirant. I look and feel like an off-duty tramp compared to these guys.

'What's going on here?' I ask Jason. 'Some sort of unofficial school reunion?'

'Nah, mate,' says Jason. 'This place is our stomping ground. The three of us are always down here on a Friday night. Have been for years.'

It turns out that all of them are divorced or separated. 'Nick split up with his missus three years ago,' explains Aaron, 'Jason's marriage ended the summer after that and I broke up with my missus the following Christmas. Between us we've got eight kids, three ex-wives, two ex-partners and six houses!'

Aaron's joke causes all three men to explode in a peal of laughter so raucous that I feel I have to join in, which disappoints me immensely. I am not like them, they are not like me and right now a night in watching my DVD collection for a seventh time is looking thoroughly appealing.

The only upside to an evening involving the consumption of a ridiculous amount of alcohol at a phenomenal pace and conversations that rarely leave the realms of football, high-performance cars and which of the many attractive women in the bar Jason and his friends would or wouldn't 'do' is that it offers me first-hand anthropological insight into a phenomenon that until now I didn't know existed: a world of young attractive women who actually thought that men who had turned forty were a catch.

I wouldn't have believed it if I hadn't seen it with my own eyes but throughout the evening a constant stream of girls in eye-poppingly revealing outfits sashayed over to Jason and his friends specifically to flirt and banter with them or (for the more coy) allow themselves to be flirted and bantered with. For someone like me, who had been in a relationship for a good portion of the last decade, it was a real revelation as I'd assumed that despite young women's propensity to date up in terms of age there was something of a cut-off point – a line in the sand – which few girls in their twenties would feel inclined to cross unless you were George Clooney; and should I desire to cross it the other way, I'd be labelled 'a bit creepy' or 'an old lech'.

But standing in Bar Babylon with Jason and his friends brimming over with the kind of self-confidence that I'd had knocked out of me this past six months it's clear that there are girls who considered these guys neither creepy nor lechy but actually *desirable*.

Stunned by this revelation and aware that with the expensive designer clothes, gym workouts and self-assurance that comes from having been back in the game for a while, Jason and his friends do indeed have edge. Nevertheless, I'm convinced that this is not a world I want to inhabit any longer.

'Listen,' I say, yelling to be heard over a thumping club track, 'I think I'm going to get off.'

Jason puts his hand to his ear. 'What? You think it's time we got off?' Jason puts his sweaty arm around my neck in a blokey, beered-up fashion. 'No problem, son! We'll be getting off once Aaron and Nick have pulled a couple of birds for us to go clubbing with.'

I'm horrified. 'Clubbing?'

'Between us we know every guy who does the door on every club in the city. Mate, I guarantee you this will be the best night ever!'

Reeling at the thought, I scan the bar for Aaron and Nick. They disappeared about twenty minutes ago and I spot them playing court jester in the middle of a gaggle of tight-dressed, big-haired, fake-tanned, high-heeled twentysomethings. Nick grins like he's just won the lottery, Aaron gives us the thumbs up, and before I know it Jason is dragging me over to the girls he's labelled 'tonight's conquests'.

'All right ladies,' bellows Aaron, tattooed arm slung proprietarily around a tall blonde with a killer cleavage, 'meet the rest of the gang: Jase and Boffin.'

As one the girls, who are quite clearly very drunk, greet us with a cacophony of giggles and a flurry of flirty kisses but it's clear that they only have eyes for Jason and his unfeasibly large biceps, so while he regales them with tales of his bench-pressing abilities I make my excuses and disappear to the toilet.

*   *   *

It's a relief to be away from the pounding music, if only for a few moments. I stand in front of the urinal and undo the buttons on my jeans and try to conjure up excuses that will allow me to go home early. It'll have to be a good one though, because Jason doesn't seem the type to let his plans go awry without a good excuse. It needs to be something involving death: possibly a grandparent or at the very least an uncle. Not even Jason Cleveland would go clubbing if his uncle had died. Just as I'm trying to decide between killing off my Uncle Roy (on the basis that no one in the family has heard from him since he left my auntie and ran off with the barmaid from his local pub) and making up an entirely fictitious uncle in case I'm tempting fate I hear the door to the gents' open and someone enters.

It's an unspoken rule at the urinal that you keep your eyes fixed straight ahead, so I'm sure I have probably stood next to someone famous while I'm about my business and been none the wiser, but when the guy next to me says: 'Having a good night are you, mate?' I can't help but turn my head to confirm my suspicions and find myself saying: 'You're Gerry Hammond.'

He gives me a quizzical sideways glance.

'That was a really weird thing to say, wasn't it?' I apologise. 'You say, "All right mate?", and I tell you who you are. I should just shut up, shouldn't I?'

He gives me a wink. 'Nah, it's cool, mate. Always nice to meet Pinfolds fans.' Zipping up his flies he turns to wash his hands.

'Funnily enough,' I say as I finish at the urinal, and wait behind him at the sink, 'I've actually met you before, quite recently. You work in that charity shop in Moseley don't you? I came in a while ago when you were playing The House of Love's first album and we had a chat.'

'You bought a Thomas Hardy novel and *Songs of Love and Hate*, didn't you,?' he says as he dries his hands under the blower.

I can't believe it. I actually inhabit space in Gerry-from-The-Pinfolds' head. The seventeen-year-old me would be over the moon. 'Yeah that's me.'

'How was Hardy?'

'Depressing.'

'And Simon and Garfunkel?'

'Pretty much the same.' I become conscious of the fact that we are now two men standing in a toilet who no longer need to stand in a toilet. 'I should stop bothering you. It's been nice to see you again.'

'You never said if you were having a good night,' says Gerry. There's a mischievous look in his eye as though he's conjuring up a plan. 'Because I'll tell you for nothing, mine's atrocious.'

'I wouldn't really have thought this was your kind of place.'

'It's a mate's birthday and he wanted to come here. But his mates are a right bunch of boring bastards. You're not a boring bastard are you?'

I think this over carefully. 'Probably.'

Gerry laughs. I've just made a joke that made Gerry-from-The-Pinfolds laugh. If I still kept a diary that would've been the entry of a lifetime.

'Let's get out of here and find ourselves a proper good time. Decent music, quality booze, and birds that haven't got it all on show.'

'Just you and me?'

'Why, who else do you want to bring?'

'No one,' I say quickly, and then I see that mischievous grin of his and realise that he's joking. 'I mean . . . you and me, we're just going to walk out of here and go for a drink just like that?'

'Well I was planning to levitate but walking will do. So are you in or what?'

'I'm in,' I say, still unable to believe my luck. 'I am absolutely in.'

23

'So how come you're hanging out with old schoolmates you can't stand?' asks Gerry as we stand drinking at the bar while a gorgeous-looking girl backed by a live band works her way through an amazing-sounding James Brown cover. We're in the Yardbird, a cool jazz bar, that until a short while ago I hadn't even known existed.

I take a long sip of my pint and meet Gerry's gaze. 'It's a long story.'

'I should bloody hope so,' say Gerry. 'Life's way too short to be hanging out with idiots for no reason.'

I tell him my story. About Lauren, the breakdown, and my forced exile to the Midlands but when it comes to the part about Ginny and Gershwin I find myself skating over the story in a bid to save my ego: 'Anyway,' I say, 'to cut a long story very short indeed, in one fell swoop a few weeks ago I pretty much managed to estrange my only two friends up here and I needed a night out and the guys I was with were the best I could come up with.'

'So what did you do to alienate your proper friends?' asks Gerry. 'Sleep with your mate's wife? I tell you what, that can really ruin a friendship.'

'Nearly . . . I hooked up with an old ex.'

'So what's the problem?'

'She failed to inform me that she'd just split up with my best mate.'

Gerry looks suitably scandalised. 'When did you find out?'

'When she got back with him after we'd made a whole bunch of plans together.' I take a long sip from my glass. 'It was serious, really serious. We were going to go travelling together and do all the stuff that we should've done when we were young. Me and this girl, Ginny, we've always had this . . . I don't know what you'd call it. A sort of thing, an attraction . . . a curse if you like. It's like we're connected but we keep doing everything we can to deny it and it's fine if we're living in different cities but put us in a room together and there's trouble.'

Gerry nods sagely. 'I've been there for sure. Some women just get under your skin and never leave. No wonder you started thinking about the ex when you split up with your missus! If you come back to Brum and . . . pow! You're back in the thick of it!'

Gerry gulps his pint. He seems enthralled by my story, which thrills me no end. I'm hanging out with my teenage hero, in a jazz club spilling the beans about my hopeless love life. It's a dream come true.

'So does your mate know what happened with . . . Ginny?'

'Nope.'

'And does he know that you know they were together?'

'We had a big face-off over it. Then the next day she turns up on my doorstep asking me to keep schtum about us being together.'

'And you agreed?'

'I had no choice. They're talking about starting a family, I can't get in the middle of all that. Having kids means everything to her.'

Gerry drains his pint. 'You're a better man than me. I would've shoved it right in his face.'

'I can't do that to her.'

'No,' says Gerry, 'You're Mr Nice guy, aren't you?' He waves a dismissive hand in the air and almost knocks over my pint. I now realise just how much drunker he is than me. 'You want my advice?'

I nod. Who wouldn't want life advice from the man who reached number eight in the indie singles charts with 'Love's Longest Letter'?

'You're better off without them. Screw your best mate, the girl, your ex-wife *and* those losers you were hanging out with tonight!' He turns to the barman who's busy pouring a pint next to us. 'Two lagers with a bourbon chaser when you're ready, fella. Me and my friend Matt have got a lot of serious drinking to do.'

Between drinks Gerry tells me all of the stuff I've been desperate to know about him but had been too afraid to ask. About how the band split up on the eve of their biggest gig in America (which is pretty much as I'd read in the pages of the *NME* and *Melody Maker* at the time). The growing tensions between The Pinfolds' two creative leads (Gerry on lyrics and Pete McCulloch on music) became so intense that they escalated into a full-blown fist-fight resulting in Gerry getting his nose broken. Vowing never to talk to Pete again Gerry split with the band's management and found himself new representation. The rest of The Pinfolds tried to carry on under a new name but didn't get beyond releasing a couple of EPs. Gerry meanwhile took six months off to write and record new material, and a year later his debut solo album, *I told You I Was Right*, reached number fourteen in the indie charts on the week of its release. The following album however, *You Made Me*, recorded following his return to Birmingham, was critically revered but commercially reviled and pretty much marked the end of his career as a solo artist.

In the years that followed he added vocals to a number of singles that charted well, produced a couple of debut albums for well-known local bands and for a while even had a stint as an Arts and Culture correspondent for the weekly 'Birmingham Calling' strand of *Central Tonight* but then eventually that work faded away and he was left to pursue 'other projects'.

He looks like he's finished talking for a while but I'm too gripped to give up without teasing just a little more of the story out of him. 'So how did you end up volunteering in a charity shop?'

'I don't volunteer. I'm the manager.'

This surprises me and my face shows it. Maybe I'd expected a loaded rock star to give his time for free. 'So how did that come about then?'

'I'd made enough money from The Pinfolds and other stuff not have to work again—'

'What? Ever?'

'We had good accountants and financial people. I've got everything I need: a nice three-bed penthouse over on the old Britannic site in Moseley, my scooter to get around on and enough cash in the bank to last me a lifetime.'

'So basically,' I reply, 'you're sorted for life?'

He nods thoughtfully. 'Yeah, basically, I am.'

'So what are you doing at the shop? Your bit to help humanity?'

Gerry laughs and allows himself to be distracted by a pretty girl approaching the bar. 'I was bored of the music thing and fancied a change, and the shop opened, I knew a few people helping out there and so I started volunteering. After a while the manager told me he was leaving and suggested that I apply for his job. I ummed and ahhed because it's not like I need the hassle but in the end I took it because I love music and I love books and well . . . I was doing something good. I upped the turnover thirty per cent in my first six months.'

'So you do it for the love?'

Gerry looks at me like I'm an idiot. 'I'm not going to do it for the money, am I? It's peanuts.'

More beers follow. I accompany Gerry on numerous trips outside for cigarettes and in between he keeps me entertained with a number of long and potentially libellous stories that are as painfully funny as they are outrageous. At the end of the set he suggests we move on and so we head over to Broad Street in search of a cab and when we reach our destination over on Queensway he practically drags me into a tiny bar packed full of youths with daft haircuts and off-putting piercings. All of them seem to know and worship Gerry and the girls especially can't get enough of him. He introduces me to everyone, but despite their standard-issue ironic geek glasses their lack of interest in me is apparent. But not even that can take the shine off my night because as Gerry nudges me in the ribs and repeats a filthy joke he's just been told through the fog of an alcohol-induced blur I realise I am having the time of my life.

24

'You need to get out of bed this instant,' says Mum, storming into my room and wrenching open the curtains. 'Anyone would think this place is a dosshouse the way you've been carrying on of late!'

As I lie squinting back the daylight from underneath my duvet it occurs to me that Mum might have a point given the time (nearly midday), the state of the room (think church jumble sale) and the smell (think men's changing room). Nothing has seemed right since my night out with Gerry over a week ago. It's as if having had a glimpse of how cool my life might have been I've faced up to the fact that I have no mates, no job, no wife and therefore no reason to get out of bed.

I turn over and look at the ceiling and in so doing get a whiff of my armpits. How long has it been since I showered? 'Leave it with me,' I tell Mum. 'I'll get up in a bit, OK?'

'You'll get up now!' she says, and gives me a look that means business. 'We've got guests coming and I need you showered, shaved and downstairs pronto.'

'Guests? What guests?'

'Never you mind,' snaps Mum. 'Just make sure you're ready!'

Mum is in the living room needlessly rearranging the decorations on the Christmas tree for what seems like the millionth time since she put it up last week, when the doorbell rings and she calls out: 'They're here,' in her loudest voice.

'Looks like it's show time,' says Dad, heaving himself out of his armchair. 'Won't get any rest until they've gone.'

'Until who's gone?' I ask Dad, but Mum overhears and scowls in Dad's direction and he shuts his lips so tight that even under duress I doubt he would've even given me his name, rank and number.

Curiosity piqued, I follow Mum into the hallway because I'm half convinced that my parents are about to spring an intervention on me. Mum's TV viewing habits include the kind of American talk shows where that sort of thing happens and I wouldn't put it past her to try her hand at creating her own version. But when she opens the door all I can see is a plump-looking woman about Mum's age and a freakishly tall man in a snow-wash denim jacket, and an Iron Maiden T-shirt.

'Look who it is,' says Mum with a flourish, 'it's Mrs Baxter and your old friend Mark!'

Judith Baxter was a friend of Mum's from way back in my nursery schools days. She and Mum had bonded because they were both nurses and had worked at the same hospital at different times and so knew people in common but mostly because her youngest son and I were in the same class. Mark was a bit of an oddball – his favourite trick in nursery used to be pulling down his shorts in the middle of story time and shouting: 'It's just like an elephant!' at the top of his voice. I hadn't seen Mrs Baxter or her son since the day I left junior school so why they were here in my parents' house was a mystery to me.

'Mrs Baxter,' I say, shaking her hand, 'lovely to see you.'

'You too,' she replies. 'And my, haven't you grown? Seems like yesterday you and Mark were playing on the swings together. When I bumped into your mother the other day and she very kindly invited us to tea I just couldn't resist the opportunity for a catch up.' Mrs Baxter nudges Mark with her elbow. 'Isn't that right, Mark? Say hello to Matthew, why don't you?'

Mark, reaches up with his left hand, tucks some stray strands of long, greasy shoulder-length hair behind his ear, nods in my direction, and utters a barely audible: 'All right?'

'Great, thanks,' I reply, as my mum smiles expectantly. 'You?'

Mark shrugs. 'I'm OK.'

I look at my mother in confusion as she ushers everyone into the living room but she refuses to make eye contact. I know something's going on but I can't think for the life of me what it might be.

*   *   *

'So Matthew,' says Mrs Baxter, as my mother leaves the room for the kitchen to make everyone's drink, 'your mum was telling me that you used to work in computers?'

'Sort of.' I notice Mark is reinserting the earphones of his iPod into his ears. Granted, as weird behaviour goes it's not quite up there with taking out your tackle during story time but all the same it's a pretty odd thing for a forty-year-old man to do. 'I was director of software development for a firm in London.'

'Oooh,' she says eagerly, 'that sounds very high flying. Was it?'

'I suppose so.'

Mrs Baxter spots the earphones and angrily mouths, 'Take those out now!' in Mark's direction before continuing, 'Our Mark likes computers, don't you Mark?'

'They're all right.' His voice is completely flat, devoid of emotion, colour or interest, a bit like a robot only without the warmth.

'You've got two of the things!'

'Yeah, but one's a laptop.'

'Don't laptops count then?'

He looks at her blankly.

Mrs Baxter and Dad make festive related small talk and when that runs out Mrs Baxter questions me in greater detail about my former career until Mum arrives with the refreshments. As Mum pours the tea and hands out coffees, I notice her hand Mark an empty glass.

Mrs Baxter catches me looking.

'Mark only drinks energy drinks, don't you Mark?' she explains, reaching into her bag to hand Mark a can of Red Bull. In one swift motion, he opens the can, takes a sip, and pours the rest into the glass.

'The drink of gods,' he says triumphantly.

I can't help myself. My curiosity is piqued. 'You only ever drink energy drinks?'

Mark nods proudly. 'No other liquid passes my lips.'

Dad and I exchange concerned glances. 'So . . . you're telling me you don't drink any other liquid? Not water, not beer, not even milk?'

'I did drink the insides of a coconut a couple of years back as an experiment,' he relents, 'but it didn't agree with me.'

I look to Mrs Baxter for further explanation but Mum intercepts her.

'Oh Judith,' she says standing up, 'let me give you that mince pie recipe you asked about the other day.'

Picking up her tea, Mrs Baxter quickly follows my mother out of the room. A moment later Dad stands and says: 'Oh, I've just remembered I've got to do that thing,' and before I can respond he too has left the room. The moment Mark and I are alone all the pieces of the puzzle begin to fit together: my mother's insistence that I get out of bed, her refusal to tell me who was coming for tea, and her sharp exit from the room with Mrs Baxter followed by my father . . .

I stand up. 'Back in a sec, Mark, just need to check something with my mum,' and I practically run to the kitchen where I find Mum, Dad, and Mrs Baxter sitting round the kitchen table whispering with each other conspiratorially.

'What were you thinking?

'What do you mean?' replies Mum, clearly acting the innocent.

I look at Mrs Baxter. Not even her presence can restrain my annoyance. 'I'll tell you what I mean! You've just set me up on a playdate like I'm a toddler with no social skills.'

'I thought it would help!' protests Mum. 'All you've done for the past few days is mope in that bedroom of yours. You don't see Gershwin, you don't see Ginny either. It's not good for a man of your age to spend so much time on his own!'

'So you thought you'd set me up with Mark Baxter?'

'Well, he hasn't got any friends either and he likes computers.'

'Just for the record,' pipes up Dad, 'I did tell her it was a terrible idea from the start.'

'Oh be quiet will you!' snaps Mum, 'I'm sure you'd be quite happy for our eldest son to spend all day every day festering in bed. Well I for one have had enough: Matthew Timothy Beckford, consider this your formal warning: either you sort your life out this very second or I will!'

'Fine,' I reply, through clenched teeth, and then I look over at Dad. 'Can I borrow the car?'

Dad hands me the keys without a word.

Heading outside without saying goodbye I start up the engine, head in the direction of the high street and within ten minutes I'm striding purposefully into the charity shop in Moseley where I first met Gerry.

'Look who it is!' says Gerry from behind the counter, 'I was thinking about you only the other day. How's that head of yours? Mine was awful for days afterwards! Are you here to shop? We've had some great new stock come in the last couple of weeks. I'm not sure but there might even be some Pinfolds stuff amongst it.'

'I'm not here to buy anything,' I reply. 'I want a job.'

'Here?'

'Yeah, if you'll have me.'

'You know we don't pay?'

'Will you give me enough hours so that I don't have to spend all day, every day with my parents?'

Gerry laughs. 'The olds driving you up the wall are they?'

'Up and over.'

Gerry holds out his hand for me to shake. 'Looks like you've got yourself a job, mate: Welcome aboard.'

Days left until I turn forty: 113

25

Although it's only been three weeks since I started working in the shop, even I can see the change it has wrought in my personality. It's not just the hopefulness and the promise of a fresh start that a new year brings that lifts my spirits, rather it's that every morning I wake up feeling positive about the day ahead and every night I go to bed exhausted (mainly because I've been out to the pub almost every night during the festive season with Gerry for 'just the one' only to reach home at two o'clock in the morning). I'd been dreading Christmas but actually ended up enjoying it, thanks to Gerry. There are no longer whole days spent in bed, playdates with forty-year-old Red Bull addicts and no reason to allow myself to regress back to childhood just because I'm living with my parents. And while the work isn't the most exciting in the world (it's mostly cataloguing stock, sorting through donations, restocking shelves and putting the good stuff we get on eBay) it is oddly fulfilling, even more so when it registers that I'm doing my bit to raise money for a charity that helps people who can't help themselves. Altruistic causes aside, what makes it one of the best jobs I've ever had is the fact that I get to spend all day, every day, hanging out with Gerry, talking about music and books with Gerry and hearing Gerry's take on life, the universe and everything in between. No matter whether the shop's full or empty, we always have a laugh even if we're just talking about our all time favourite 'B' sides or alternative uses for the fifty-odd dog-eared copies of the *Da Vinci Code* stacked up in the corner of the stockroom.

'What exactly are you going to do with these?' I ask Gerry as I add to the pile from the latest batch of donations.

'That,' says Gerry, 'is a good question my friend. I only started it a couple of weeks ago because Jean, one of our Saturday volunteers, bet I couldn't get a stack higher than my desk within a week. Once I won I kept on going just because I could. I've thought about starting a breakaway branch purely to get rid of them but I'm not sure it would go down well with the regional manager. Chances are I'll bag 'em up and drop them outside the Cancer Research shop up the road. Maybe some hippy types will get hold of them and make themselves a nice eco home.' He looks at his watch. 'Time for lunch. Where do you fancy?'

'I'm in the mood for a touch of fine dining,' I say, thinking back to my old life and some of the top-notch meals I used to enjoy on expenses. 'Maybe sautéed calves' liver on a bed of braised fennel followed by dressed crab, tortellini of lobster, caramelised scallop with a scallop velouté washed down with a nice chilled bottle of Viognier.'

'So that'll be two cheese and ham toasties and a pot of tea from Annabel's as usual will it?' says Gerry.

'Yeah, I mean if it ain't broke why fix it?'

Leaving the shop in the capable hands of Anne, a retired music teacher from a local private girls' school who tends to look after the classical music, and Odd Owen, a bearded part-time mature student who according to his own CV only ever reads books about World War II, we head next door to Annabel's.

Over lunch Gerry tells me about his plans for the evening: he's meeting up with his girlfriend Kara for a curry at the Diwan. Kara's the girl I saw him with in Selfridges, a Dutch postgraduate student half his age. They met at a club night he goes to occasionally. She's dropped into the shop a few times and even though she's a bit too trendy for my liking with her retro hairstyle and clothes, there's no denying that she is utterly stunning. Gerry tries to sell the curry to me by mentioning that one of Kara's mates is coming along too but it sounds way too much like a double date. 'I can't,' I tell him once he's started employing emotional blackmail. 'I promised my mum I'd take her to my sister's tonight.' It's a lie and Gerry knows it. 'Listen,' I say finally, 'all I want to do is go home, eat my tea and maybe watch a couple of DVDs in my room. I don't even want to think about women, let alone be around them.'

The rest of the afternoon goes by in a blur. I spend an hour finishing off the donation sort, another hour putting new stock on the shelves before finally heading to the tills to take over from Anne, so that she can have her tea break. I've barely been at the tills a minute when a young woman with dark hair and an amazing smile walks into the shop, heads straight to the till and asks me a question that sounds like: 'Have you got any elephant-dung paper?'

'You want to what?'

The young woman laughs self-consciously. 'I was asking about . . . erm . . . elephant-dung paper. Have you got any?'

'Elephant dung?'

'Paper. As in paper made from elephant dung. I was told you sell it.'

'By who?'

'A friend at work, she bought some for her brother as a sort of jokey Christmas present.'

I look around the room, scanning for a hidden camera. My gaze returns to the young woman. She really is quite stunning.

'We're a second-hand music and bookshop. Elephant-dung products aren't really our thing.'

The young woman looks confused. 'Are you absolutely sure?'

'Absolutely,' I reply, but just to be on the safe side, I shout for Gerry.

'I'm just in the middle of something.' he calls from the stockroom door. 'Is it urgent?'

'I've got a customer here who wants to buy some *elephant-dung paper*,' I tell him, my voice dripping with ironic detachment.

'It's on the rack by the door,' shouts Gerry. 'Anything else?'

Abandoning the till I check the rack by the door. There, along with the birthday cards, packs of discounted Christmas cards that still haven't shifted and a children's make-your-own pirate hat kit, is indeed an elephant-dung writing set.

'I'll take it,' says the young woman, now standing next to me.

'I honestly had no idea that we sold this stuff. You must think I'm an idiot.'

'Not really,' she says kindly. 'If the truth be told I wasn't entirely sure that my friend wasn't winding me up for a laugh but I know my mum'll get a real kick out of it. She's pretty much the last person in the universe who handwrites letters.'

'Now there's a lost art form!' I say, hoping to sound clever and erudite. 'Everything's emails and texts these days.'

'I can never really be bothered with them,' she replies. 'Are you a big letter-writer then?'

'I wouldn't say big exactly.'

'So what would you say?'

'I'd say you could probably describe it as small . . . tiny, if you want to be pedantic. In fact one might almost say, given that I haven't written one in about a decade, that I'm not actually a letter-writer at all.'

It's excruciating. I want the ground to open up and swallow me whole. Why did I exaggerate my fondness for letter-writing to a complete stranger? What could I possibly gain from saying such a thing? Why didn't I just sell her the dung paper and shut up? Thankfully she laughs and so I quickly scan the item and bag it up for her.

She hands me her credit card. Her long and slender fingers are perhaps the most lovely I've ever seen.

'You can take your card out now,' I inform her once the transaction has gone through and then I hand her purchase to her.

'Shouldn't you have asked me if I actually wanted a carrier bag?'

'I can take it back if you like.'

She shakes her head. 'Maybe I'll drop it back in once I've finished with it,' she says in a manner that if I didn't know better I might have described as flirtatious. 'You know, do my bit for the environment.'

'I'll look forward to it,' I reply.

I watch carefully as she leaves the shop and once she's gone I ask Odd Owen if he wouldn't mind covering the till for a moment while I take a tea break.

'Did you see any of that?' I say to Gerry as I enter the stockroom.

'What, with my X-ray eyes?' replies Gerry, who's sitting at the computer. 'You sound like something's wound you up a bit. Was it the elephant-dung paper thing? Everyone gets caught out with that. Until we received the first shipment I was convinced it was a wind-up.'

'No it's not that . . . well it is, but it's sort of more. Did you see the girl who asked for it?'

Gerry shakes his head. 'Wasn't paying attention. Why, was she pretty?'

'Very.'

'And?'

'And well, the thing is I started talking about letter-writing with her which was a really stupid thing to talk about because who talks about letter-writing with an attractive woman but the thing is . . . I was flirting, Gerry . . . me, Matt Beckford, flirting with a member of the opposite sex.'

'Didn't you just tell me over lunch that you were done with women?'

'I know,' I reply, 'which goes to show the right one can make all the difference.'

At home that night I catch up with my parents in the kitchen. Now that I'm working we all seem to be getting on better and even though I know Mum has her doubts ('But I don't understand, why are you pouring all your energy into something that doesn't even cover your bus fare?') and Dad has his too, ('Tell me son, how are you going to explain this on your CV?') they can both see that working at the shop has brought about a positive change in me.

I go for a run and even though I only manage ten minutes before I'm too shattered to go on it still feels good. Maybe I've turned a corner, perhaps this is where things start to improve for me. Reaching home I hit the shower and afterwards eat dinner with my folks and not even Mum's incessant worrying about my nephew and nieces ('I'm sure they should all be taller than they are!') can spoil my good mood.

After dinner I leave my parents to *CSI Miami* and head upstairs to watch an Adam Sandler DVD on my laptop but I end up idly surfing the internet instead. First a couple of IT websites just to see what's new, then over to eBay to check on the bidding on a couple of out-of-print text books I'd listed and then finally I check the newspaper headlines and accidentally mis-click and find myself staring at the home page for an upmarket broadsheet's online dating site.

I attempt to correct my mistake but then the picture of the site's 'member of the day' attracts my attention. She's got dark hair and a wicked smile; likes 'glamping' ('camping with a touch of glamour' she explains), literature and walks in the park on cold winter afternoons; she's recently separated, but doesn't have kids and is looking for a long-term relationship with a man between twenty-five and thirty-five. Her final demand is that her suitor must be solvent as she has no interest in men still looking to 'find' themselves. She calls herself MBA_girl_77 but I know her as Lauren, my soon-to-be-ex-wife.

26

It's the following morning. The shop's not open for another five minutes, Gerry and I are in the stockroom and I've just finished telling him the story of how I'd spotted Lauren on a dating website, to which his first response is: 'Did she look hot?'

I look at Gerry askance. 'What kind of question is that, you nutter?'

'A valid one if you still dig her.'

'Which I don't.'

Gerry raises a sceptical eyebrow. 'Obviously.'

'What's that supposed to mean? You think I still have feelings for Lauren?'

'I don't think anything. I'm just here to watch you vent.'

Neither of us speaks for a moment and then I realise how ridiculous I'm being. 'To answer your question: she looked stunning and do you know why?' I take out my wallet and pull out the exact same photo. 'I took it when we were on holiday in Dubai two years ago. It's the best bloody photo I've ever taken. She looks amazing.'

He places a consolatory hand on my shoulder as I tuck the picture back into my wallet.

'I don't know what to say mate . . . other than that this is the best thing that could have happened. This is the kick up the backside you've been waiting for! Newsflash, Matty boy: your ex-missus and that Ginny bird have both moved on and so should you.'

He's right of course. There is no point in me holding a candle for either Lauren or Ginny now they've both made it clear that I am surplus to requirements, but this leaves me out on a limb. At least if I'm sitting around feeling sorry for myself I know exactly what to do. This securing my own future stuff is too go-getting for my current frame of mind.

'I'm fine as I am,' I reply.

'Then I'd hate to see you when your life is really falling apart. You're not fine, you're not even close to fine. You need to get out there and you need to do it now. What about Elephant-Dung Paper Girl from yesterday? You fancied her didn't you? Didn't she tell you she'd come back into the shop?'

'She won't,' I reply. 'I guarantee it.'

'Well couldn't you Google her or look her up on Facebook or something?'

'And say what? I've been cyber-stalking you, please date me?'

'Well Kara's got a ton of girl mates I could introduce you to.'

I briefly imagine what kind of 'girl mates' Kara might have and shudder involuntarily. The last thing I need is a bisexual goth Ph.D student with a penchant for bloodletting.

'Thanks,' I tell him, 'but no thanks. Honestly, I'm fine the way I am.'

For the rest of the morning I struggle to focus on customers as I try not to obsess about my wife being back on the dating scene, but just before eleven something happens which throws me completely. A man wearing a scruffy-looking tracksuit with stains down the front, greasy hair and a patchy beard comes in, catches sight of me and heads straight towards me.

'Beckford, is it really you?'

'Harrison.' I shake his hand. 'Good to see you, mate.'

Back in my secondary school days Andrew Harrison was a byword for the opposite of sexual attraction. If you happened to have the misfortune to fancy one of the gobby girls at school and she wanted to make it clear that you had absolutely no chance with her she'd tell you that she'd sooner snog Andrew Harrison than you just to drive the point home. If it was the evening of the school disco and you'd spent a whole afternoon trying to make yourself look cool and your mates wanted to take you down a peg or two they'd tell you that you looked like Andrew Harrison's uglier twin. In fact if there was any derogatory point that needed a character to illustrate the ultimate in revulsion then Andrew Harrison's name was it.

He'd lived in a council tower block on the edge of Kings Heath with his mum and her ever-changing litany of boyfriends. He came to school wearing odd socks, his school uniform always smelt faintly of cats and stale urine and if ever there was an outbreak of head lice it went as read that he was ground zero.

It wouldn't have been so bad if he had been bright because at least then there would be some hope of future improvement; but although he started out well enough, between looking after his mum during her various bouts of depression and bunking off school whenever the bullying from characters like Jason Cleveland became too much, it wasn't long before he was in the bottom set for every single subject and by the time we came to take exams he had long since stopped coming to school.

'How long have you been working here?' he asks.

'Not long. I've only recently moved back to Brum. How about yourself? What are you up to?'

He shrugs. 'On the dole, have been for years. Used to work down the Rover, just as a cleaner mind. It was an OK job, but then they closed it. End of.'

'I'm sorry to hear that.'

'Ah, he says dismissively, 'could be worse. Where are you living?'

'Back with my folks. You?'

'Got a flat in one of the tower blocks near the Maypole, it's only small like, but it does for me, the missus and the nipper.'

'You've got a missus?' The words spring from my lips before I have time to consider them and I feel terrible. 'I mean, how long have you been together?'

'Five years. We met on the internet. We both love horror films and we used to talk about them all day to each other on a forum. Then we just started talking about other stuff and then one day we decided to meet up and that was it. She moved down from Sheffield the week after.'

'And your kid? Boy or girl?'

'A girl, Shona, she's a cracker. In fact that's why I came in here today: someone told me it was good for kids' books.'

'It is.' I lead him over to the children's section and help him pick out a few things. Between us we choose *The Very Hungry Caterpillar*, *The Gruffalo* and a Charlie and Lola story, which he carries over to the till.

'What's the damage?' he asks.

'Nothing.' I hand him the books in a bag.

'You can do that?'

'Consider it my present to Shona.'

'Cheers.' He holds out his hand and I shake it firmly.

'Good to see you, mate,' I reply.

'Who was that?' asks Gerry, as I open the till and slip some coins from my pocket into the drawer.

'Just an old mate who seems to have his life more sorted than I ever will.'

Instead of heading to Annabel's with Gerry at lunchtime I nip out for a sandwich from the Sainsbury's Local across the road and eat it sitting at the desk in the stockroom thinking about my encounter with my old schoolmate. He'd met the love of his life through the internet; might it be possible that I could too?

Keeping an eye out in case Gerry returns from lunch early I log on to Lauren's dating website and begin the registration process. The easy bit is outlining the sort of women I'm hoping to meet. The most difficult is the 'about me' section and I can't seem to write anything here that doesn't make me cringe. It's not a natural thing to do, sum up your entire personality in a witty paragraph, and even attempting to do so is alarmingly sobering. Thwarted, I consider giving up but then it occurs to me that if I swallow my pride and involve Gerry in the process I'd have access to the man whose words have literally moved thousands to tears. Surely he could write something that didn't make me sound like a closet serial killer.

'You want me to write your profile for you?'

I stare at him. He's enjoying torturing me. 'Only if you're not going to make a big deal out of it.'

'Of course I won't,' he says, pushing me out of the chair. He cracks his knuckles before hitting the keyboard in a flurry of activity. I look over his shoulder but he tells me in language that causes Anne to reprimand him sharply from her position behind the counter to stay away. Fifteen minutes pass before he beckons me over to the screen.

He gets up and stretches. 'This, my friend, is a masterpiece of understated genius and when you score off the back of this you will owe me a pint or two by way of a thank-you.'

I take his seat, peer at the screen and read the following:

Hi, I'm Matt and here are my cards on the table:

1. I'm recently separated.
2. But I did like being married.
3. I recently resigned from a well-paid job.
4. But I love working hard.
5. I'm looking for a new beginning.
6. And I'd love it if it could be with you.

Gerry watches for my reaction and when my face cracks and a grin appears, we both start to chuckle.

'It's genius,' I say, patting him on the back. 'Absolute genius. Moving without being mawkish . . . and yet funny, and honest too – and full of integrity. Have you done this before?'

'Never. I just let the songwriter in me out for a minute. Granted, it might scare away a few of the fluffier ones and some will read the marriage stuff and assume quite rightly that you're damaged goods but the rest of them – the free spirits – I reckon they will flock your way. Have you got a photo?'

'Only the one that you used for my photo ID.'

'Even better. You look seriously trustworthy in that photo.'

I upload the photo to the site, double-check my entry, press return and it's done. My profile has gone live: I am officially internet-dating.

27

The way this particular dating site works is that every time I log in, a box in the corner of my screen tells me a) who's looked at my profile and b) how many direct messages I have. On my first day I get a resounding fifteen 'looks' and no messages; on the second day I get seven 'looks' and zero messages; and then on the third day seventeen 'looks', but still no messages. I am baffled by why I am doing OK on the 'look' front but so appallingly on the 'message' front where I assume the real action takes place. It's only when Gerry concludes: 'They're birds aren't they? They're waiting for you to make the first move!' that it even occurs to me that my 'lookees' might be waiting for me to direct-message them. Focusing my attention on my three favourite profiles I channel the spirit of Gerry and contact: Lou_bee_Loo (a forty-one-year-old nurse), Flirtythirty_GH (a thirty-nine-year-old teacher) and NewtoBrum76 (a thirtysomething graphic designer).

And then I wait.

And I wait.

And I wait.

And then finally just as I'm wondering if I should cast my net wider I get the following message:

From Newtobrum76: Dear Matt, thanks for your lovely message the other day. Sorry I didn't get back to you straight away but it's been absolute madness at work. Could I get your number and text you some time soon? Have a great day, Abi.

Message from me: *Hi, Abi! Here's my number! Just thought you ought to know that there's a typo on my profile. Where it says that my favourite film is Fellini's 8½ it should actually read – anything with Jason Statham in it. Cheers, Matt.*

Message from Abi: *Hi Matt, Funny you should say that! Where my profile says 'I love theatre and classical music' it should actually read 'I love everything Katherine Heigl has ever done and the music of Abba.':—)*

We carry on like this for the rest of the week with barely a couple of hours going by without one of us texting the other, but whenever I suggest meeting up she always finds a way to sidestep the issue. If it had been any other lifetime I'd have given up by now but the truth is I'm loving the diversion, plus if her profile photo is anything to go by she's actually pretty damn hot.

'So what's with all this texting?' asks my sister the following Sunday as my parents lead her husband and the kids into the living room having demolished one of Mum's legendary

Sunday dinners. 'You've barely stopped looking at your phone the entire time we've been here.'

'It's complicated,' I say.

Yvonne isn't fooled for a second: 'It's a woman isn't it? What's she like?'

'Nice.'

'Nice?' Yvonne looks at me like I'm mad. 'What's wrong with her?'

'Nothing.'

'So why are you saying she's nice?'

'Because she *is* nice.'

'So why do I sense there's a problem? She's not married is she?'

'No, of course not!'

'Then what's the problem?'

'There is none . . . other than the fact that I haven't actually met her yet.'

'How can you not have—?' Yvonne stops herself quickly, lowers her voice and whispers. 'This is an internet date, isn't it?'

I wince. 'Don't say a word to anyone!'

'Oh, come on, Matt!' says Yvonne, 'It's the twenty-first century! Everyone internet-dates! In fact it's good to know that there are nice guys getting in on it. Have you got a photo?'

I show Yvonne Abi's profile on my phone. It's the first time I've shown anyone what she looks like and while I'm keen to get another opinion I'm apprehensive in case I've missed something obviously off-putting about her like the fact that she's got a horn growing from the middle of her forehead or a tattoo of her favourite singer running down her neck.

'She's absolutely gorgeous!' says Yvonne.

I let out a huge sigh of relief. 'I really landed on my feet with this one.'

'Don't sell yourself short,' says Yvonne, grinning. 'If anyone's landed on their feet it's her.'

Once my sister and her family have gone I escape to my room to text Abi:

Message from me: *Sorry for the text silence this afternoon. Had family around. x*

Message from her: [Two minutes later] *No worries! Family is important to me too even if you do want to strangle them sometimes! Hope it went well. X*

Message from me: [one and a half minutes later] *It was fine. My nephews think I am the coolest uncle ever. X*

Message from her: [One minute later] *My nieces think I'm great too. We should compare notes some time.*

Message from me: [Ten seconds later] *How about this weekend? Maybe Friday night? X*

Message from her: [Thirty seconds later] *Would love to but have a 'thing'. How about Saturday afternoon?*

Message from me: [Ten seconds later] *Sounds great. Where?*

Message from her: [Thirty seconds later] *The café at the MAC is always good for people-watching. See you there at 2 p.m.?*

Message from me: [Eight seconds later] *Definitely! X*
Message from her: [Eight seconds later] *See you there!!!*

Bingo. So there it is. It may have cost me a couple of callused thumbs but finally I have my first real live date with a complete stranger in over seven years.

As is typical of weeks when you have something to look forward to mine drags like no other week has ever dragged before. Even work, which up to now has always made the days go quickly, seems so sluggish that I have to check that the 'open' sign on the door is actually on display. By the time that five o'clock on Friday evening comes around, I'm so desperate not to spend my evening counting down the hours until meeting up with Abi the following afternoon, that when Gerry asks me whether I fancy a quick pint after work I practically leap down his throat in order to say yes and so we head straight to the Fighting Cocks.

'So,' says Gerry once we've got a couple of pints in front of us, 'feeling nervous about tomorrow?'

'No, should I be?'

'You'll be fine mate. Sounds to me like it's pretty much in the bag.'

'And there speaks someone for whom it is always "in the bag". You have no idea what it's like for mere mortals, do you?'

'And you'd know this how exactly? Because of what you read in the music press when you were a kid?'

'What? Are you telling me it's not true?'

Gerry chuckles. 'It's like all things isn't it? It depends how deep you dig. I'm not saying that I haven't had my fair share of groupies and the like but if you think that everything's always gone my way you'd be way off the mark.'

'You're telling me the great Gerry Hammond has had his heart broken?'

'Where do you think lines like: "She lifts me up, and puts me down, I'm broken glass inside her now?" came from? You can't make any art unless you've had your heart broken a few times. It's the law.'

'So who last broke your heart?'

'Me,' he replies. 'I'm so bloody careless you wouldn't believe it.'

I sense there's more to the story but even though I press him for the rest of it he just changes the subject and then Kara and her cronies turn up and start talking about a party over in Balsall Heath that one of them has been invited to and Gerry asks me if I fancy going.

'What are you going to do instead?' he chides. 'Go to bed? Come to the party, have a laugh with me, and if it's terrible, Scout's honour we'll leave within the hour.' He drains his pint. 'It's way too early to think about going home and there's no way I'm spending the night getting trapped in a corner talking about how great the bloody Velvet Underground are with Kara's mates again.'

It's after midnight as we finally pile out of the minicab we'd ordered to take us to Balsall Heath.

'Whose party is it anyway?' I ask Gerry as we walk up the path of a dilapidated double-fronted Edwardian house that had spent so long being passed down from one miserly landlord to another that it was now a mere ghost of its formerly glorious self.

'I don't know for sure,' he says, raising his voice to be heard over the music coming from the house. 'Whoever it is she's a friend of a friend of Kara's and it's to celebrate her thirtieth birthday.' He chuckles. 'Thirty . . . those were the days. I don't remember anything about my thirtieth which I'm guessing means I had the best time ever.'

I look at Gerry and feel the urge to ask him something that's been on my mind for a while. 'Does it bother you being in your fifties?'

Gerry thinks for a moment. 'Nah.'

'You're not even the slightest bit bothered?'

'Why should I be?'

'I'm not saying you should, it's just . . . I don't know. Sometimes I find the whole getting older thing a bit weird, especially as I don't feel any different now to when I was thirty.'

'That's the thing though, isn't it? Inside no one feels any different to the way they felt when they were young. I mean look at me, I might be fifty-one on the outside but mentally I'm twenty-three.'

I can't help but laugh. 'And you say that like it's a good thing.'

'Because it is! Why would I want to be like all the other boring gits my age sitting around in their cardigans talking about the fuel consumption on their executive cars and how their kids are getting on at university? Do you want to be that guy?'

'I dunno,' I reply. 'It doesn't sound that bad.'

'So why did you give up your job?'

'Because it was sucking the life out of me.'

'And don't you think that doing the family thing would be the same? Weekends stuck in freezing cold parks entertaining ungrateful hyperactive brats? You'd have to be mad to do it.' I shrug and Gerry immediately picks up on it. 'Don't tell me you actually bought into all that?'

I nod. 'I did . . . for a while, but it was all a bit like a car crash. I took my eye off the road for a split second and the next thing I know I'm being pulled out of the wreckage.'

'That's the kind of accident that will be the making of you.'

'I bloody hope so,' I sigh, 'I really do.'

We step inside. There are four young guys in the hallway smoking. They deliberately give us the once-over as if to underline the fact that in addition to being old we're unwelcome. The hallway smells of dust and old carpet and the music is horrible. I want to go home. I want to be in bed.

We walk into the front room. It's packed full of people dancing. Kara and her friends are talking in a corner and I follow Gerry over to her but then I feel a tug on my hand and turn round to see a pretty dark-haired girl in a sparkly top and jeans. Only when I adjust my eyes to the light do I see that it's Elephant-Dung Paper Girl. She leans in towards me and instinctively I lower my head. She presses her lips to my ear: 'It's my birthday!' she says. Before I can respond her arms are round my neck, her tongue is down my throat and all I can think is: 'Well, I certainly didn't see that coming.'

28

As I break away from the kiss my head is full of wonder as I think of how little I understand women despite having reached the age of thirty-nine. Every time I think I've got them sussed one does something so off the wall, so unexpected that all I can do is scratch my head in a gormless fashion. I know I've been off the market for a while but is this really how young women act these days? Do they all just come up to blokes they met once buying elephant-dung stationery sets and start kissing them?

'Hi,' I say, holding out my hand in a deliberately formal fashion. 'I'm Matt and up until a few minutes ago in my head at least you were Elephant-Dung Paper Girl.'

Overcome with embarrassment she ignores my hand and covers her face with those slender fingers of hers. 'I can't believe I just did that.'

'So that was a first? I'm impressed.'

'They dared me.' She glances over to a small group of young women on the opposite side of the room pretending not to look at us.

I look over at them. 'Do you always do everything they dare you to do?'

'Never,' she replies. 'It must be the cocktails we were drinking earlier . . . or maybe the shots, I don't know . . . it's not even my birthday.' She hangs her head in mock shame. 'I'm so drunk it's not even funny. What are you doing here anyway? Who do you know in the house?'

'I came with that lot over there,' I say, gesturing to Kara and her friends.

'She's not your girlfriend is she? You know, the pretty one. She keeps looking this way.'

I think she's referring to Kara. 'Nope, not my girlfriend, but a mate's. He should be round here somewhere.' I scan the room for Gerry but he's nowhere to be seen. 'His name's Gerry. You probably know him. He's the kind of guy everyone knows.'

'Never heard of him,' she says and she looks over at Kara again. 'You're definitely sure that's not your girlfriend?'

'Positive. I couldn't be more single now if I tried. And anyway, she's not my type.'

'And what would your type be exactly?'

'I used to belong to a pretty broad church but recently I've decided to focus purely on women who buy elephant-dung stationery. They're a select bunch but they really get my motor revving.'

She laughs. 'What was your name again?'

'Matt.'

She holds out her hand. 'Well Matt, I'm Rosa, and I'd really like to get you a drink. Will a beer do? I think there are some in the kitchen.'

'Beer sounds great. But let me get it. It's the least I can do after you've made me so welcome.'

'Too late,' she says, peeling away from me. She stops and points a finger at me in mock menace. 'Don't you dare move!'

Rosa doesn't head to the kitchen. Instead she makes a beeline to her friends on the other side of the room, who erupt in cheers as they throw their arms round her. Through the hugs she sneaks a look in my direction. Her face is the very picture of embarrassment and I begin to wonder if she'll ever return. But then she breaks away from them and heads towards the kitchen and as she does so I feel a rush of excitement go through me. I have no idea how this night will end but it feels good to be this free.

All feelings of liberation are curtailed however when my phone vibrates. It's a text from Abi: *There's nothing on telly, entertain me Beckford! Really looking forward to coffee tomorrow, Abi xxx*

Abi. Somehow in the time that it's taken me to arrive at a party and kiss a virtual stranger I have forgotten that I am supposed to be seeing her tomorrow. This is typical of the kind of luck that always comes my way. I go weeks without so much as a sniff of interest and then the one weekend in which I have a date with a funny, pretty and charming woman I have to walk into a party in Balsall Heath of all places and get jumped on by a girl like Rosa.

The best I can do in the circumstances is to make the courageous decision not to make any decisions and so I tap out the following message: *Can't entertain you right now, am getting seriously hard stares from the people I'm out with who think it's rude to text gorgeous and funny women when I should actually be soaking up the riveting anecdotes about their trekking holiday in the Himalayas.* As I press send I look up in time to see Rosa returning holding a plastic beaker of wine and a bottled lager.

'Texting your other lady friends are you?' she teases, handing me the lager.

'Hardly,' I reply.

She raises an eyebrow. Clearly I'm a much worse liar than I thought. 'Are you sure you haven't got a girlfriend?'

'Hand on heart, guv, there is no lady in my life. But in the interests of transparency and because I'm a lot more drunk than I intended I have to tell you that I do have a sort of ex-wife.'

'Sort of?'

'We're separated.'

'I'm sorry to hear that. How long were you together?'

'Long enough.'

'But you don't live together?'

'She's in London selling our house and I'm up here licking my wounds.'

'I knew you were damaged goods the moment I saw you in the shop,' says Rosa and she touches my hand briefly. It's an unconscious act of pure tenderness that makes me want to kiss her all over again. 'You just had that look about you.'

* * *

She leads me to the hallway to get away from the music and we sit and talk in earnest. She tells me that her academic parents named her Rosa after the America civil rights icon Rosa Parks and I tell her that my parents named me Matthew because it was the only name they could both agree on. I also learn that Rosa's a visual arts relationship manager at the West Midlands office of Arts Council England and when I ask what that is she explains that she OKs funding for visual arts projects and then checks in on them from time to time. She loves her job and I tell her that it's good to love your job because otherwise it can really rain on your parade. Inevitably she asks me a few questions about the shop and what I'm doing in Birmingham. In the light of my date with Abi I try my best to keep it all vague and she seems to get the message. Before long we've left all the autobiographical stuff by the wayside and are getting stuck into films, music, places we've visited and places we're desperate to see. Suddenly she stands up, and asks me if I want to dance.

I've only ever been passable at dancing, just enough sway to look like I'm enjoying myself but nowhere near enough to be eye-catchingly cool. The last time I really danced was the night of my thirty-ninth birthday when after an evening in various bars with Lauren and our friends we ended the night in a club in the West End. Although my recollection is impaired I'm sure that I'd danced pretty well that night, all things considered, but given that nearly a year has elapsed who knows what might have happened to my dancing skills? And more to the point, now that I am nearly forty there's every chance that I might inadvertently start dancing 'from the knees', and now is certainly not the time to debut my 'dad' dancing to the world.

I briefly think about searching out Gerry but if I do this there is a danger that I will break the spell between Rosa and me. I need this girl to like me. I need for her to want to take me home. I need for her to believe that I'm not completely damaged goods and if dancing is what I've got to do to make that happen then dancing is what I'm going to do.

'OK, you're on,' I say, and I allow her to lead me back into the living room. I have no idea what the song is. To me it sounds like twelve different songs being played simultaneously. I look over at Rosa and she flashes me a heartfelt grin as though my fulfilment of her request has satisfied something deep in her soul. Moving to the music I try to channel the spirit of my eighteen-year-old self who used to be a lot less self-conscious about this sort of thing and I think it works. Because while I'm not in receipt of a standing ovation when the song comes to an end on the plus side no one's pointing and laughing. More importantly, Rosa's fingers are now firmly entwined with my own and she looks blissfully happy. It feels like for ever since I've been able to make someone happy just by holding their hand and I find myself wishing that I might always be able to make her feel this good.

29

Rosa tells me that her head is feeling a bit light and that she could really do with some air. I suggest that we go outside and she tells me to wait by the front door while she gets her coat. I'm about to leave the room when Gerry intercepts me. His grinning face says it all. 'All right, stud? What's going on here then?'

'The truth? I have no idea.'

'I couldn't believe it when she just pounced on you like that. I had to be in a band to get that kind of attention! Who is she? Do you know her?'

'About as well as you do. She's Elephant-Dung Paper Girl.'

Gerry raises a knowing eyebrow. 'And she was on you like that just because you sold her novelty paper? I'll have to man the tills more often!'

'You, wish! I'll have you know that Rosa and I have really good chemistry. Plus, she's drunk a bucketload so I'm guessing her judgement's not up to much.'

I look over my friend's shoulder and spot Rosa. She's wearing a bright red coat and carrying two bottled beers.

Even drunk she looks amazing. I look back at Gerry. 'I'll see you later, mate.'

Gerry gives me a wink laden with innuendo. 'I doubt it.'

We walk down the front path past a group of smokers talking, laughing and joking with each other. One of them, a cool-looking young guy wearing a trilby, nods in Rosa's direction as we pass calling out: 'All right, Ms Logan?' but she barely acknowledges him. He reminds me of a mannequin I'd seen in Top Man when I'd tried to update my wardrobe. It too looked as though it had dressed in the dark.

'Who's your friend?' I ask as we sit down on the wall across the front garden.

She hands me one of the beers. 'You don't miss a trick, do you?'

'I'm oblivious to most things but this was impossible to ignore given the daggers being thrown in my direction. When did you split up?'

'A while ago. This is his party and this is the house he and his friends rent.'

'What did he do wrong?'

She studies me carefully. 'What makes you so sure he did anything wrong? It could've been me.'

'Again, I refer you to the daggers. Guys don't throw looks like that when they're in the right. He wants you back because he did something for which you won't forgive him. The daggers are for your benefit as much as mine. Yes, he'd like to punch my lights out but he's actually more interested in letting you know that he knows you're trying to make him jealous and it's working.'

'You're pretty good at this, aren't you?' she says.

'Not really, I've just been around the block a few times.'

Rosa smiles mischievously. 'And how many times would that be?'

'For the sake of argument, let's say forty. After all, what's a month or two between friends?'

It feels good to have got the age thing off my chest. I'd been wondering when it would come up. I had thought it might raise its head when I mentioned I was separated but it almost felt like she was deliberately avoiding the question, perhaps because she feared the answer. Anyway, it's out now, and there's nothing I can do to put the genie back in the bottle.

She looks at me disbelievingly. 'You're really forty?'

'Just about.'

'You don't look it.'

'I'd say thank you but the truth is it's less about how you look than how you feel. And I feel old.' I take a swig of beer. 'How old are you, if you don't mind me asking?'

'What if I do?'

'Then I suppose I'll have to guess.'

She puts the beer bottle up to her lips and for a moment I think about following my current line of questioning with a kiss but having studied her youthful skin these past few minutes under the unflattering xenon glow of a Balsall Heath street lamp I have a horrible feeling that she's much younger than I'd like her to be.

She takes another swig of her beer and then sets it down on the wall: 'Be my guest,' she says.

'I want you to be older.'

She arches one of her carefully maintained eyebrows. 'Why?'

'Because then it wouldn't feel so weird. I was hoping you might have a really youthful face but be in your late twenties but you're not, are you?'

'How old would you like me to be?'

'In an ideal world, you'd be over thirty-five and I'd fall in love with you right now . . . but in the real world I'd settle for anything over twenty-five. Please tell me I'm right.'

She rests her head on my shoulder. Her hair smells unapologetically feminine. I inhale and hold my breath even though I know her answer is going to break my heart. 'Looks like you're out of luck. I'm twenty-three.'

Twenty-three. Between her birth and my own there's a whole seventeen-year-old who's halfway through their A levels. No matter how much I like her it's way too much of a gap for me to contemplate this going any further. After all I'm not Gerry. Or Jason Cleveland. Or for that matter Hugh Hefner.

She kisses my cheek. 'The age thing, it's freaking you out, isn't it? '

'Just a bit.'

'You shouldn't let it.'

'Why not?'

'Age is just a number.'

'And that right there is why this right here would never work. No one but the seriously deluded believes age is just a number. It's not a number, it's an incontrovertible fact. Like, I don't know, being tall . . . having red hair . . . or being allergic to oysters.'

'You're allergic to oysters?'

'Actually, no, but that's not really the point.'

Rosa laughs. 'All night I've been thinking about what you remind me of and I've just realised that it's a passage in *The Velveteen Rabbit*. Have you read it?'

'Never heard of it.'

'I used to have it years ago but I lost it somewhere along the way. I'd love to read it again.'

'I'll look out for a copy in the shop if you like.'

'You'd do that for me?'

'I like to look after my customers. What does it say?'

'There's no point in my half remembering it and spoiling the effect. When you find it, I'll read the passage to you and you'll see how right I was.'

Rosa leans in and kisses me. It's a good few minutes before either of us comes up for air and even then I'm less bothered about breathing than I am about wanting to kiss her again.

'Look,' I say, trying to come to my senses, 'I'd better be going.'

'Before you do something you'll regret?'

'Yeah, something like that.'

'I'm like forbidden fruit to you, aren't I? You have no idea how fantastic that makes me feel. I feel positively goddess-like. Is this some kind of reverse psychology trick that you learned from your twenty years in the dating world? Because if it is, it's working.'

'Sadly, it's not a trick,' I reply. 'I really ought to go.' As I stand up I catch a glimpse of Trilby Boy and his hard stare. 'He's still looking.'

'That's because he's still jealous.' She pats my jacket pocket, pulls out my phone and adds her number to my address book. 'You know the Cross in Moseley? Well, I'll be there next Friday with some mates, you should come along – you know, just as friends if that's all you can handle right now.'

'Friends?'

She crosses her heart with the index finger of her right hand. 'Why? Is that illegal too?'

'You're not making this easy.'

'It's not my job to. Having semi-seduced you once I sort of want to do it again. It was fun.'

This is killing me. 'And on that note. I'll take my leave.'

We head back inside, past Trilby Boy and his daggers, and she doesn't let up with the flirting even for a second. I wonder briefly if her behaviour tonight hadn't been about putting Trilby Boy in his place but decide against it. Even from the little that I know of her I can tell she's not like that. Whether I want to believe it or not, there's a good chance that she actually likes me and this knowledge alone makes me feel a million feet tall.

I look around for Gerry while Rosa waits in the hallway but he's nowhere to be seen. I think about calling him but all I want to do is go.

'So,' says Rosa putting her arms round me. 'This is it then?'

'Looks like it.'

'We would've made a great-looking couple.'

'Absolutely. We would've been the best.'

'And I would have been an amazing girlfriend.'

She leans in and we kiss briefly. If there ever was a kiss that had the power to change a mind, this is it. I can feel my resolve crumbling and if I'm not careful then anything I have even close to a conscience will be crushed.

'So about next weekend . . .' she says as we part.

'Somehow I don't think that's going to happen.'

'I can't say anything to change your mind?'

'I'd prefer not to take the chance.'

Rosa smiles. 'You should never say never, Matt. Who knows what you might miss out on in life with an attitude like that?'

30

Gerry greets me the following Monday morning with a round of applause as he opens the door to let me into the shop. 'And here he is – the man of the hour – the one, the only, Matthew Beckford!'

The other volunteers all stop what they're doing and look perplexed.

'Is it his birthday?' asks Odd Owen.

'I think he must have pulled over the weekend,' says Steve the Student.

'Gerry's just having his little joke,' I reply, keen to keep news of my love life away from the other volunteers. 'Morning all!'

I dump my bag in the office and return as Gerry calls a morning meeting.

'First order of business—'

'We're out of milk,' says Odd Owen.

'No we're not,' says Gerry. 'I looked in the fridge just this morning. There's at least two-thirds of one of those big bottles in there.'

'It's gone off,' says Odd Owen. 'I smelt it.'

Gerry looks confused. 'But you don't drink tea, do you Owen?'

Owen shakes his head. 'Just Pepsi for me, thanks.'

'So why are you smelling the milk?'

Owen looks down at the floor and Gerry's momentarily lost for words.

'Right, well . . . I'll definitely look into the milk situation.'

Gerry soldiers on with the morning meeting. There's a new notification about being on the lookout for dodgy twenty-pound notes, a warning that the card machine has been playing up again but the man won't be out to fix it until next Monday, a memo from head office praising the shop for hitting its targets in the last quarter and the announcement that a new work rota has been pinned to the board in the stockroom.

'Are you quite finished?' asks Anne, in her usual no-nonsense manner, just as Gerry is about to wrap things up. 'Only some of us have got quite a lot of stock to get through.'

With that the meeting falls apart as Anne marches back to the stockroom, Steve opens the door to a large bearded man banging on the window and holding up several bags of donations and Odd Owen wanders over to the shelves, picks up a Stephen King novel, positions himself behind the till and begins reading.

Gerry looks at me. 'It's going to be one of those days isn't it?'

'I think you may be right. Coffee break?'

'I thought you'd never ask.'

We leave the shop and head to Annabel's. I can see Gerry wants to ask about the weekend and much to my surprise he restrains himself until after we've been served and are sitting down at a table.

'So come on then. How was it?'

'How was what?'

'Friday night! With that girl!'

'Nothing happened.'

'What do you mean, nothing happened? She was all over you!'

'And she was twenty-three!'

'So what?'

'What do you mean, "So what?" She would've been two years old the year *Newhall Lovers* came out. Doesn't that freak you out?'

'Of course it doesn't! Kara's only twenty-six and you don't hear me making a big deal about it. Age doesn't matter. It's people that count. I've met women my age that aren't even half as mature as Kara. The thing you should be asking yourself is, did you like her?'

'I thought she was amazing. We didn't stop talking the entire time we were together. But that doesn't change the fact that it's like the biggest cliché in the book, does it?'

'So you don't want to see her because you're afraid of being a cliché? I had no idea you were so fragile.'

'It's got nothing to do with being fragile and everything to do with not wanting to be the bloke that tries to hang on to his youth by dressing like a teenager and hanging out with girls half his–,' I stop myself quickly. 'Not like you, of course, you're different. You can work it somehow and not make it look sleazy or desperate because it's not a pose. I think what I'm trying to say is this whole being young when you're not actually young is a bit like being able to pull off wearing a hat without looking like an idiot. Some people can do it, others can't and I am definitely not a hat man.'

'You're a mug if you believe that.'

'And if I don't I'll be a creepy bloke dating a girl seventeen years my junior. I've done the calculations! I am technically old enough to be her dad! Which is why I've decided to give things a go with Abi instead.'

Gerry looks confused. 'Abi? Who's Abi?'

'Keep up, will you? She's the woman from the dating site I was texting all last week. We had about half a dozen conversations about her. I was meeting up with her on Saturday afternoon.'

'And how did that go?'

'It was perfect. Could not have been better. And she is definitely the girl for me.'

In reality my date with Abi was easily one of the worst I have ever been on. To begin with she was an hour late (something to do with her cat going missing) and when she did finally turn up for the first five minutes her sole topic of conversation was how far away she'd had to park her car. Over the course of our date it became clear that despite the obvious chemistry of our text messages, in person we couldn't have been less in tune with each other. Everything I loathed she liked and everything I liked she hated. More off-putting than that, however, was her odd habit of attempting to finish my sentences and also the realisation that she was still clearly working her way through a number of unresolved issues to do with her ex. But for the fact that she was as attractive as her online profile picture had led me to believe, her near-constant reassurances that this was the best date she had been on in months and the fact that like me she too was turning forty this year I probably would've given up on the date altogether. And, because of this, when she texted me the following morning to thank me for the date and ask if I was free on Friday night, instead of going with my gut and declining I went with my head and said yes because of late my gut decisions had been letting me down badly.

Leaving my parents' house on the night of my date with Abi, smelling of freshly sprayed deodorant I decide to walk to Moseley rather than catch the bus because it will give me time to conjure up a plan of action for the evening ahead. I want this thing with Abi to work. Not just because Lauren's moved on, or to exorcise the ghost of Ginny or even because being with her might make turning forty easier. I need it to work because by choosing to pursue things with Abi rather than Rosa I feel like I'm giving up someone I felt a real connection with in order to make a point that no one seems to believe in apart from me.

I reach the Bull's Head, a former boozer of the old-men-in-flat-caps variety now transformed into a cool pre-club hangout for a much younger crowd. I order a beer at the bar and wonder how Abi and I can conduct any kind of conversation when there's a DJ in the corner right next to where I'm standing. Maybe we'll just have the one drink here and move on or maybe this will be the excuse I'll need to lean over and talk into her ear and establish some sort of intimacy.

The barmaid brings my drink. I take a sip and my phone buzzes. It's a message from Abi: *Sorrrrrrrry!!! Running half an hour late. Promise I'll be worth the wait!!! xxx*. This leaves me feeling uneasy. Was I making a hideous mistake here? Rosa was fun, and feisty and being in her company made me feel really alive. OK, so I didn't want to be the guy who thinks having a young girlfriend is the answer to everything and so what if she didn't get my references to *Tiswas* or *Moonlighting* but did I really want to be the guy stuck in a dead-end relationship because he was too short-sighted to see a good thing when it came his way? Pushing aside my drink, I run out of the bar, cross the road (only narrowly avoiding being run over by a minicab) and head into the Cross in search of Rosa.

My heart racing like I've run a marathon, I scan the faces, groups of girls, drinks held aloft, laughing, joking, preening and posing. Had this always been my plan? Was it just a coincidence that I had chosen a venue to meet Abi that was less than a hundred metres away from where I knew Rosa would be on the same night? But now I can see Rosa it doesn't matter because she's exactly as gorgeous as I remember her.

She spots me straight away and her expression seems to freeze. I wonder if she has met someone else. Someone her own age. Someone more suitable. But after a moment she walks over to meet me, buries her face in my chest, then looks up and we kiss.

'A week ago you seemed pretty insistent that this was a bad idea,' she says. 'What changed your mind?'

'You did,' I reply. 'Just when I least expected it. Speaking of which I've got something I need to do and it just might take me a while.'

Rosa smiles. 'Take as long as you like,' she says. 'I'm not going anywhere.'

After one last kiss I head back over to the Bull's Head to do one of the hardest things I've ever done: break up with a woman who I'm not even properly going out with and whose only crime it appears was setting our first date twenty-four hours too late.

Days left until I turn forty: 64

31

'You're going to be late.'

'I know.'

'But you were late yesterday too.'

'I know, but I heard on the radio that it's the wettest February since records began and you're all nice and warm. Maybe I'll call in sick. Will you do it for me?'

'Like I did last Wednesday? Don't you think they'll see a pattern forming? Rosa's got herself a new bloke and now all of a sudden she's got a cold every other day.'

Rosa sighs. 'This is torture. The only way I'm going to make it through a whole day of not seeing you is if you give me something to look forward to tonight.'

'What do you want?'

'I don't mind as long as you're there.'

'How about the theatre?'

'Nope. Not special enough.'

'How about we go out for a meal?'

'Still not special enough, plus we've been out so much in the last couple of weeks that I'm nearly as broke as you are.'

'OK, well how about I cook you dinner?'

Her face brightens. 'Now you're talking! There are few things sexier than a man cooking for his lady. What'll you make?'

'My signature lady-impressing dish: fish fingers on a bed of sliced white bread adorned with a dollop of ketchup.'

'Sounds delicious,' she whispers, 'I can't wait,' and right on cue the bedside alarm goes off again. As I watch her naked form exiting the bedroom I realise two things with perfect clarity: first, that I'm happy and second, my only ambition right now is to make this woman as happy as she is making me.

It's hard to describe the past fortnight without trotting out all the usual superlatives, but being with Rosa really has been amazing. After the night at the Cross she invited me back to her place and late the following morning we walked hand in hand down to the centre of Moseley, bought a couple of newspapers, ate a leisurely breakfast at the French café across the road from the shop before taking a stroll down to Cannon Hill Park where we fed the ducks, pushed each other on the kids' swings and generally acted like fools in love.

Neither of us wanted the day to end so we made sure that it didn't. I made a brief appearance at my parents' but before my mum could open her mouth to ask me what I wanted for dinner I had showered and changed and was back out of the door on my way over to Rosa's where I stayed until the Monday morning when we finally both had to go to work.

Despite having resolved over the weekend not to spend Monday night together neither of us had the willpower to resist and soon a pattern emerged where I would stay at her flat every night, pop over to my parents' (normally while they were out) for a shower and clean clothes before going back to Moseley and the shop where Gerry would mock me remorselessly for being so ludicrously happy.

And I don't fight it because I *am* happy.

Rosa and I just click. We get each other and instead of being a barrier the age thing seems to be something that draws us together. It's almost as if when I'm with her I stop being thirty-nine, she stops being twenty-three and somehow we meet in the middle. I haven't had a great deal to do with her friends and I haven't exactly got any friends around other than Gerry to make her feel weird, so for the most part it's just me and her and that seems to be pretty much all we need.

Gerry's Lambretta is already parked on the pavement by the time I arrive at the shop and as I press the buzzer and peer through the window, I can just make out the outlines of Gerry, Anne and Odd Owen chatting in the back office.

'Morning, sunshine,' says Gerry, opening the door, 'who's looking even more loved up than usual?'

I can't help but laugh. On the walk down this morning even I had noticed a big soppy grin on my face.

'What can I say?' I reply, 'I'm a happy man.'

'So it's going well?'

'It's going better than well, it's going brilliantly. She's amazing.'

'And all this from the man who thought it was doomed from the start. You've certainly changed your tune.'

I'm not going to be drawn. I say my hellos to the other volunteers, take a look at the list of tasks on the wall, hang up my jacket and get the kettle on for the first brew of the day.

The morning passes quickly: I spend an hour on the tills, another creating a window display of children's books and the remaining time before lunch putting new stock on the shelves. As the shop has more than enough cover today Gerry and I decide to head next door to Annabel's and we're just getting our coats when there's a sharp knock at the rear door. I open it expecting to see someone carrying one of those huge blue IKEA bags weighed down with donations but instead there's a tall, lean guy wearing sunglasses, a black velvet jacket, denim shirt and jeans.

'I'm looking for Gerry,' he says in a well-spoken voice with only the faintest hint of a Midlands accent. 'Is he about?'

I open the door wider to reveal Gerry. The two men stare at each other and neither says a word. I sense I'm surplus to requirements so I tell Gerry that I'll meet him at Annabel's when he's done.

I realise there's something familiar about Gerry's guest but it's not until half an hour later when Gerry sits down opposite me that I find out for sure.

'Who was that?'

Gerry picks up his sandwich. 'And there was me thinking you were a real Pinfolds fan.'

'So that really was Pete McCulloch?'

'The very same.'

Pete McCulloch was a legend in his own right as well as being Gerry's former songwriting partner and The Pinfolds' lead guitarist. After The Pinfolds split up, Pete had moved to New York and joined a succession of moderately well-known bands before finding success as a music producer on two platinum-selling albums in a row, which made him one of the most in-demand producers in the world. And while he wasn't famous enough to be stopped in the street by your average punter, I'd seen enough photos of him hanging out with people who were globally recognisable, and read the back pages of enough CD inserts, to be impressed that he'd crossed the threshold of our little charity shop in Moseley.

'What did he want?'

'What do you think?'

The first answer that pops into my head is too huge to contemplate. 'He wants to get the band back together?'

'Bingo!' says Gerry, pointing his right hand at me like a gun. 'Apparently the bastard's got the other two on board and now he thinks I'll just fall into line.'

I can't believe what I'm hearing. 'You're not going to do it?'

Gerry grimaces. 'Of course I'm not going to do it! The man's scum! I swore twenty years ago that I'd have nothing more to do with him and I can't see a reason to change my mind.'

'What happened back then? What did he do?'

'You don't need to know,' replies Gerry firmly. 'It's just one of those things that is never going to happen. Not for the sake of old times, not for the fans and least of all for the money.'

It's clear that he doesn't want to talk about it any more and so I try to change the subject but he doesn't seem to want to talk about anything and he stays that way for the rest of the afternoon, only venturing out of the office with a face like thunder when the credit card machine breaks down.

Even though I'm supposed to be making dinner for Rosa, I invite him for a quick pint across the road, but he mumbles something about meeting Kara in town so I leave him to his own devices. As I'm about to leave the shop Rosa texts saying she has finished work early and to hang on at the shop until she arrives. Minutes later there's a knock at the door and I see her face at the window.

'No need to ask if you've missed me,' she grins as we part from our embrace.

'No need at all.' I grab my coat and shut up shop as quickly as I can.

We cross the road to Sainsbury's Local, pick up a basket and wend our way along the aisles with me throwing things in for the meal and her adding stuff she needs for the flat. I know what she's thinking because it's exactly what I'm thinking: *This is good. It feels comfortable. It feels right.*

When we get to the till I pull out my credit card even though I can't afford it, but this moment seems too important to let a little thing like debt get in the way and so with fingers crossed I hand over my card. It's only when I actually have our goods that I allow myself to exhale in relief but then we walk out of the shop and heading straight towards us, hand in hand, are Ginny and Gershwin.

32

I really had tried to avoid this moment. I had deliberately steered clear of Pat Kav's where I had met Gershwin for a drink; hadn't been back to the Sainsbury's where I'd first bumped into Ginny; and deliberately avoided the café on York Road where Ginny and I had once breakfasted. In short I had given my two former friends practically the whole of Kings Heath in return for my never having to see either of them in public again, but it seemed that the whole of Kings Heath wasn't enough.

I greet them both as warmly as I can, which, given the fact that I still want to punch Gershwin and can do little more than look daggers in Ginny's direction, isn't all that warmly. It doesn't help that they had looked so happy together (Ginny's head was turned towards Gershwin listening intently and Gershwin was clutching her left hand in a proprietary fashion).

'What are you up to?' asks Ginny, trying to look and sound normal.

I raise the carrier bag in reply. 'Just picking up a few things. How about yourselves?'

'We're on our way to the Thai place next door to Kav's.'

'You'll love it,' says Rosa. Ginny and Gershwin turn to look at her as though they hadn't noticed her before. 'A group of us went from work a while ago and we had a great time.'

'We've been before,' says Ginny, 'but thanks for the recommendation.'

Was it my imagination or was there a hint of acerbity in Ginny's voice? I glance from Ginny to Rosa and decide to get the introductions over with. 'Rosa,' I say, 'this is Ginny and Gershwin, some old school friends of mine, Ginny and Gershwin, this is Rosa, my girlfriend.'

It's hard to know which of us is more surprised by the use of the word 'girlfriend'; my former friends certainly seem staggered by my revelation but Rosa's eyes widen too. In fact I'm the one most in shock even though I do a pretty good job of hiding it.

'Well,' says Ginny after an awkward pause, 'we'd better be getting off if we're not going to lose our reservation.'

'Of course,' I reply, 'it was good to see you.'

Ginny glances over at Rosa. 'Nice to meet you.'

'You too.'

I look at Gershwin and he looks at me but we don't say a word.

As Ginny and Gershwin walk away I count in my head using 'elephant' seconds trying to guess how long it will be before Rosa questions me about our encounter. I barely get to two.

'Who was that?'

'Two old schoolmates.'

'But why were they being so weird? The guy didn't say a word and you were throwing lethal looks in his direction.'

'It's complicated.'

'She wasn't your soon-to-be ex-wife was she?'

'Of course not, Lauren is in London, I told you.'

'So who was she then?'

'Another ex, a sort of more recent ex . . . Look, do we really have to do this? The last thing I want is to go over it all again. Can't we just go home, crack open a bottle of wine and chat while I make you the best fish finger sandwich you've ever tasted? The art lies in getting the ketchup to cheap white bread ratio just right.'

It's a nice try but I can tell from the searching look in Rosa's eyes that she's not going to let it go that easily. 'You called me your girlfriend.'

I feign confusion. 'Did I?'

Rosa stops, stares at me as if trying to size me up and then pulls back her fist and hits me square in the chest.

For a reasonably small person she actually packs quite a punch. 'What's that for?'

'For taking me for an idiot. I'm not stupid, Matt. You said it to make her jealous.'

'Why would I want to make her jealous? Up until a couple of months ago I hadn't seen her for years.'

Rosa shrugs. 'People are weird like that.'

'Well, not me.'

'So why did you call me your girlfriend then? You've never called me that before.'

'I've never had a reason to until now. It's not like we're bumping into a continuous stream of people for you to meet, is it? We barely go out, who am I going to introduce you to? Your next-door neighbours?'

Mellowing, she reaches out a hand and rubs the spot on my chest where she struck me. 'I'm sorry. I shouldn't have done that. It's just I don't think you should go bandying about words like "girlfriend" unless you mean it.'

'And who says I don't?' I'm glad to have our first argument behind us. I feel the same rush of affection for her as this morning when she left for work. 'You are my girlfriend, aren't you? I don't want to be with anyone else and I don't want to be anywhere else.' I dig around in my bag, pull out a book and hand it to Rosa.

'*The Velveteen Rabbit*,' she says, 'you remembered.'

'I've been hunting for it ever since you mentioned it at the party. A copy came in last week and I was going to keep it to celebrate our one-month anniversary but now will do just as well.'

'I love it,' she says and kisses my cheek. She flicks through as if searching for something. 'This is the part I was telling you about, the part that reminds me of you: "Real isn't how you are made," says the Skin Horse. "It's a thing that happens to you . . . It doesn't happen all at once. You become. It takes a long time. Generally by the time you are Real, most of your hair has been loved off, and your eyes drop out and you get loose in the joints and very shabby. But these things don't matter at all, because once you are Real you can't be ugly, except to people who don't understand." '

She looks at me. 'You've been battered, bruised and pretty much neglected Matthew Beckford, but you're real and don't you ever forget it.'

Ordinarily I'd make a joke about losing my hair but feeling oddly moved by the quotation, I just say, 'OK.'

The rest of our Friday night goes well. Rosa declares my fish-finger sandwiches the best she's ever tasted and once we've cleared up the kitchen we drink wine, talk until late and fall asleep on the sofa in each other's arms.

The following morning I find myself lying next to a beautiful partially dressed woman snoring softly at my side, with a whole work-free Saturday stretching ahead of us and not a worry in the world. Life really doesn't get any better.

And then my phone rings.

I see that it's my parents. I switch the phone to silent and set it back down on the table.

Rosa rouses herself and gently rubs her eyes. Her just-woken-up face is as beautiful as her everyday made-up face. 'Who was that?'

'My mum most likely.'

'Is she OK?'

'I couldn't bring myself to answer it. I already feel guilty enough that I haven't seen much of my folks these past few weeks. She's probably fed up that I've been spending all my time here and is trying to coax me home with the promise of a meal. She's called about half a dozen times and not left a message.'

Rosa frowns. 'I feel bad. Maybe you should see her then.'

'What? And spend a night away from you? No thanks. I'll drop in sometime on Sunday. They'll be fine.'

'And will you take me?'

I eye her suspiciously. Surely we weren't at this stage quite yet. I know I'd called her my girlfriend but wasn't this usually a few more months down the line? 'I wasn't planning on it but if you want to . . .'

'No, not really, not unless *you* want to.'

The relief I feel is palpable. My parents would take Rosa's presence in my life as further evidence that I wasn't taking the breakdown of my marriage seriously enough and was more than likely having some kind of mid-life crisis.

'There's no rush is there?'

'Well, my parents have been asking about you quite a bit and I've been putting them off, but yesterday they bullied me into bringing you to their house tonight for supper.'

'Supper?' Having never had a great deal to do with people who called their 'dinner' 'supper' until I reached university, I still found the word amusing whenever I heard it used.

Rosa pulls a throw around her and sits up, revealing the very beguiling tops of her naked shoulders. 'You hate the idea, don't you? I'll just call and tell them you're not well.'

I'm still thinking about her naked shoulders. 'Sorry?'

'I said you hate the idea.'

'I don't love it.'

She looks crestfallen. I hate seeing someone with shoulders this beautiful looking crestfallen. It's a million different kinds of wrong.

'But that doesn't mean that we shouldn't go, it might be fun.'

Rosa laughs. 'It won't be fun, they'll ask you a hundred and one questions and make a big deal of the fact that they're not making a big deal that you're thirty-nine.'

'Which I'm guessing is better than them making a big deal about it?'

'Only just. Are you sure you feel up to this?'

I'm not at all sure. Rosa's dad is only five years older than Gerry and her mum is only twelve years older than me. They're both academics working in the English department at Birmingham University. Her dad likes Bob Dylan and her mum is a world expert on the poetry of Christina Rossetti and I know for a fact that unless I Wikipedia both this could easily end up being the longest meal of my life. But whether I succeed in entertaining her parents or not I want to do this because I know how much it will mean to Rosa and if it makes her happy then – fingers crossed – it'll make me happy too.

'What time do they want us?'

She fixes me with a stare that smoulders with intensity. I genuinely can't remember the last time a woman looked at me like that.

'Have you any idea how much I fancy you right now?'

'Why don't you show me?'

33

'Rosa tells us that you're between jobs at the moment,' says Rosa's dad halfway through dinner. So far we've discussed London house prices, the best place to buy free-range chickens, TV chefs in general, Jamie Oliver in particular and how much we all miss old style *Master Chef* when Loyd Grossman was presenting it. Having worked through so many topics I am more than a little disheartened to find myself back here again. 'That's certainly one way of putting it,' I say and thankfully everyone laughs. 'Right now I'm doing some voluntary work.'

Tony nods. 'Decided to do some giving back.'

'Something like that,' I reply.

'And what are your plans for the future?'

Arabella leans forward and Rosa reaches under the table and squeezes my hand.

'I'm not sure.'

'Bit of a free spirit, are you?'

'I'd love to say yes,' I reply, 'but I'd be lying. I've just come to a bit of a crossroads and I haven't quite worked out which path to take.'

'What are the options?'

'Go back to what I was doing before or find something new. Given how much I hated the former that isn't really an option so I'll just keep searching until I find what I'm looking for.'

'That sounds like an excellent plan,' says Arabella, coming to my rescue. 'I think we've all been in that place where we're not sure what the next move to make is. Rosa was exactly the same when she left Cambridge.'

I look at Rosa. 'You went to Cambridge?'

'And got a double first in the History of Art,' adds Tony.

'I just worked hard,' says Rosa dismissively. 'Dad thinks that makes me a genius.'

'It most certainly does,' interjects her father proudly. 'You can do anything you want with your life.'

'I know I can,' says Rosa, tensing, 'that's why I'm doing what I'm doing right now.'

I joke that perhaps Rosa ought to give me some careers advice and the laughter lifts the tension long enough for us all to move on and finish our meal without any further discussion about my job prospects.

Despite my earlier anxiety, my visit to Rosa's parents appears to be going reasonably well. Tony (a tall, thin man with such a bookish air that even if he'd been naked rather than wearing a tweed jacket and mid-brown cords could not have been mistaken for anything other than an academic) turns out to be quite a laugh and though I feared we'd have nothing in common we end up bonding over a love of *Seinfeld* and early

Curb Your Enthusiasm; meanwhile even though Arabella (a strikingly beautiful woman who looks more like an ex-model than an academic) and I have little in common I still manage to get on with her mainly because after years of making small talk with strangers in offices around the world it turns out that I'm a pretty good conversationalist.

Even when they bring up the fact that I'm still married ('Rosa's told us about your situation. It must be so difficult for you.') I handle it really well, ('Obviously I'm not exactly thrilled about it, Arabella, but these things do happen,') and then I move the conversation swiftly on to an article I'd read on the internet about the current state of university teaching in the UK, and that was it, they were off talking about their world and I didn't need to pick up the conversational reins again until long after dessert.

Thinking back to all the times I've worried about such encounters, whether it be a girlfriend's parents or a third round of job interviews, suddenly I wish I could go back and face them all but this time with the benefit of age and experience to calm me down.

We stay at Rosa's parents' long after midnight and despite their invitation to stay in one of their many spare bedrooms the look of mortification that spreads across my face the moment the idea is mentioned is enough to send Rosa straight to her phone in search of a minicab firm.

'Well, that was a lucky escape,' I say once we're safely ensconced in a cab heading back to her flat. 'Were they serious about me staying?'

Rosa nods. 'My parents have never made a big deal about me bringing boyfriends home. I think Mum just likes to see the house full. Didn't you ever have girlfriends stay at your parents' house when you were younger?'

'Never. It would have been my worst nightmare and would've put me off sex for life. We've lived such different lives you and I, we really have.'

'Maybe,' says Rosa, pulling herself closer to me, 'but none of that matters now does it?'

'No.' I say and I'm pretty sure I mean it.

The next morning I wake quite early and even though it's a Sunday and I'm not due in the shop until Monday I'm overcome by the urge to get up and go back to my own parents'. Maybe having spent an evening with Rosa's parents means I find myself missing my own. I just really fancy an afternoon of their kind of normal: talking sport or local politics with Dad; hearing Mum's news about my nieces and nephews and engaging in the mundane conversation that I've known all my life and never bothered cherishing.

'What's up?' asks Rosa, sensing I'm awake.

'I'm going to get up and head back to my folks for a bit.'

'This early? Why don't you go later so we can have the morning together?'

'I feel bad that I haven't seen them properly for so long.'

She kisses me. 'Are you sure?'

'One hundred per cent.' I kiss the top of her head. 'I'll see you tonight though if that's OK? Maybe we can go to the cinema or something.'

'Sounds like a plan. Promise you'll text me later to let me know how your day's going. It'll be weird spending a whole Sunday without you.'

I'm up, showered and dressed in fifteen minutes and I make my way back over to Kings Heath. Opening the front door, I call out to let my parents know I'm back. They're in the kitchen, Dad dressed in the old clothes he wears for gardening and Mum, surrounded by open bags of flour, sugar and currants, looks to be halfway through making a cake.

She turns off the mixer. 'And it's only now you finally remember where you live?'

'It's good to see you too, Mum,' I say, laughing. 'What have I missed?'

They exchange wary glances.

'Listen son,' says Dad. 'We've got some news that might come as a bit of a surprise.'

'OK.' I take a seat at the kitchen table, bracing myself for the news that they're getting a divorce, which is the only reason I can conjure up for them acting so oddly. 'Fire away.'

'We've sold the house,' says Mum. 'We're moving.'

'You've done what?'

Dad shakes his head in dismay. This isn't the way he'd wanted to do things. 'We've sold the house, son.'

'This house? Eighty-eight Hampton Street?'

'Of course this house,' snaps Mum. 'What other house have we got?'

'But I don't get it. There hasn't even been a For Sale board outside.'

'It all happened so fast,' says Dad.

'It's not like we haven't been trying to get hold of you,' adds Mum defensively. 'You're like the invisible man these days. Where have you been spending all your time?'

'With a mate.'

Mum raises an eyebrow sceptically. 'Which . . . mate is this then?'

'Look Mum,' I say in an exasperated tone, 'it doesn't matter, does it? There's more important stuff going on right now. I mean, how could you possibly have sold the house this quickly?'

'A property developer bought it.'

I feel like the mother in Jack and the Beanstalk, about to blow her cork because her clueless son has sold the family cow for a bag of magic beans. 'A property developer? What does a property developer want to buy our house for?'

'He doesn't. We've done one of those part-exchange things.'

I feel sick. This is getting worse with every second that passes. I always knew my parents would need looking after eventually but I never imagined that it would come so soon. 'You've part-exchanged our family home for what exactly?'

'A two-bed bungalow ten minutes away from your sister in Worcester,' says Dad, and he looks at Mum as if seeking encouragement.

And then it all makes sense. They had been serious about wanting to do the grandparent thing properly after all. They were serious about there being more to life than acting as the collective guardians of my childhood memories.

'You know your mum and I have been wanting to be closer to Yvonne and the kids? Well, a couple of weeks ago we went to see your sister and your mother was distracting me with all of her talk about the woman at sixty-seven who's just moved a new bloke in and I missed the turning I usually take and we ended up getting a bit lost. Anyway, we come round the bend and notice a sign for a new retirement development that's just been completed. Your mother's always got her eye out for things like this so she notes down the number, we make some enquiries when we get to Yvonne's and the sales people invite us round to take a look that very afternoon. Long story short, we fell in love.'

Mum nods her approval eagerly. 'You should see them, Matthew, they're only two-bed bungalows but they're so lovely. Fully double-glazed, a spacious kitchen-diner, a living room large enough to fit the whole family at Christmas, a purpose-built utility room, a master bedroom with an en-suite plus a decent-sized family bathroom, a double garage for your father and a garden which while not exactly finished to our tastes will be sorted out in no time.'

'And don't forget the views,' adds Dad.

'Oh, the views,' says Mum. 'Matthew you should see them. Just trees and fields for as far as the eye can see.'

'So anyway,' continues Dad, 'after we'd looked around the sales lady asked us about our situation. We told her and straightaway she said that she thought part-exchange would be the way forward. Their valuer came a few days later, we got a chap in a few days after that and it's been with the solicitor ever since.'

'And they think it's going to be done in three weeks.'

Dad nods, his face the picture of guilt. 'We signed the papers yesterday, son, the date's set and the removal men booked for the first Friday in March.'

'We can go over this afternoon if you like,' says Dad. 'We might not be able to see the actual bungalow if they're too busy in the sales department but there's a show bungalow that you can look around to get a feel for the place. And I promise you, your room has got one of the best views of the whole house.'

'My room?'

'Well, you'll be coming with us won't you? I mean, it's not like you've got anywhere else to live.'

I don't reply. I can't. My brain absolutely refuses to process the information.

'We didn't do this lightly,' says Mum. 'I know this place has got a lot of memories for you, it has for all of us, but it's like I said to your father only yesterday: You can't keep living in the past. You have to look to the future.'

34

I don't go out for the rest of the day. I spend what's left of it on the phone to my siblings venting about the crazy nature of my parents' plan. Even though I put my case as even-handedly as I can (given the circumstances), pointing out that none of us has looked over the contract, investigated how much they've paid to secure the house or indeed (with the exception of Yvonne) even seen the bungalow, all of them think that this is the single best thing Mum and Dad could have done and I am insane for believing otherwise. 'If you'd seen how happy Mum looked when she saw the views from the kitchen,' said Yvonne, 'you wouldn't doubt that they've made the right decision.' My brother Tony was equally effusive: 'Bruv, they are going to be so happy in the place,' and finally in his typical diplomatic style my brother Ed observed: 'This isn't about them, it's about you and the hard time you're having with everything that's going on in your life. I get it, it's tough, but if you took the time to look beyond your world for a minute or two you'd see how right this move is for them.' I didn't think much of Yvonne's and Tony's comments or even Ed's half-baked pop psychology, and I left them with the most important issue at hand: 'Once the house is sold that's going to be it, a whole chapter of our lives closed for good, with no chance of it ever being reopened. If you're going to make a decision like that you have to think it through, you have to be sure, because if you're not the moment might come when you'll regret it and by then it will be too late.'

Later I get a text from Rosa asking what time I'll be back. I text her straight away and tell her that I'm coming down with a bug. She offers to come over and look after me. As lovely as this idea is I'm simply not in the mood, so I tell her that I'm going to attempt to sleep my way through my illness. I promise to text her in the morning and then I turn off my phone.

The following morning I make myself get up and go into work even though all I want to do is stay in bed. I arrive just after ten and try my best to be upbeat but within five minutes of my arrival Gerry picks up on my mood.

'Girl problems is it?' he calls from the biography section.

'Parent problems,' I reply, thankful that the shop is empty apart from the two of us.

'What's up?'

I tell him everything. He is visibly shocked. 'What are you going to do? Go with them?'

'They're moving to a retirement bungalow! I can't be living in a retirement bungalow at forty!'

'So what then?' he asks. 'Are you going back to London?'

'And live with my online-dating estranged wife? I can't imagine there'd be any problem there, can you?'

'Well I suppose you could stay here, couldn't you?'

'And live where? I'm broke. Of course, I suppose there is one other alternative . . .'

Gerry looks alarmed. 'You know I'd love to but I can't, mate.'

'Why not? You're always telling me how big your place is . . . it'd be a laugh. And it's not like I'd need a bedroom. I'd kip on the sofa and it'd only be until the house in London gets sold. It's been getting loads of viewings recently, I only need one of them to turn into an offer and I'll be out of your hair for good.'

'I can't mate – sorry. Kara's round at mine all the time these days and she's always walking about the place half naked – I think it's some kind of Dutch thing – I can't do anything to make her put on clothes. You don't want to be around that, it'd be embarrassing for all of us. Haven't you got any other mates you could ask?'

The image of Ginny and Gershwin holding hands outside Sainsbury's flashes up in my head and immediately turns my mood black. 'No,' I say, 'not any more.'

Gerry pats me on the back. 'Listen mate, if I was you I wouldn't panic. Something will turn up, I'm sure of it. Something always comes up for people like me and you.'

The rest of the day goes by in a blur. I put some of the top-quality stock on eBay where it will get a better price, rummage through donations, discourage two of the world's most hopeless shoplifters from helping themselves to CDs, field multiple texts from Rosa, get into an argument with a guy demanding a refund for the two Jim Carrey DVDs that he bought at the weekend because he allegedly hadn't realised that they both starred Jim Carrey, enter into a very weird conversation with Odd Owen about a book he's reading about Stalingrad, get told off by Anne for not keeping the classical section in order while she's been away on holiday, tell off Steve the Student after discovering him attempting to circumvent the firewall I'd put in place so he could update his status on Facebook, and spend three hours manning the till.

By the end of the day I'm exhausted, and all I want to do is go home, go to bed and not think about anything but just as we're about to shut up shop, the bell jangles and I look up from the till to see Rosa walk in.

'Hey you,' I say once I've packed the last customer off with two Lee Childs and a Dan Brown. 'How are you doing?'

Rosa's smile fades. 'I was going to ask you the same question. Is there any chance we could have a quick chat?'

'Yeah of course.' I nod to Odd Owen to take over the till while I head to the office to find Gerry.

'Do you mind if I get off a bit early?' I ask. 'It's just that Rosa's here and she looks pretty annoyed.'

'Maybe she's come to tell you she's pregnant,' says Gerry, chuckling to himself. 'I've heard it's the sort of thing that can get even the most placid of women worked up.'

I look at him incredulously. 'Why would you even joke

about such a thing when you know my life is falling apart around my ears?'

'Mate,' he says emphatically, 'if I don't pull your plonker who will?'

I head back into the shop to collect Rosa and take her across the road to the Fighting Cocks because I'm desperate for a pint.

'So,' I say once we're firmly ensconced at a table, 'what's on your mind?'

'You,' she says. 'I don't like playing games, Matt. If you're not into this any more I wish you'd just be a man and say rather than stringing me along.'

'What've I done?'

'You've been distant ever since you left on Sunday morning. I text you and I only get a single line back, I call you and you barely say a word. Is it something to do with your ex, are you getting back with her?'

'No, of course not!'

'So what then? Is it me? Is it the age thing?'

'Of course it's not you. You're the best thing in my life right now. It's just that I've got some stuff going on with my parents and it's freaking me out a bit.'

'They're OK aren't they? They're not ill or anything?'

'No, it's nothing like that. It's just that I finally found out why my mum has been trying so hard to get hold of me: she and my dad have sold their house and bought a place in Worcester near to my sister. They move in a few weeks and they want me to go with them.'

'To Worcester?'

'Exactly. I can't be doing that. It's a retirement bungalow. I'll be the youngest person there by about thirty years. I've asked Gerry if I can stay at his but he's got stuff going on with his girlfriend and there's no way I can afford a place on my own without a job so—'

'Move in with me,' says Rosa firmly.

'You what?'

'I said, move in with me.'

'You?'

Rosa laughs. 'You know how to make a girl feel wanted, don't you?'

'We'll it's just that, you know, we haven't exactly been together all that long.'

'What does that matter? You've just told me I'm the best thing in your life right now and I think you're fabulous, you need a place to stay and I've got a one-bedroom flat that feels empty without you in it. I think this is what's called in the trade "synchronicity". So what do you say?'

I think it's the absolute worst idea I've ever heard. What we have works precisely because there are no plans for the future. There's only now. Moving in together, even on an allegedly temporary basis, would change everything, and she needs to know this. I clear my throat and look into her eyes ready to tell her the truth but she looks so genuinely happy, so utterly thrilled that I might even be considering it, that I just can't bring myself to do it.

'I think that sounds great,' I tell her. 'I can't think of anything that I'd want more.'

The following morning, I get out of bed once she's gone to work and while the kettle boils for my morning coffee I open up her laptop and start looking up IT recruitment firms. Given what I'd told her last night it feels like a real betrayal but I have no choice because if I've learned anything during my thirty-nine years on earth it's this: moving in with Rosa will be a mistake. Living together so soon when things are going so well is asking for trouble. My life has been so up in the air and my head is so all over the place that I'm bound to make a mess of things. No, I need to get some cash, and fast, so that I can get a place of my own and the only way I can do that is by returning to the job that I promised myself I'd never do again. I search out the number of a recruitment firm that I used when I was at my old company. If anyone will be able to get me work at short notice they will.

I ring their top sales guy and he picks up straight away: 'Forward IT Recruiting. Damon Hunter speaking.'

My heart starts to race like it did that day in the car park at Heathrow.

'Forward IT Recruiting. Damon Hunter speaking. How can I help today?'

My palms begin to sweat like they did in the car park at Heathrow.

'Hello, Forward IT Recruiting. Damon Hunter speaking. Can you hear me, caller?'

I finish the call before I end up like I did in the car park at Heathrow.

That night when Rosa comes home I present her with a plate full of luminous cup cakes from the baker's on the high street each with a letter on top so it spells out: I LOVE YOU.

My cake message makes her cry and she tells me this is the happiest she's ever been but all I can think is: I am so terrified of going back to work that I'm prepared to risk the only good thing in my life right now just to avoid it for a little while longer.

35

They say that the three most stressful things in life are bereavement, changing jobs and moving house, and while I am in agreement with this I can't help but feel that the last category (for reasons of accuracy) needs a hierarchy of its own. Moving house is indeed a highly traumatic activity (I should know, having moved both houses *and* entire continents in recent years) but helping your parents to move out of the house in which they've both lived and raised a family for over forty years is the stuff of nightmares.

'And what do you need a book on ornithology for right now?' barks Mum, frantically scrubbing the inside of the kitchen cupboards as I come in from clearing out the shed. 'We're moving house today. Can't you do something useful for once?'

'I said I'd lend it to George at number seventy-three before we left,' says Dad as though this sentence makes perfect sense in the current circumstances. 'He's got this dark-brown bird with a white head that keeps coming into his garden and he wants to know what it is.'

'Can't he just take a picture and be done with it? Anyone would think that you don't want to move the way you've been messing about all morning. The removal men said that they would be needing to leave by eleven if they were going to get the job done and at this rate we'll be here until midnight.'

'Is there any need to exaggerate?' asks Dad. 'It's just one box and they've cleared virtually everything from upstairs, so I can't imagine it's going to take them more than an hour to clear the back room of boxes once the sofas are out. I know it's in one of the boxes in the living room, I just want to know which one.'

'Have you tried the one marked "books"!' exclaims Mum. 'Or is that too much for you?'

Dad departs muttering under his breath, leaving me to ask Mum what it is she's doing.

'I'm washing down the cupboards,' she explains. 'You should have seen the state of some of them. I really ought to have done a spring clean much earlier than this.'

'But what's the point, Mum? You know the developers are going to rip them all out. You told me yourself they're going to refurbish the whole place.'

'I can't have them thinking that I don't care about dirty cupboards!' she says, scandalised. 'I've always done things properly and I'm not about to change now.'

There is no point in attempting to counter my mother's argument because she does not allow things like logic to penetrate her world and so instead I take myself back outside to finish the shed and think about how in just a few hours I'll officially be living with a woman other than my wife.

Having had the past few weeks to get my head round the idea of Rosa and me living together I have to say that I've started to warm to it. So far as both a flatmate and a partner she's been pretty easy-going and I can't see any reason to see why things shouldn't continue this way once the move happens. The only problem that I can envision is what Lauren might have to say if or when she finds out but for the moment at least I have decided to simply shove my head in the sand and carry on as normal.

It's ten thirty on the dot when the foreman of the removal company pops his head round the door in the kitchen. I'm boxing the last of the cleaning equipment to put in Yvonne's car so that when she takes them over to the bungalow Mum and Dad can immediately commence Operation Clean-up Part 2. The removal guy informs me that everything is in the back of the removal van and that they're ready to go when we are and so I give him the nod and tell him that I'll let my parents know.

As I walk through the empty rooms I feel like the bearer of momentous news. The beginning of the end is about to commence, great change is afoot. Nothing will ever be the same again.

I spot Dad in the garden with Yvonne and walk down to them.

'I was just reminding your sister about the time she climbed on the roof of the shed and couldn't get down again,' chuckles Dad as I reach them. 'She bawled her eyes out. I thought the tears would never stop.'

Yvonne rolls her eyes in exasperation. 'Only because Tony and Ed kept telling me that the roof was rotten and that I'd fall through it and break my neck. That pair could be really evil.'

'You could be just as mean though,' I add, pointing to the Bramley apple tree we used to climb as kids. 'Do you remember when Ed climbed up to the top of this using Dad's old ladder and while he was up there you took the ladder away and left him stranded?'

'Do I ever?' laughs Yvonne. 'Once Mum rescued him she chased me round the house with a slipper yelling, "You'd better run because if I catch you you'll be seeing stars!" ' Yvonne pats the rough bark of the ancient tree.

Yvonne and Dad head back into the house and while they load up the car I go upstairs to my parents' bedroom where Mum is busy hoovering the grey swirly carpet that is over twenty years past its prime and which will certainly be dumped the second the developer walks through the door.

'So that's it then, Mum,' I say, as she turns off the vacuum. 'The removal guys are all done and Dad and Yvonne are waiting for you in the car.'

'But there is still so much to do.'

It's apparent that her desire to clean has less to do with wanting to impress the developer and more with wanting to keep her mind occupied. 'Not any more there isn't.'

She unplugs the hoover and I can see she has tears in her eyes.

'I know it's tough, Mum,' I say, putting my arm round her, 'but you're doing the right thing. Just think, you'll be able to see Yvonne and the grandkids whenever you want, take long walks in the countryside with Dad and get plenty of exercise, make tons of friends and maybe start a few new hobbies. You'll be living the dream.'

'I know,' she says, wiping her eyes, 'but I won't have this place any more, will I? Not the bedrooms where you kids slept, or the living room where we spent so many Christmases or the kitchen where I've made so many dinners.'

'But you'll still have the memories, won't you?' I reassure her. 'Leaving somewhere doesn't change that.'

We go downstairs and head outside. I load the vacuum cleaner into the back of the car while Mum climbs in.

'Are you sure you're going to be all right, Matthew?' asks Mum as I poke my head through the open window to give her a kiss. 'You know you don't have to stay with this friend of yours, it's not too late for you to come with us.'

'I'm good thanks. All my stuff's in the front room ready for when Rosa arrives to pick me up. I'll be fine.'

'And you won't forget to drop off the keys at the solicitor's?'

'No Mum.'

'Or to shut the front door properly and lock the back gate?'

'I'll do everything on the list.' I pull out the sheet of A4 she had handed me first thing this morning. 'Now, are you sure you don't want me to come and help at the other end?'

She shakes her head. 'I've told you a million times the removal men will do all the unpacking. You need to sort out yourself.'

'Fine,' I reply, 'you have a good journey and I'll call you tonight and see how you're settling in.'

Yvonne starts up the car and as they pull away I return their waves before disappearing back into the house to attend to Mum's list.

Closing the windows takes the longest as some of them have long since stopped working properly and having been opened for the express purpose of giving the house a 'good airing' now refuse to close. While I'm struggling with the most troublesome of these the doorbell rings and when I peer out of the window I see Rosa looking up at me.

'Are you going to let me in?'

She's wearing jeans and a black jacket and her hair is tied back in a loose ponytail. She looks beautiful and I tell her so.

'Why thank you,' she says, planting a kiss on my lips. 'So how's it been?'

'Tougher than I thought. Mum got a bit upset just before she left.'

'I'm not surprised. It must have been a real wrench for them and for you.'

I give her a guided tour of my empty family home, covering the front room that was only ever used for best, the back room where we watched TV, the kitchen where I calculate with the aid of my phone that Mum probably made the best part of forty thousand meals, my parents' bedroom where I used to sleep if I got scared in the night, my sister's bedroom that she would never let me or my brothers into because she said we made it smell, the bedroom I shared with my brothers and finally the garden where I and my siblings spent thousands of hours during the long summer holidays making our own entertainment and nearly killing ourselves in the process.

'I wish I could have seen it before all the life was taken out of it,' says Rosa. 'You make it sound like it was the best place in the world.'

'It was.' I search in my coat for the front-door keys. 'It was the absolute best.'

There's no reason to stay and so I get Rosa to open her car and I start loading my stuff into the back. It doesn't take long although I'm surprised how much stuff there is: all my old vinyl records from the loft, a cardboard box full of my school exercise books, carrier bags filled with comics and old music magazines and a framed picture of me, Ginny, Gershwin and the rest of the gang taken outside the school front gates on the last day of our A levels.

'You look really young,' says Rosa, taking the picture from my hands as I finish loading the rest of the stuff into the car. 'Very young and very handsome. Who are these guys with you?'

'Just some friends.'

'Do you see any of them?'

'Not in years,' I reply, 'that's what happens when you get older. People move on.'

She stares hard at the picture and points to Ginny. 'Why does she look familiar?'

'Because you met her,' I reply. 'We bumped into her and this guy,' I say, pointing out Gershwin, 'a little while ago in Moseley.'

'You were friends even then?' she asks and I can see her replaying the moment she and Ginny came face to face.

'Yeah.'

I brace myself for further questions but they don't come. Relieved, I put the last box into the car and then ask Rosa to wait while I do one final lap around the house as per my mother's instructions. Everything's fine of course, all the windows are closed and doors locked, so there's nothing left but to leave. As I shut the front door for the last time I have to choke back tears before getting into the car. I'm going to miss this place, the bricks and the mortar, the wood and the glass, but more than anything the life it once contained.

Days left until I turn forty: 29

36

'No one really wants to do nothing on their birthday,' says Rosa matter-of-factly as she opens the oven to take a closer look at the dish currently bubbling away inside. She pokes the cheesy cornbread topping of her chilli con carne with a sharp knife, pulls it out and examines it carefully before turning off the oven with something of a jubilatory flourish. 'It's just the kind of thing you say when you secretly want people like me to organise a big party and are just too proud or stubborn to come out with it.'

'Is that so?' I set down the glass of wine in my hand on the kitchen counter and begin laying the table.

She pulls a large bag of salad out of the fridge and calls for the salad bowl from the sideboard. 'You know it is,' she says, 'so let's just cut to the chase, shall we? Your birthday is in two weeks and there is no way I'm going to let it pass without some kind of celebration so the choice is this: you leave it up to me and just turn up on the right day at the right time and look surprised or you tell me what you want and I'll make it happen. But that's the only choice you're getting, and just so you know, Mr Beckford: this "I'm not really all that into birthdays" shtick that you keep peddling my way is getting really old, so just put it away and be happy.'

I'm about to defend myself when the front-door buzzer goes. Relief makes me generous. 'I'll finish up here, you go and welcome our guests.'

Having braced myself for the worst, the past few weeks with Rosa in her tiny flat have been the happiest since coming back to Birmingham. I had predicted conflict at every turn and problems round every corner but instead there had been unexpected harmony and joy, to the extent that I almost wished I'd moved in sooner. When I'm with Rosa I forget about everything that might bring me down – my employment status, Lauren, my lack of direction and looming birthday – and all I can think about is: if I can keep this going for another forty years then I'll die a happy man. Even so, I have been dreading tonight because while dating a twentysomething has turned out to be easier than I imagined, hanging out with her mates will undoubtedly be harder.

Rosa's friends Josh, a housing officer at the university, and Victoria (Tory), an arts administrator, are nice enough people and even though it's apparent in minutes that we're never going to be the best of friends (Josh seems intimidated by me while Tory is one of those people who isn't happy unless they're sharing their opinion on *everything*) for Rosa's sake I try to make the best of the evening, which means allowing Tory to dominate the post-dinner chat in the living room and not asking Josh too many questions when the women excuse themselves under the guise of making coffee to talk about us in the kitchen.

Just after midnight, when most guests my age would be calling a minicab, they get out the Sambuca and I find myself in the kitchen searching for a notepad and paper for some drinking game that Rosa and Josh are desperate to play when in walks Tory.

'Rosa says forget the pad because she's forgotten the rules of the game and anyhow she and Josh have plugged his phone into the music player so it'll be just like uni: those two screeching away all night while everyone else looks on. Still, it will give me the chance to have a proper chat with you.'

I look around nervously. 'Why would you want to talk to me?'

Tory laughs. 'Calm down, dear, I'm not after your body. I just wanted a chat.'

'About what?'

'About my sweet, sweet, Rosa,' she replies. 'You know all she talks about these days is what an amazing guy you are.'

'That's nice to hear.'

'I haven't seen her this happy since she and Jonny split up.'

It's the hint of smugness in Tory's voice that alerts me to the fact that I'm being tested. She knows something I don't and wants to be the one to tell me. Under normal circumstances I wouldn't have gone anywhere near so obvious a trap but it's late, I'm tired and a little too drunk to even think about not taking the bait.

'OK,' I say. 'I'll bite: who's Jonny?'

'You don't know?'

I shake my head.

'I know you don't because she told me that she didn't tell you.'

'So why are you telling me?'

'Because I know Rosa better than anyone, and if she hasn't told you it's because she wants you to think that she's as tough as she is funny and daring, when the truth is she's anything but. She's human, she's been hurt before, badly let down by someone who should have known better, and I think that you should know so you can make sure you never do the same.'

The story isn't anything new if you've had your heart broken before. This guy Jonny was her first love. They met as teenagers, did the long-distance thing throughout university and when their respective courses were over he talked her into moving back to Birmingham where he'd landed a job as a runner for a local TV production company when she wanted to move to London to begin the next chapter of her life. They got a room together in a shared house, kept each other sane when times were tough by making plans to go travelling and then one day she finds out that he's been seeing someone else. She confronts him with the truth and moves out the following day. Five years down the drain; a virtual lifetime of happy memories permanently tainted; a wound that feels like it will never heal.

'Where was the shared house?' I ask. 'Balsall Heath?

Tory nods, surprised. 'How did you know?'

'And the guy who cheated on her? I'm guessing he's still there?'

'Yes,' she says. 'Do you know him?'

'No,' I reply, carefully retrieving from my memory banks the image of the idiot in the trilby at the party where Rosa and I first kissed. 'Not quite.'

The following morning I text Gerry to see if they can do without me in the shop and once Rosa has gone to work I do a little research on the internet before heading into town on the bus and making my way over to the Mailbox.

For the uninitiated, the Mailbox is a large shopping and restaurant complex housed on the site of what used to be the central sorting office for Birmingham. Like other historic locations around the city it has been transformed by fancy architects and truckfuls of money into the new home of all manner of designer stores, shops, galleries and eateries. I haven't been near the place during my stay in Birmingham so far but today I make an exception on Rosa's behalf.

'How much is it to get your haircut by the man himself?' I ask the girl behind the desk in the reception of the Nicky Clarke Hair Salon.

'You want your hair cut by Nicky Clarke?' she asks, looking at my closely cropped locks.

'It's not for me,' I explain, stunned that she might even think for a second that I would spend more than a fiver on a haircut, 'it's for my girlfriend. I think she'd really like it.'

'Oh, I see. I'll need to go and check, just a moment.'

The idea had come to me after mulling over what Tory had said about Rosa's ex-boyfriend. I wasn't going to bring up the subject with her, but I felt I needed to do something in order to show Rosa just how unlike her ex I was. I started off thinking that I'd take her for an expensive meal or even for a posh weekend away but as I was taking a shower this morning I thought that if I was going to put myself into a huge amount of debt it ought to be for something a little less predictable and that's when I noticed the rows of hair products lined up in Rosa's shower.

Rosa took her hair very seriously indeed. Her regularity at the hairdresser's ('I go the first Saturday in the month without fail'), her armoury of products ('You might mock but a good serum is worth its weight in gold,') and the copies of *Hairstyle Monthly* nestled in amongst issues of *Frieze* and *Art Monthly* attested to this. So, as I saw Nicky Clarke's name looking back at me from the side of his own-brand hair products, a lightbulb lit up in my head. If my girlfriend enjoys using this guy's products, went my interior logic, how much more would she enjoy having the man himself cut her hair?

The receptionist returns with one of the senior stylists in tow who explains that although Nicky does occasionally cut hair in Birmingham there's a three-month waiting list for his services. The real bombshell is the price. While I hadn't expected it to be cheap neither had I expected it to be quite so expensive and, while Rosa was worth the money, my credit card would spontaneously combust if I handed it over to pay for it.

'That's certainly food for thought,' I say, taking the card and leaflet I've been offered and trying not to look horrified. 'I'll be certain to let you know as soon as possible.' With what little that remains of my dignity I exit the salon and walk straight into Ginny.

37

'You can just carry on walking if you want, pretend you didn't see me.'

I'll grant you this is a pretty mean-spirited way to greet a woman who you used to believe might approximate to the somewhat hackneyed soubriquet of 'soulmate' but I don't care any more. I'm done with being nice for the sake of it, I'm done with pretending that everything's fine when it's anything but, and I'm certainly done with making small talk with someone that I have absolutely no respect for. Right now I could not be more over it.

'You really hate me, don't you?' Ginny looks like I've just slapped her in the face. I see that she has tears in her eyes.

'Yes. There's no point in us going over old ground again, is there? Let's just go our separate ways. Have a nice life.'

'After all we've been through that's the way you want to leave things?'

'Yes, it is.'

She starts walking towards the escalators that lead to the upper levels of the shopping complex. I am determined not to follow her because I am 99 per cent sure that I am in the right and she is 110 per cent in the wrong but at the last moment I feel my resolve slip away. I never could stand to see her upset. I call out her name but it's only when I catch up with her and put my body between her and the escalator that she finally stops and after a moment of resistance allows me to comfort her.

'Look, I'm sorry, OK? I shouldn't have said I hate you.'

'But you meant it, didn't you?'

'I honestly don't know what I'm going on about half the time. Only last week I was trying to tell a mate of mine about this Stephen King book I was reading, only I kept referring to Stephen King as Clive Barker because there was a Clive Barker book right in my eyeline. What's next? Am I going to end up only being able to hold conversations about stuff that's right in front of me?'

Ginny smiles weakly. It's a relief not to be responsible for her tears. She scans my face with all the prowess of an expert poker player looking for a tell and says: 'When you say "mate" I take it you actually mean "girlfriend"?'

'No, when I say "mate" I actually mean "mate".'

Her brow furrows; I've intrigued her. 'Who are you hanging out with now?' she asks. 'I thought you barely knew anyone here?'

'Come and have a coffee and I'll tell you,' I say by way of a peace offering. 'You'll never guess in a million years.'

We go to a café opposite Nicky Clarke's, one of those trendy café/deli affairs that would totally confuse my parents, all posh cheeses and designer coffee.

'So come on then,' she says as we sit down at a table near the window, 'who's this new friend of yours?'

'Guess.'

Ginny pulls a face. 'OK, it's got to be someone really unlikely but equally someone we both know so I'm going to say . . . Jason Cleveland, or failing that one of those two Neanderthals he used to hang out with at school, what were their names again . . . that's it! Aaron Baker and Nick D'Souza.'

'You're pretty good at this, aren't you?'

Ginny's eyes widen. 'Don't tell me you're really hanging out with those guys. I saw that sleazebag Cleveland in the Cross a while back with some girl barely out of her teens! It turns my stomach just thinking about that muscle-bound idiot strutting around like he's irresistible to womankind!'

'Easy now,' I say, holding my hands up in defence, 'I said you were good, I didn't say that you were right.'

'So who is it then?'

'Gerry Hammond.'

Ginny's face takes on a look of confusion, like she's trying to convert inches into centimetres and back again. 'Gerry Hammond from The Pinfolds?'

'The one and only! He manages a charity shop on Moseley high street, not for the money, because he's minted, but you know, I guess he wants to give back if you know what I mean. I went in there a while ago and we got talking and then I bumped into him – and here's an irony for you – when I was out with Jason Cleveland and his cohorts. Gerry sort of took me under his wing and we've been hanging out ever since.'

Ginny looks properly stunned. 'He must be in his fifties at least now. Does he still look the same?' She sighs comically like a lovelorn schoolgirl. 'I can't tell you how much I used to fancy him. I had a whole wall of my bedroom covered in pictures and interviews with him from the music mags.'

I take out my phone and show her a picture of me and Gerry drunkenly leering into the camera lens while trying to perfect our Elvis sneer.

'That's him,' she screams, 'that's Gerry Hammond and that's you! I can't believe you're mates. Is he nice, is he fun to be around? Don't you feel weird being mates knowing how much of a super fan you used to be?'

This is good, this is exactly what I have been missing all the time Ginny and I haven't been speaking. We are old hands, veterans, survivors of the battles of our teens, twenties and thirties. It has always seemed wrong giving up on so much shared history when so few know our full stories, almost like I was setting fire to the only other copy in the world of *The History of Me* and as I'm already set to lose my last six years with Lauren, can I really afford to get rid of any more?

'So come on then,' says Ginny as our drinks arrive, 'what else has been going on that I might have missed?'

'Other than my parents moving to Worcester?'

'You're kidding me! When are they going?'

'They've gone. They got a part-ex on their place and that was it, they were off.'

'So you're living in Worcester now?'

I shake my head. I know I have no reason to feel guilty about telling her that I'm living with Rosa but the last thing I need is her trying not to look all judgemental when she hears the news. No one in their right mind would think I was doing the right thing here. I just want to keep this light and fun. She can drag the truth out of me some other time.

'I'm crashing with Gerry at the moment.'

'The fun never ends, does it?' she laughs. 'The eighteen-year-old you would absolutely die if he knew that one day he'd be sofa-surfing with one of his all-time heroes. What's his place like?'

Despite dropping regular hints to Gerry that he should invite me and Rosa around to his flat I have yet to set a single toe in Gerry's bachelor pad, so the only description I can give Ginny is the one he always gives me: 'Think twenty-first-century shag-pad meets Moore-era Bond-villain lair with a touch of IKEA.'

'Sounds exactly the kind of place a guy like Gerry would choose to live in. I'm green with envy. Promise me that you'll get me his autograph.'

'Maybe,' I reply. 'If you're lucky.'

The rest of the hour we spend together goes more smoothly than I could have hoped. I tell her about working in the charity shop, update her on the sale of the house in London, and even let her in on my total lack of plans for life after I've turned forty. When we prepare to say our goodbyes outside the café it feels like we're back to being friends again and it's only when she puts her arms round me I realise that neither of us has made a mention of our respective partners.

I wonder if I should feel guilty. After all, Ginny had originally been the reason that I'd come back to Birmingham and given our complicated history was it really a wise move spending an hour with her now that I had a girlfriend? But it wasn't as if I'd planned our meeting was it? And it wasn't as if I'd welcomed our meeting (at least not initially). And while yes, the fact that I had lied to her about where I was living probably did signal that I wasn't being totally honest it also showed sensitivity to her feelings. It wasn't as if she didn't know about Rosa.

It'll probably all come out the next time I see her if that ever happens. For now it is good that we no longer hate each other.

When Rosa comes home just after seven I present her with a bouquet of flowers in lieu of her celebrity hairdresser haircut and she's overjoyed. It's a really sweet moment, a girlfriend reduced to tears by an unexpected gift from her adoring boyfriend, and should have been the beginning of a great night; but as she's arranging the flowers and talking to me about her day, she asks me what I've been up to and, compelled by the spirit of what, I don't know, I tell her about my coffee with Ginny and immediately wish that I had kept my big mouth shut.

38

'She crops up a lot this woman, doesn't she?'

'How do you mean?'

'Well, you bumped into her yesterday, we saw her in Moseley that time and of course there's the little fact that you have a framed photo of her.'

'It's a framed photo of me and a bunch of mates taken when I was eighteen! I didn't even remember I had it until I cleared out the loft.'

'I'm just wondering what's so special about her.'

'There's nothing special about her.'

'Really? So what is she to you exactly?'

'She's a mate.'

'Who you've slept with.'

'Yeah . . . but . . .'

'But what?'

'Nothing. Can we just drop it?'

'No, we can't. I don't understand why you're being so evasive.'

'I'm not. I told you it's complicated.'

'Why was that guy we saw her with so frosty with you that night? Is it that you want her back?'

I can't believe she's asking me this question, let alone expecting a response. I voluntarily tell her the truth and now she wants to use it as evidence for the prosecution. 'Why would you even ask me that? It was just coffee. I bumped into her, I told her I didn't want to talk and was needlessly rude, she got upset, I felt bad and decided to patch things up by taking her for a coffee. That's it, that's everything. There were no stolen glances, there was no *moment* between us, and I most certainly don't want her back. I just didn't want to waste any more energy on hating people I don't need to hate. You must get that surely?'

Rosa looks at me sharply. 'What, because of Jonny?' I look surprised, Rosa's never used his name before and I know I'm not supposed to know. 'Tory told me that she talked to you about him – she never has been able to keep a secret.'

'But why would you want to keep it a secret? We talked about him that night at the party, remember?'

'But we didn't go into all the details did we? I never asked too many questions about your exes and you never asked about mine and that's the way I wanted to keep it.'

'It's not like it's a big deal. I've got exes, you've got exes, who cares?'

'I do,' she sighs, 'and besides, this one is different isn't she?'

'We've known each other a long time if that's what you're getting at.'

'How long?'

'Since we were seventeen.'

273

Rosa shakes her head as if she was beginning to wonder what she's doing with me. 'I really do care about you, Matt.'

'And I care about you.'

'But I think I care more and I'm fine with that, I really am. And I don't make a big deal about not knowing what you'll do once your house is sold, and I don't make a big deal about you having to stay in touch with your ex-wife either, but your being friends with Ginny is just a step too far. I've never wanted us to completely air our pasts because mine is nothing like yours. You're thirty-nine, Matt, I don't need a long line of your exes parading around in my mind making me feel inadequate and I certainly don't want to give them room to play in my reality.'

'And they won't. Seeing Ginny today was as much a shock for me as it was for you. You saw how I reacted when we saw her that time. She's not someone I want to spend a lot of time with and like I said before, today was about trying to make peace. If I had an ulterior motive why would I tell you that I saw her in the first place?' Rosa doesn't answer and so I take a second stab at it. 'Look, I'm sorry this has upset you, it was a one-off, I don't expect it to happen again . . . in fact there's no reason for it to happen again. So why don't you let me try and make it up to you? Let's go out, see a film and have something to eat afterwards?'

'That would be really nice,' she says, and I breathe a sigh of relief, 'but we still need to sort out this problem.'

'There's nothing to sort out,' I reply. 'I just won't see her.'

Rosa shakes her head. 'With my hand on my heart, I want to promise you that Jonny will never play a part in my life again, not even for a second. From this moment on, he's history.'

I have no idea how to respond to this but eventually say, 'Fine, if that's what you want to do.'

She looks at me. 'What about you?'

'You want me to say that Ginny is history too?' Rosa nods. 'Well, fine. It's highly likely given that she's about to marry my ex-best mate.'

'That's not enough. I want you to promise you won't see or talk to her again.'

'There's no need for you to be like this.'

'Well, I think there's every need.' I can see that this is a deal-breaker. All I have to do is say the wrong thing and she will jettison everything we have together.

'Fine,' I say, 'if it's what you want I won't see her again.'

'That wasn't about you,' says Gerry at work the following morning. 'That was all about the ex, Mr Hatwearer.'

'Yeah,' I look over at Odd Owen who is standing on a chair with one foot balanced precariously on the back of the seat, cleaning the tops of the shelves. 'I had sort of guessed that but it freaked me out. Rosa's a great person but it really felt like I was being put in my place.'

'That's because you were. She's staked her claim. You're hers now and she wants everyone to know it.' Gerry laughs and tugs at the back of my shirt, trying to expose bare flesh. 'Just looking for the mark where she's branded her name on you!'

Later, as Gerry and I are moving one of the shelves back into place that Odd Owen had knocked over during his cleaning attempt, I feel a tap on my shoulder.

'Matt? Matt Beckford? How are you, mate?'

Gerry laughs. 'Is there anyone you don't know?'

I do the introductions. 'Gerry, this is Craig Fowler. Craig Fowler, meet Gerry Hammond.'

Back in my school days Craig Fowler was the very definition of Mr Average. He wasn't cool (at least not if you considered Dungeons and Dragons role-playing games the height of sophistication), he wasn't the least bit athletic (I was once ordered to sit with him while he recovered from an asthma attack brought on by a cross-country run) and out of a year group of two hundred pupils he wasn't even in the top one hundred and ninety-nine vying for a spot as the class clown. He was just sort of there, academically able but middle of the road, and it was clear he was never going to shine. So when we do the catching-up thing and he tells me he's got a place in London and makes his living as a club DJ I'm more than a little stunned.

'I know,' he says, looking at my face. 'Weird isn't it?'

I leave Gary to sort the shelves as Craig gives me the low-down on the last twenty-odd years. Heading to London to do a law degree he ended up 'falling in with the London party scene'. While still doing his degree he started running various club nights in Brixton, got his girlfriend pregnant, began DJ'ing to make extra cash on the side, then split up with his girlfriend after three years. The DJ'ing took off and he moved to Ibiza for a decade, bought a bar, was made to sell the bar at gunpoint by drug dealers then returned to London and started running club nights around the city.

If I'd heard this kind of story from any of the other kids I'd gone to school with I wouldn't have believed a word of it, but seeing the transformation from who Craig was to Craig now convinces me that anything is possible.

'So now you do what exactly?' I ask as he concludes his tale.

'I'm only up here for a few days seeing my mum, she's not very well at the minute; just had an operation. Back in London my day to day stuff is DJ'ing, promoting, the occasional bit of producing but basically, mate, I just have a laugh. How about you?'

'I work in the IT industry,' I explain, feeling a bit inadequate, 'I'm taking a sort of sabbatical at the minute.'

'What sort of thing in IT?'

'It's dull,' I replied. I hate talking about what I did for a living if only because I hate seeing people's faces when I tell them.

'Try me.'

'I oversaw the design, implementation and maintenance of software for financial systems.'

Craig's laugh says it all. 'I'm trying, mate, I'm really trying but I can't find a way in.'

'Believe me, there isn't one.'

'But you enjoy it?'

I shake my head. 'Not for a long time.'

Craig nods sagely. 'Life's too short to be doing stuff that doesn't fire you up.'

'You're telling me.'

'So you've got a plan then?'

I recall my dad asking me that very same question on our trip to my sister's. 'This is it, sort of. I handed in my notice a while back, my house in London is on the market, I've moved back here and now I'm just taking it easy for as long as I can and then . . . well, something should spring up.'

'You'll be all right mate,' he tells me, 'I was a bit like that when I got back from Ibiza. Takes a while to get up to speed.'

When I get home that night I tell Rosa about bumping into Craig Fowler and when I tell her that he's apparently a famous club DJ now, she looks at me as though I'm joking and then sits at her laptop, pulls up a picture of him (the front cover of a dance music magazine with the headline: THE KING OF IBIZA RETURNS!!! and asks me if this is him.

'That's Craig,' I reply, looking over her shoulder at the screen.

'He's one of the biggest DJ names in the country and you went to school with him!'

I feel more than a bit weird. Was nondescript Craig Fowler really the most famous out of all the people I went to school with? I feel like I'm trapped in an episode of *The Twilight Zone*. 'Not only did I go to school with him but today I sold him two Kraftwerk albums on vinyl, and some mid-eighties Grace Jones.'

*   *   *

Craig Fowler's story stays with me longer than I want it to and for the next few days a dark cloud of despair comes over me as I begin thinking about how close my fortieth is, how I am nowhere near being where I thought I'd be at this landmark age and how I'm heading for a divorce. Just when I'm at my lowest, as I sit on the sofa in front of my laptop watching a YouTube video of some pop star I've never heard of singing the praises of Craig's remixing skills, I get a text from Ginny: *Could really do with a friend right now. Any chance we could meet tomorrow?*

There are many reasons why I should say no, not least of which is Rosa who is sitting less than five feet away from me at the dining table. I'd promised her that I wouldn't see Ginny and I meant it. But there's something about Ginny's message that sounds desperate, and for all I know she could really be in trouble; as much as I want to do right by Rosa I don't think I could live with myself if something was really wrong with Ginny and I'd ignored her. I'll see her, hear what she's got to say and that will be that. And Rosa, thankfully, will be none the wiser.

39

The following day I'm in the middle of telling Gerry about Rosa's plans for my fortieth birthday when Ginny enters the shop. It's a bright but fairly cold day and her clothing – a black quilted jacket, jeans and boots – reflects that she is a grown up, a fully fledged member of society, and I feel in comparison like a student at best and a dosser at worst.

'So this is what you've been doing with yourself,' she says, walking over to the till. 'It's a really nice set-up, isn't it? I've often walked past and thought about popping in.'

'Gerry, this is Ginny, an old school friend of mine.' I turn to Ginny. 'This is Gerry Hammond.'

Gerry shakes her hand and I can see from the impish grin on his face that he fancies Ginny.

'So you're a friend of Matt's are you? He hasn't got many, has he?'

'He's got a few,' Ginny laughs, 'and I hear you've been taking good care of him.'

'Someone's got to, haven't they? Who knows what kind of trouble he'd get into otherwise.'

'Has Matt told you how much we both used to love The Pinfolds when we were students? We must have seen you play at least a couple of dozen times in Birmingham alone, and then of course there was that amazing gig at the Astoria – do you remember that, Matt? – we all went down to London by coach and didn't get back home until three in the morning. There was barely anyone at sixth form the next day because we were all too busy sleeping off our hangovers.'

Gerry laughs. 'I got pretty trashed that night too but even I can remember it being one of the best gigs we ever played. I looked out into the crowd and thought: This is it, we've finally made it. You should come out with us one night . . . once I've had a few the old Pinfolds stories just keep pouring out.'

'That would be amazing,' says Ginny, 'a real teen dream come true. It's completely mad that Matt knows you so well and that you're sharing a place.'

'We'd better be off,' I say quickly, in the hope of diverting Ginny from the look of confusion on Gerry's face, 'I've only got an hour.'

'Well,' says Ginny over her shoulder, 'it was really nice to meet you.'

'You too.' Gerry throws me a quizzical glance. 'Hopefully we'll meet again soon and have a proper talk.'

'Where do you fancy eating?' asks Ginny as we step out on to the pavement.

'I've already got it sorted,' I reply, 'follow me.'

I lead Ginny part way down the high street before coming to a halt in front of a dubious-looking alleyway sandwiched between a tapas bar and a Subway. It looks like the kind of alley you'd go to only if you had a limited amount of time and a body to dump.

Ginny grins. 'I know where this is! Have you actually got keys?'

'One of the volunteers lives just round the corner, so she's got some, and she lent them to me this morning.'

We are standing in front of the entrance to Moseley Park and Pool: eleven acres of parkland that once belonged to a huge manor house and which was saved for posterity by a group of wealthy businessmen in the late nineteenth century. Surrounded by shops and houses on all sides it's invisible to the casual passer-by but to those residents who pay a nominal annual subscription for a key it's a blissful escape from an increasingly urban sprawl.

We walk in silence down a muddy path with brambles on either side that gradually opens up into a wide, tree-lined clearing. Taking a moment to get our bearings we walk along a path that leads off to the left down a slight incline until we reach our destination, the focal point of the whole park: Moseley Pool. We stand at the water's edge and watch a family of ducks going about their business before making our way to a bench a few feet away.

'How long is it since we last came here?' asks Ginny as I take two pre-packed sandwiches and two bottles of water out of my bag.

I do the calculations. It was our friend Elliot's family who had the keys and it would probably have been when all of us were home at the same time and the weather was decent so . . . 'I think we're probably talking the summer break of our second year at university.'

'That long?' Ginny shakes her head in disbelief. 'It only feels like yesterday since we were all working in rubbish temp jobs to whittle down our overdrafts.'

'I think I was working in the Unspoilt By Progress that summer. Do you remember you all used to come and see me on a Friday night and I'd sneak you the odd free beer.'

'Just like I used to filch free crisps and chocolate for Bev and Kat when I was working at that sandwich shop over in the jewellery quarter. I feel guilty now that I think about it. Bev and Kat were in there all the time, the poor owner must have gone broke with the amount of stuff I gave away.'

I offer up the sandwiches. 'Chicken salad or Brie and grape?'

'You first.'

I take the Brie and grape knowing full well that's the one Ginny wants, pretend to open it and at the last moment snatch the chicken salad from her hands.

'I thought that was too weird to be true,' she says, opening the packaging, 'I would've bet good money that the chicken salad was yours. It's all you ever ate in sixth form.' She takes a bite of her sandwich. 'This is delicious.'

We sit quietly munching for a few moments. A woman with two pre-school kids, a boy and a girl, passes by and the boy waves and asks what's in our sandwiches, forcing his mortified mother to apologise on his behalf.

'It's OK,' I reply, and turn to the boy, 'Mine's ready salted slugs on cheese and hers is crushed butterflies and bacon. You can have a bite if you like.'

The children writhe in paroxysms of laughter and ask me to say it again but their mum tells them to stop bothering people trying to eat their lunch.

We watch them trundle off down the path and Ginny takes a sip of her water. 'How are things going with your new girlfriend? You didn't mention her the other day. Is everything still OK?'

'She's good, thanks,' I reply, relieved that this is coming out. 'She's in Wolverhampton all day today taking meetings with a gallery there.'

Ginny seems impressed. 'What does she do?'

'She works in arts funding. I suppose you'd call her a project manager.'

'Sounds like a great job.'

'It is,' I reply, 'and she's good at it too, really dedicated.' I reason that I should probably ask after Gershwin if only out of politeness. 'How's Gershwin?'

Ginny sighs. 'Not great really. He's under loads of stress at work. Last week they announced that they're making everyone on his pay grade reapply for their own jobs, and of course they're cutting positions at the same time so you can imagine how horrible the atmosphere is.'

I want to say something along the lines of: 'That's karma for you, love,' because I'm a long way from forgiving Gershwin, but what I actually say is: 'I'll keep my fingers crossed for him.'

We fall into a comfortable silence until Ginny sets down her food, takes another sip of water and wipes her lips on a serviette, making it clear that the time to talk has arrived.

'My gran died.'

'I'm sorry to hear that,' I reply. 'How old was she?'

'Eighty-four. We weren't close. It was Dad's mum so it's not like I've had a great deal to do with her or the rest of his family over the years. My Aunt Louise called me last week – it's been so long since we spoke that she wasn't even expecting the number to work let alone that I'd answer – and she apologised for all the family arguments that got in the way of us seeing each other and ended up inviting me to the funeral.'

I make the connections in my head: if Ginny's gran has died, chances are that her dad will be at the funeral and Ginny hasn't seen or heard from him since she was ten, when he walked out on her and her mum. 'And you're not sure whether you should go because your dad's going to be there?'

'According to my aunt he's been living in Ireland. She didn't say whether he'd got a new family, but it wouldn't surprise me.'

'So how did you leave it?'

'How do you think? Why would I want to see him after all these years? What could either of us possibly have to say to each other? I told her I doubted I'd come but that I'd definitely send flowers.'

'And now you're having second thoughts?'

Ginny nodded. 'Is that weird?'

I shake my head. 'You've probably got more to say to him than you think. What does Gershwin say about it all?'

Ginny doesn't reply which I take to mean she hasn't told him yet.

'Any particular reason?'

'He's got enough on his plate with work – he doesn't need all my mental baggage in his lap right now.'

'You should tell him,' I say, trying to be charitable. 'If I was him I'd want to know.'

'What would be the point? He's up in Glasgow fighting for his job. I just want to know if I'm doing the right thing in going or not. Every time I convince myself I should stay away I change my mind and want to go; and then just as I think I'm settled I find myself shaking at the thought of seeing him again.'

'And where are you now?'

'Wanting to go.'

'Then I'll come with you.'

40

'So are you going to tell me what that was all about then?' asks Gerry as we sit in the pub for our first after-work pint.

'What what was all about?' I ask innocently.

Gerry sighs like I'm a five-year-old trying his patience. 'So you don't want to talk about it? That's fine by me, but we do need to talk about something because you haven't said a word in over five minutes and as much as I enjoy the comfortable silence that only male company can provide, truth is it's not even the good kind.'

'What's that supposed to mean?'

'It means that when you asked me if I fancied a pint after work I didn't think it would involve me watching you stare listlessly into your drink. Now, either you start talking about whatever's on your mind or I'm going to take my pint back to the bar and do the crossword until Kara arrives.'

'All right! All right!' I hold up my hands in surrender. 'I think I have what's called in the trade a dilemma.'

'And what might that be? It's not like you disappeared for an hour today with a right cracker who you categorically promised your live-in girlfriend that you'd never see again, is it?'

I take a long sip of my pint and let the taste of the beer roll around my tongue. How long had I been drinking this stuff? Twenty-five years? More? Would I still be drinking it in another twenty-five? What would the world look like then? Who would I be with? Where would I be living?

'I've volunteered to go to a funeral with her.'

Gerry raises an eyebrow. This wasn't what he'd been expecting. 'Whose?'

'Her grandmother's. Gershwin's away with work and it's a bit of an awkward one because it's her dad's mum who's died, and Ginny hasn't seen him or any of that side of the family since she was ten and he walked out on her mum.'

'Can't she find someone else? A female friend or something?'

I shrug. 'I'm guessing that if she could've she would've. The bottom line is I've volunteered my services.'

'And what are you going to tell Rosa?'

'That's the million-dollar question. I can't tell her the truth and I don't want to lie to her.'

'So you're going to say nothing,' says Gerry, thankfully reaching the same conclusion that I had moments earlier.

'What else can I do?'

'Nothing,' says Gerry, 'it is what it is.'

I limit myself to just the one pint and leave within the hour as Kara and her mates turn up. As I start walking home I wonder if Gerry is as happy with the life he leads as he makes out. With the girls and the drinking and the being out all the time it seems like he's never stopped living in his twenties, but as I think about going home to Rosa and the meal we'll share and the evening we'll spend together the thought of Gerry's evening exhausts me. I don't want to relive my twenties, I don't even want to revisit my thirties. I want this next stage to be the one where I finally get my act together so I can start living the life I was meant to.

It's quiet inside the flat and for a moment I think that maybe Rosa's not in but then I hear her laughter coming from the kitchen, and I find her leaning against the counter with the phone pressed up against her ear, chatting animatedly into the receiver.

'I know,' she says into the phone.

And then, 'That's exactly what I always say to him.'

And finally, 'He won't listen, and he thinks he knows it all, but we know better don't we?'

That is when I realise that she is talking to my mother. *My mother!*

'Why are you talking to my mum?' I mouth in silent anguish at the thought of how long this conversation may have been going on.

Rosa waves and turns her back on me.

'Stop this madness now!' I mouth once more having circled round so that she can see me, 'Stop before it all goes too far!'

Ignoring me, Rosa turns again and says into the phone, 'Oh no, not at all . . . it has been an absolute pleasure talking to you Cynthia . . . Of course! Can't wait to meet you and the rest of the family either . . . and you must let me bring something along . . . I make a really mean pavlova . . . of course, it goes without saying I'll make sure that he's there on time . . . I can't stand it either . . . take care . . . no, I don't mind you calling . . . you can ring any time.'

She returns the phone to the charger with a flourish. 'How was the pub?'

I narrow my eyes at her. 'Why are you talking to my mother?'

'Because she called.'

'I only gave her this number for emergencies! I told her a million times that if she needed me she could call my mobile.'

Rosa pulls her very best comically patronising face, the one she uses to put me in my place. 'Matt, if you knew Cynthia like I know Cynthia you'd know that she doesn't really like mobiles.'

'You're loving this aren't you?'

'Why wouldn't I?' She plants a kiss on my lips. 'She loves me, Matt, she adores me, she said I'm a good influence on you.'

'She actually said that?'

Rosa scrunches up her nose and shrugs. 'She might as well have done for all the praise she was passing my way.'

'How long did you talk for?'

'Half an hour, maybe forty minutes, who knows? All that matters is that we're having lunch at your mum and dad's on your birthday and so I will get to see them in person and wow them even more.'

Clearly amused to have one over on me Rosa exits the kitchen, leaving me alone to ponder once more my decision not to tell her about Ginny.

Later that evening as Rosa's lying on the sofa with her slender limbs stretched across my lap as she reads through half a dozen reports she's brought home with her, while I plough my way through a Rolling Stones' biography that Gerry recommended, it occurs to me that I should come clean. Young as she is, in many ways she's more mature than I am and if only I can find a way of explaining why I'm helping Ginny, she might understand there's nothing in it, that this is simply one old friend helping another in their time of need. I take a deep breath, prepare for her reaction and open my mouth ready to give birth to the words, but it's as if I've lost all power to communicate.

'What's up?' Rosa looks up from her papers. 'You look like a man with something on his mind.'

'You know the other day when you said that you thought that I didn't feel the same way about you that you do about me?' She nods and puts her papers down, giving me her full attention, 'Well, that's not true. This is going to sound like something inside a Hallmark card but I love you, I really love you, I think I have for ages but just haven't known how to get the words out.'

The interesting thing about this unexpected moment, the thing I hadn't seen coming, is that despite half a lifetime during which I've seen, done and felt everything there is a million times before, these words feel as fresh and as new as the first time I said them on the day that Elaine moved into my apartment in New York all those years ago. How can something so clichéd and jaded feel so newly forged? I feel like no one in the history of the world has ever said these words and meant them with the intensity that I mean them now, and as Rosa leans in to kiss me, I know that she feels this too.

The morning of the funeral Rosa's up and out of bed early as she's got a meeting in London she has to attend in lieu of her boss who is off work with the flu. It's the first meeting of its type that she's ever been to and the opportunity to network with people she doesn't usually get to see means that she's a bundle of nerves.

'What if I say something stupid?' she asks as she sits on the edge of the bed. 'What if I just dry up and nothing comes out?'

'It'll all be fine,' I reassure her, 'I used to get like that when I first started chairing meetings but the more you do it the better you get. Just talk like you know your stuff – which you do – and they will all fall into line.'

'Can I call you if I panic? I probably won't but it would be good to know that you're just at the end of the line if I really need talking off a ledge.'

'Of course you can, but you won't need to because you are going to be amazing.'

She seems suitably reassured, and after one last kiss she picks up her bag and leaves. For a moment after I hear the front door slam, I lie in bed as though I'm expecting her to return having forgotten some key item for the day ahead but she doesn't. Even if she had my lying still wouldn't have made any difference to the tang of deceit in the air. As I stand at the bathroom mirror waiting for the shower to heat up I study my face and while the steam starts to obscure my expression it does little to make me look less guilty.

41

'How do I look?'

Standing on Ginny's front doorstep I give her a twirl. I'd only got one black suit and that was in London. The only one I have with me in Birmingham is a dark grey Paul Smith that I'd only packed on the off-chance that if my resolve caved and I needed to go back to work I'd have an interview suit. 'It's not black but you have to admit it is pretty smart.'

Ginny smiles but it's clear from her eyes just how much effort it's taken. 'You look very handsome,' she says, 'and I'm sure any woman would be proud to be seen with you. Good enough?'

'You look really nice.' It is the blandest of bland comments but given that my gut response had been to tell her that she looked incredible, I reason that for now nice will just have to do.

'Thanks, it's hard trying to work out what to wear to things like this. I always think about the day of Mum's funeral and how I ended up in jeans and a top I'd been wearing for two days in a row because I couldn't make up my mind between the three dresses I'd bought.'

I try to make conversation to distract her but if her half-mumbled answers to even the most basic of questions ('What plans have you got for the weekend?') are anything to go by she's more than distracted enough so I leave her to her thoughts and she leaves me to mine until we find ourselves approaching our destination. It dawns on me when I was last here at this very cemetery.

'This is where Elliot's buried isn't it?' I say of our old friend.

Ginny pulls the car over and turns off the ignition. 'That didn't even register with me. What kind of person am I that I can't even remember something like that?'

'I forgot too.' I'm aware we both tend to feel guilty about Elliot. 'I don't think he'd mind. I think he might even find it funny. Maybe we can go and see him later?'

'We haven't any flowers.'

'Doesn't matter.' I squeeze her hand. 'He was never all that keen on flowers anyway.'

We park on the gravel car park between a white panel van and a yellow digger and as we climb out of the car Ginny looks towards the stream of mourners heading inside the chapel.

'You worried?'

She shakes her head. 'I've just told myself to grit my teeth and get on with it.'

'The daily mantra for everyone our age.' Ginny manages to raise half a smile. 'Sometimes my jaw aches so much from gritting my teeth I think they might fall out.'

We enter the chapel behind a couple in their fifties who are walking with their arms round the shoulders of their two tearful teenage daughters. Ginny doesn't recognise them. In fact she doesn't recognise anyone at the funeral at all. We plant ourselves in the only space available on the third pew from the back. The elderly woman next to me smiles and offers me a Polo mint. I take one because it feels rude not to.

Ginny's hand tightens round mine when the congregation rises to its feet as the coffin, followed by the immediate family, is brought into the chapel by pallbearers, one of whom must be her dad. How difficult it must be for her to see these relations after so many years, a relationship with them denied by circumstances brought about by her father. How odd it must feel to be at the funeral of your own grandmother and not feel a thing.

The service commences with 'All Things Bright and Beautiful', and as we stand I remember that my phone's still on. I reach into my pocket and switch it off. After the hymn the vicar begins reading from the Psalms and this leads me to think about my own funeral, who I'd want there and what sort of music I'd like played. I make no firm decisions other than the following:

1. Even if I die at eighty I still don't want Gershwin at my funeral
2. I'd like my casket to enter to The Rolling Stones' 'You Can't Always Get What You Want', thereby summing up the whole tenor of my life

3. If I die single (which let's face it is highly likely given my track record) then I'd like Ginny to give the eulogy because she'd make a good go of it and at least wouldn't get any of the salient facts wrong.

Twenty minutes into the service the vicar instructs Terry Pascoe to come up to the lectern to give the first of three eulogies and if he wasn't obviously Ginny's dad from his colouring, Ginny's involuntary shudder would have given the game away. Terry Pascoe is a big man, bigger than I'd expected, and he looks uncomfortable in his suit as though he isn't used to wearing one. His eulogy is heartfelt and I'm moved by the love for his much-missed mum that he conveys to the congregation. I wonder if he knows that Ginny is here too, and if so whether he is aware of the irony of a child talking about the love of a parent when he himself has made such a mess of loving his own flesh and blood. Part of me would take great pleasure in informing him because even though I'm not looking at Ginny I know that every word this man is saying is breaking her heart, reminding her of his absence from her life these past thirty years.

When the service is over the old lady offers me another mint.

'Lovely service, don't you think?'

'Yes it was.'

'How do you know the family? Are you related to them or is it on your wife's side?'

It takes me a moment to realise that she's talking about Ginny. 'She's not my wife.'

The old lady nods sagely. 'It's what people do nowadays.'

There's no real point correcting her and anyway, I can feel Ginny tugging at me like she wants to make a quick exit and so I make my excuses to the old lady.

'Are you OK?' I ask Ginny, as we stand in the side aisle while people leave the chapel.

'I've been better,' she says. 'But at least we can go now.'

'Are you sure?'

Ginny nods. 'I don't know what I hoped for from today but I don't think I'm going to get it. Sorry Matt, to put you through all of this.'

'You haven't put me through anything,' I reply. We join the queue and file outside.

It's a little after three by the time we pull up in front of Ginny's house. She'd asked me several times if I wanted dropping off at Gerry's but I insisted that I had some errands to run on the high street and that it would be easier if she took me to hers. I feel bad carrying on this lie now that we're properly back to being friends but this doesn't seem the right time for revelations. I'll tell her about Rosa soon, and it'll all be fine, and maybe if the stars and the moon are aligned correctly and I'm feeling sufficiently lucky I'll tell Rosa about today, and I can get that off my chest too. How did my life get this complicated? How did I end up being involved with so many people who needed protecting from the truth?

'Are you sure you won't come in? Not even for a cup of tea or something?'

'OK, go on then,' I tell her and just then a silver Fiat Uno passes by and I catch the eye of its driver long enough to see that she's female but I can't remember where I know her from. Ginny calls me into the house and ditching all thoughts of the car's driver I head inside.

42

Standing in Ginny's kitchen as she brews two mugs of tea I scan the room for evidence of Gershwin's occupation but instead discover signs that Ginny has been thinking about the future more than she has been letting on.

'Are you putting your house on the market?' I point at the large brown manila envelope on the counter in front of me emblazoned with the name of a well-known local estate agent.

Ginny glances at the envelope guiltily. 'I was going to tell you, Matt, but it never seemed like the right time. Gershwin's moving out of his place at the weekend and we're seeing a guy about a mortgage Monday night. I can't believe it's all really happening.'

'Have you found somewhere or have you just started looking?'

'We've got our eye on a place in Kings Norton. It's quite a big house compared to most we've seen – four bedrooms and a loft – and needs a lot of work but even once you factor in all the renovations it's still going to be loads cheaper than, say, Bournville.'

I don't know what to say. Places like Kings Norton feel like the suburbs, where you go to start a family, where you go when you're done being young and all you want are good schools, decent gardens and off-road parking. I'd put good money on everyone in Kings Norton having a shed. It's the sort of place that having a shed would be practically obligatory.

Ginny sets my tea down on the table opposite.

'You look disappointed,' she says.

'Not at all, I think it's a great idea.'

'Do you really? I'm so excited about it all. I feel like I'm only just learning to live life properly.'

'That's good,' I say. 'I'm pleased for you.'

Ginny lifts her cup to her lips and blows across the surface. She takes a sip. 'Have you decided what you're doing for your birthday yet?'

'Rosa's sorting it all. Nothing too flash. I think we're going to my parents' on the day and then to the pub in the evening.'

'Sounds nice.' Ginny takes a sip of her tea. 'I'm sorry we won't be there, that's all. Do you think things will ever get back to normal?'

'I don't know,' I reply sincerely.

'Can I be honest with you about something?'

I look at her uneasily but hear myself saying the words: 'Fire away.'

'That evening that Gershwin and I bumped into you and Rosa – I don't know how to say this – I felt jealous seeing the two of you. You both seemed so happy, so together, I don't know . . . it just took me by surprise.'

'I don't know what to say,' I reply.

'Because there is nothing to say. I made my choice and you made yours, and I don't think either one of us would change things. It's just a shame, that's all. We were so close to getting it right that it's hard not to feel a little sad at how it all ended.'

I don't say anything after this and neither does Ginny. It's as though having introduced reality into the proceedings there's no way forwards and so we finish off our tea and I repeat my excuse about needing to go to the high street and gradually we make our way to the hallway to say goodbye.

'What a day,' sighs Ginny, putting her arms round me. 'I would have been lost without you.'

'I didn't do anything. You were really strong all the way through and you stayed true to yourself and did the right thing.'

Ginny doesn't seem too sure. 'He's my dad,' she says. 'The only close relative I've got left and I've just walked away from the only opportunity I might ever have to make things right between us.'

'And why are you the one who has to make things right? He left you, not the other way round. Being a dad isn't about having money, it isn't even about getting things right all the time; it's simply about being there for your kids when they need you. That's all.'

Ginny hugs me tighter. 'You'll make someone a great dad one day, you know.'

'And you'll make a great mum, and if that's what you want you should make it happen. Me and you, we're the same. We've spent too long waiting for life to happen to us and not enough bringing things about through sheer force of will. We can't be spectators any more, we have to get stuck in and start playing the game.'

'Just what a girl needs,' grins Ginny. 'A nice sporting analogy! You're right though, I do need a kick up the backside. I don't know what I'm waiting for but if I wait too long I'll miss it.' She looks up at me. It's a moment of intimacy, a moment of connection, but rather than speaking of sexual attraction it speaks of friendship and loyalty.

'I couldn't have got through today without you, which goes to show that some things remain true even after all these years.'

'Like what?'

'That when you've got your mates in your corner shouting for you, anything's possible.'

It's a little after four by the time I reach home. Taking off my suit I bury it at the back of the wardrobe before taking a shower. The best part of half an hour later I feel like a new man and throwing on my jeans and a top I begin work on the story of my day for Rosa while I prepare a vegetable pasta bake from a recipe in one of last weekend's newspapers.

It's difficult to calculate which of the two occupations is the more taxing but once the pasta bake is in the oven the lie seems to fall more easily into place and I decide that the easiest thing for me to do is base it entirely on my last full day at the shop minus the lunchtime visit from Ginny.

Feeling on top of everything I check my phone for texts from Rosa but as I find it nestled amongst my wallet, loose change and keys on the table in front of me I remember that the phone I had promised Rosa I would be contactable on all day has been switched off since the beginning of the funeral service.

I can barely breathe as I switch on the phone, frantically hoping that there won't be any messages. No such luck: six unopened texts, five missed calls and two voicemails.

I read the texts and listen to the voicemails and piece together the story of the day. Everything that could go wrong for Rosa, had gone wrong, and not just common or garden wrong either but spectacularly, cringe-makingly wrong, the kind of wrong where the one thing that might help is a call from your boyfriend telling you that he loves you.

Rosa's train had been an hour late into Euston; there had been delays on the Northern Line and the Victoria Line; even though I'd printed out a Google map for her she got lost trying to find the building where the meeting was being held; she was asked at least half a dozen questions which despite all of her preparation she didn't know the answer to; over lunch she discovered that she'd lost her purse and had no choice but to cancel all three of her bank cards, a process which took her entire lunch hour. If that wasn't enough then there were the texts of which the final one held the real bombshell:

Have managed to get earlier train. Arriving at 16.30. Have no money for taxi. Any chance you could leave work early and pick me up? My car keys are on the table next to the bed.

I look at my watch. It's ten minutes past five. Even if I got in the car now in rush hour traffic I'd be lucky to be there in twenty minutes by which time I'd be nearly an hour late, but it doesn't seem right to do nothing and so I grab my coat and the car keys but before I reach the front door it opens and in walks Rosa, closely followed by Tory.

'I've only just this second got your messages,' I tell her. 'I left my phone at home and it's been mental in the shop all day so I didn't notice.'

'Oh, so you've been in the shop all day?' she asks, hands on hips.

'Yes. A couple of the volunteers didn't turn up so I was pretty much chained to the till.'

'Liar,' says Rosa, her voice breaking with emotion. 'You absolute liar!'

'I'm sorry. I left my phone at home, and I'm sorry you've had such a terrible day. You worked so hard and I know you must feel I've let you down, but please let's talk!'

'Don't say another word if it's going to be a lie.' She gestures to Tory. 'She saw you this afternoon, Edmund Road, wearing a suit, talking to a woman who sounds an awful lot like your ex.'

The penny drops. The woman at the wheel of the silver Fiat Uno. That must have been Tory. I feel as if an explosion has gone off somewhere near the centre of the earth and right now the very ground beneath my feet is being sucked down into the cavernous space below. 'I can explain,' I tell her.

'Are you going to tell me it wasn't her?'

I don't reply.

'Maybe you're going to tell me she's not the reason you've had your phone off all day?'

Still no reply.

'Maybe you're going to tell me that a short while ago you didn't promise me you'd never see her again?'

I shake my head for what I know is the last time.

'I don't want your explanations,' spits Rosa, 'I don't want to know why you were with her or what you were doing. You promised me, Matt, you stood right here on this spot and you promised, and while I might put up with a lot, I don't put up with liars. I'm staying at Tory's tonight and I'll be there until the end of the week. But when I get back I expect you to be gone.'

43

'Look Mum, I'd better be going. I'm heading into the shop in a bit.'

'Are you sure you should be working? You don't sound like yourself.'

'It's just a cold, I'll be fine.'

'Will you promise to call if you need anything? I know you've got that lovely girl looking after you but I'm still your mum, you know.'

'I know you are and yes, if I do need anything I'll call, I promise.'

'And you'll pass on my best to Rosa and let her know how much I'm looking forward to seeing her on your birthday?'

'Definitely.'

There's a long pause and then: 'I love you, son.'

These words have formed the first part of an automatic 'call and response' type ending to every telephone conversation we've had with each other since I first left home and yet today I catch my breath and have to swallow hard to counter the swell of emotion that's seeking to engulf me.

*　　*　　*

It's been three days since Rosa walked out, during which time I have all but forgotten about the deadline she imposed on my staying in the flat and focused on drinking myself into a stupor while supplying Rosa with enough ammunition for a city-wide restraining order should she apply for one. I left multiple messages on her mobile; bombarded her email with increasingly incoherent rants; and had long and involved conversations with Tory, during the last of which she took care to explain as carefully as she could that if I didn't stop calling she would involve the police. In every message the core content was the same because the way I feel is always the same: I'm sorry and I want her back. And it's true. I miss her more than I thought possible and I feel her absence like an energy-devouring, all-consuming black hole.

I've lost count of the times that I've run over that day in my head and I'm still shocked at how easily I'd betrayed Rosa for a friendship that with the gift of hindsight I now see is doomed. Ginny is never going to give up Gershwin and Gershwin is never going to give up Ginny, and my presence in their lives even as a friend is always going to be a source of disquiet. So why had I so quickly chosen the option that would be wrong for Rosa?

I don't have any answers. Just questions piled on top of questions, and as I gaze at a silver-framed photograph of Rosa and Tory, and drink in Rosa's delicate features, I find a rage boiling up that is aimed squarely at my own self-destructive tendencies that have seen me give up on people I loved, sabotage career prospects and destroy a marriage from the inside. Rosa was my last chance to get things right, my final opportunity to learn from past mistakes before I cast myself for good as a no-hoper.

I take a shower and get ready for work, pausing only to look in the mirror to register, for the benefit of my liver, exactly the kind of toll three days of drinking can wreak on the face of a soon-to-be forty-year-old. My eyes are bloodshot, my skin feels dead to the touch and with three days' worth of stubble plastered across my chin the combined effect is to propel me into the centre stage of middle age. It's a truly horrible sight. I don't look worn in like Gerry, or mature and sophisticated like George Clooney, I look worn out, clapped out, knackered, like I've run a marathon or climbed a mountain when the most strenuous activity that I've undertaken is getting out of bed for a five-minute chat with my mother. I can't carry on like this; I have to get a grip.

There is another motivating factor to consider today: I have run out of time. Having wasted three days of Rosa's deadline feeling sorry for myself there are now little more than twenty-four hours before both I and my possessions are put out on the street. Thus, my plan consists of the only options available to me: I'm going to ask Gerry to let me crash at his for a while and then call up Lauren and talk her into lowering the price of the house for a quick sale and maybe, just maybe, I won't end up totally screwed.

'Ah, mate,' says Gerry, 'not this again!'

'Oh, come on, I'll have my place sold in a matter of weeks and then I'll be out of your hair for good.'

'If I could, I would, you know that, but I can't.'

'Pleae, mate. I don't need much, just somewhere to kip. You'll barely notice I'm there.'

'I told you before, it's Kara,' says Gerry. 'If it was up to me that spare room would be yours. But since Kara moved in she calls the shots and well . . . we're going through a bit of a tricky phase at the minute so having someone else around wouldn't pan out well. You can dump your gear here in the office, though, that won't be a problem. You box it up and I'll help you bring it over so at least you'll know it's all in a safe place.'

'And that's all you can do?'

'My hands are tied mate, sorry.'

There's not a great deal more to be said, and although I suspect that Gerry's not telling me the truth (since when did he and Kara move in together? And even if they were living together I can't imagine any scenario in which Gerry played the hen-pecked husband) I am grateful for somewhere to keep my stuff and so after work we collapse as many boxes as we think we'll need and get Steve the Student to drop us at the flat.

I pick up the pile of post from behind the door and shuffle through it hoping none of it involves me, but three letters down is the official-looking white envelope I've been dreading. I tear it open and scan the contents:

Dear Mr Beckford,

According to our records you have now reached your official overdraft limit and therefore need to make an appointment to see a customer care consultant as soon as possible. Any attempt to take out further monies from your account (including direct debits) will result in it being frozen until as such time as significant repayments have been made and may also result in your incurring multiple charges.

'What's that?' asks Gerry, trying to get a look over my shoulder. 'A love letter?'

'Nothing.' I tuck the letter in my pocket and focus on the task in hand. It takes me just over an hour to pack my things and the best part of half an hour to ferry the boxes down to the shop in the back of Steve the Student's car and afterwards the only thing I'm good for is the pub which given my three-day bender isn't exactly the best idea in the world.

'You can't stay in,' says Gerry, when I tell him of my plans for the evening, 'you'll end up drinking anyway but you'll do it alone and drinking alone is the first sign that things are starting to go really wrong.'

I have to laugh. 'How much worse can things get? My girlfriend hates me, I turn forty next week and as of tomorrow I'm officially homeless.'

'Oh come on mate, you're being melodramatic. You can always stay with your folks can't you?'

'You don't get it, do you?'

Gerry puts a gentle hand on my shoulder as though he's afraid I'm losing the plot. 'I do, mate, I really do,' he says soothingly. 'Listen, let's get a drink and see if we can't sort out this problem between us.'

I haven't got the strength to resist so once the shop is locked up we head across to the Fighting Cocks, grab a pint (even though it's standing room only), push our way through the hordes and lay claim to three square feet of unoccupied space on the far side of the bar. Gerry tries to keep the conversation light but I only have one thing on my mind and so he asks the million-dollar question.

'So do you think she'll change her mind?'

'I've no idea, but she means it when she says she wants me out by tomorrow.'

'I don't know what to say, mate.'

'It's fine,' I say, 'something will come up.'

'I can probably let you kip in the shop for a couple of nights. You'd have to keep it quiet from the other volunteers though.'

'That's better than nothing.' I'm grateful even though I know how cold the back office can get when the heating isn't on. 'Anything that buys me a bit of time has got to be a good thing. I've reached my overdraft limit but if I catch Lauren in the right mood she just might lend me enough for a room in a house share for a while.'

Gerry's phone buzzes from inside his jacket. 'That'll probably be Kara, she's gone to the cinema with her mates but she might drop in afterwards.'

I'm reminded of Gerry's weirdness earlier in the day and his refusal to let me stay at his place. Just as I start piecing together a theory based on him having turned his flat into a marijuana factory he interrupts my thoughts by shoving his phone under my nose so that I can read the last bit of the text: *128 Whitehouse Lane, Balsall Heath.*

I look up at Gerry, confused. 'What's that?'

'Your new home if you want it. Kara's been on the case for me. Apparently if you turn up there midday tomorrow with a deposit and a month's rent there'll be a double room with your name on it.'

'Why does that address seem familiar to me?'

'Because it's the address of that party we went to, the party where you and Rosa got together.' Gerry looks at me resignedly. 'Do you still want it?'

I try to imagine myself living with my parents in a retirement bungalow in Worcester.

'Doesn't look like I've got much choice, does it?' I reply. 'Tell the landlord I'll be there at midday.'

44

The dilapidated facade of 128 Whitehouse Lane, with its broken guttering, peeling paintwork and overgrown front garden in the grubby light of a truly grey and horrible Balsall Heath rainy day reminds me of every craphole of a student house that I've ever lived in. Twenty-three Charlotte Street, for instance, where I lived for most of my first year of university and which had a kitchen wall so damp that water would pool daily at the base of it; or 228 Manton Avenue, where our next-door neighbours would regularly break into our house and steal our stuff; or 91 Lingham Street where I discovered a family of cockroaches living in the airing cupboard; or finally 218 Bristnall Street, which although damp- cockroach- and burglar-free, was so cold come winter that I used to have to sleep fully clothed under three heavy-weight winter duvets. The day I moved out of Bristnall Street, I vowed that I was done with sub-standard rental accommodation. Never again would I hand over my hard-earned money to crooks and swindlers in return for a roof over my head and with the exception of the first place I lived in London (a house-share in Kensal Green with no running water) I stayed true to my word. So 128 Whitehouse Lane represents the biggest backwards step I've taken in the last twenty years. It's the real-life equivalent of being three squares from the end of a game of Snakes and Ladders only to roll the die, and land on the longest snake on the board.

A full tour of the house by the landlord's sportswear-adorned, headphone-wearing son, Kamal, disabuses me of any hope that 128 Whitehouse Lane might not be as awful as I recalled from the party. The kitchen, with its ancient and frankly dangerous-looking electric cooker, formica work surfaces and walls covered in brown 'tiling on a roll' wallpaper, looks like something left over from 1984; the green carpeted bathroom with full avocado suite and stick-on-the-mixer-taps showerhead looks like the before picture in a renovation project; and the living room is furnished with a number of sofas and armchairs (none of which match) that have clearly been picked up from a Salvation Army charity shop some time in the last fifteen years. Finally there is my room: an eight foot by eight foot magnolia box, with walls dotted with abandoned Blu-Tack, a cheap IKEA wardrobe that smells of old pizza, a pine chest of drawers that looks like it is held together with Sellotape and nautical-themed curtains framing the filthy windows.

'So do you want it, boss?' asks Kamal as we conclude our tour in the hallway. 'Because if you do my dad says you need to stump up the readies now.'

Part of me wants to walk out of here without another word to Kamal, because a) he's annoying and b) the house is obviously a dump, but with Rosa coming back to the flat today and the prospect of sleeping in the shop too awful for serious consideration, this is beginning to look like my only option.

'Can you just give me a minute?' I walk out of eavesdropping distance and dial Lauren's number.

'Hi, it's me.'

'Matt, how are you?'

'Not too bad.' Kamal is playing some kind of game on his phone while nodding his head in a studiously cool manner to the music blaring through his headphones. Lauren is my only hope for a life free from any further interaction with this man. Is it too much to ask for a minor miracle? Is it too much to hope that in the last twenty-four hours she's found a cash buyer for the house and hasn't bothered to tell me? I could last three weeks in the shop if I knew that I'd have a stack of cash in the bank at the end of it.

'Listen, I know it's a long shot but I'm just wondering . . . any news about the house?'

' 'Fraid not,' she replies. 'There was a couple who came for a second viewing and seemed really keen but the agent got back to me yesterday and said that they've made an offer on the place next door.'

'The place next door's up for sale too? What's happening in Blackheath? A tribal exodus?' It was meant to be a joke but it comes out wrong. I sound angry, bitter. This is as horrible as it gets. I'm going to be stuck in this run-down hovel full of students for ever.

'Matt, are you OK?'

'No.'

'What's wrong?'

This is going to kill me. 'I need to borrow some money.'

There's a silence. I feel my last drops of dignity ebb away.

'How much do you need?'

I can barely get the words out. 'A grand.'

She doesn't miss a beat. That's how guilty she feels right now. 'I'll call the bank and get it to you straight away.'

I return to Kamal who removes just enough headphone from one ear to hear me over the racket that he's listening to.

'What's the score, bruv?'

'I'll take it.'

'Always nice to do a deal, innit?' Kamal tries to shake my hand, gangster style, but I don't engage. He looks at me, disappointed, while I wonder what Lauren is thinking right now. She used to respect, even look up to me and now I'm just some bloke who leeches money off her.

Kamal shifts uncomfortably. 'Something wrong, bruv?'

'No,' I reply. 'Everything's just wonderful.'

Returning to the relative civilisation of well-heeled Moseley I stand in the communal gardens of Rosa's flat finishing off the remains of a ham and cheese baguette I'd bought in lieu of breakfast. Screwing up the bag which the sandwich had come in, I drop it into the pocket of my jacket and fish out the keys to the main entrance acutely aware that I am making this journey for the last time. Now that most of my stuff is at the shop all that's left inside is my holdall, and a jacket or two, and even with the half an hour I've factored in to tidy up the flat I'll be long gone before Rosa arrives to reclaim what is rightfully hers.

My mind still churning over my decision to return to the crap housing circuit, I open the front door and hear a noise from the kitchen. I'm not alone.

'I didn't realise you were coming this early,' I say as Rosa and Tory appear in the hallway. They're still wearing their coats and boots, which suggests they've only just arrived.

'Obviously not. How could you leave the flat like this?'

'Look, I'm sorry. Just give me an hour to clean up and I'll be out of your hair.'

Rosa shakes her head. 'Just go, I'll sort it myself.'

'Please,' I reply, 'let me do this one thing, OK?'

'No. I don't want you here any longer than you need to be.'

'Rosa,' I plead, 'is this really the way you want to leave things?'

'What other way is there?'

I shift my gaze to Tory. 'Any chance you could just give me a minute to talk to Rosa alone?'

Tory ignores me and looks enquiringly at Rosa, who nods and says, 'Why don't you make us a cup of tea and I'll give you a shout in a minute?'

I need to deliver something worthy of having asked for Rosa's undivided attention. I take a deep breath, take aim and pull the trigger on what could be my final round of ammunition. 'I do love you, you know.'

'They're just words, Matt, unless you mean them,' says Rosa, with a look of disappointment. 'They're not some kind of sticking plaster that makes everything better.'

'I know you love me.'

'I did, more fool me because you don't love anyone but yourself.'

'You don't get it.' I think about the Jason Clevelands, Aaron Bakers and Nick D'Souzas of this world, 'I'm actually one of the good guys.'

'Maybe and maybe not. Who knows? But this time around you just weren't good enough.'

Days left until I turn forty: 7

45

The first thing I do when I wake up the following Monday morning is swear loudly. Not because I'm developing a case of Tourette's syndrome, or because I've stubbed my toe, or because I'm depressed that it's Monday morning. No, the reason for my expletive is because for a few brief seconds I am fully convinced that I am lying in Rosa's warm bed, in Rosa's warm flat, with Rosa's beautiful long naked limbs curled around my body. It is a wonderful sensation. I feel secure and loved, I am happy, blissful even, nothing can touch me. But then I open my eyes and see the once-white, now grey dust-laden Chinese lantern-style light shade that hangs over my bed, which draws my eye to the cracked ceiling, which takes my gaze to the thickly painted woodchip wallpaper on the walls and the awful truth: I am a recently separated, about-to-be forty-year-old man, living in a house-share with a bunch of twentysomething 'young professionals' and like I've just been jabbed in the eye with a blunt stick, I give birth to an expletive-ridden, anguish-laden outburst, that would shock a sailor. That is how miserable this place makes me.

I resolve to get out of bed and take a shower but not before checking that the coast is clear. I've been here two days and although I've heard my fellow housemates, I have yet to see a single one of them, having set about a deliberate tactic of avoidance (showering early, eating late and staying in my room) and although on Sunday afternoon someone did knock on my door, I pretended not to be in. I don't want these people to become my friends. I don't even want to know their names. All I want is to get out of here as quickly as humanly possible because I'm beginning to fear that the damage this stay is doing to my psyche may be irreparable.

Double-checking the landing for signs of life I make my way to the shower and emerge ten minutes later fully dressed and ready for work. Although I don't much feel like doing it even I can see that a distraction like work is going to come in handy. I grab a slice of toast, down half a carton of orange juice and console myself that with a friend like Gerry I won't have to return here until after the pubs are shut. This lifts my spirits but after half an hour of trudging through the rain despair returns as I approach the shop and see all the volunteers huddled outside.

'What's going on?' I ask Anne, deeming her the person most likely to give me a sensible reply.

'The shop is still shut,' she says briskly, 'and there's no sign of Gerry.'

'Has anyone called him?'

'I've tried three times and Owen has sent him several text messages.'

'Maybe he's not well.'

'It's a possibility,' concedes Anne, 'although I've been volunteering here for a good year and a half now and any time he's not been able to turn up he's always arranged for a key to be dropped off with me so that we can at least keep the shop open.'

Odd Owen nods in agreement, 'It's just not like him. What do you think we should do?'

Everyone looks at me as though I will have the answer and no one has done that since I gave up my job. I find it disconcerting. 'I don't know,' I reply, 'what does everyone else think?'

The responses are split between those who think we should stay and those who think we should go. As a group we decide on a compromise and opt to wait next door at Annabel's taking it in turns to pop our heads out from time to time to see if he's arrived. I try his mobile but after an hour without any sign, people begin to head home, until just after eleven thirty, all that's left is me and Odd Owen (who for the best part of an hour has been extolling the virtues of the *Tenko* box set that he bought from the shop the week before).

'I think I'm going to get off, Matt,' he says eventually. 'I've got an essay that needs to be in soon and I could do with the extra time to work on it.'

'Of course,' I reply, 'I think I'm probably going to stay a little longer just to be on the safe side. Just out of curiosity though: I know Gerry's place is where the old Britannic Insurance building used to be but do you know exactly what number he lives at? I might take a walk down there if he doesn't turn up.'

Odd Owen shakes his head. 'Not a clue, but do you want some company? I'm always up for a bit of amateur detective work.'

'What about that essay?'

'Who cares? Gerry could've been robbed by masked raiders looking for his millions. Right now he's lying in a stairwell outside his flat bleeding to death praying that we're about to come to his rescue.'

I throw Odd Owen my best 'What did you just say?' look.

'That was too weird wasn't it?'

'Just a bit.'

Britannic Park is a development of upmarket apartments for monied professionals keen to avoid the city centre. It looks from the outside like a slice of 'loft style' living without the downside of being more centrally located like finding pools of vomit outside your front door or abandoned doner kebab innards on your windowsill. Essentially it's a very large ornate building set in beautifully maintained lawns and a penthouse apartment here is exactly where you'd expect to find Gerry living out the bachelor pad dream on behalf of men everywhere.

'This is amazing,' says Odd Owen as we look through the window of one of the apartments and take in the stripped oak floors, white walls and large, expensive-looking works of art. 'How much do you think places like this go for?'

'No idea, but I'm pretty sure you wouldn't be able to cover the rent with your student loan.'

I realise that the kind of people who live in places like this are unlikely to answer the door to random strangers and so rather than ringing doorbells I suggest that we wait until we see someone coming in or out and ask if they know Gerry.

The first three we approach practically run away as if we're about to mug them but then Owen gets chatting to a young couple out walking their dog and he calls me over. We show them a picture of Gerry on my phone and although the woman from the couple recognises him (she too had been a Pinfolds fan in her youth) she claims never to have seen him around the building. It's a similar story with everyone else: even those who aren't into music claim that a man as striking as Gerry would stick out a mile in a complex that is mainly populated by accountants, lawyers, doctors and dentists.

'So what do we do now?' asks Odd Owen, as the last of our respondents walks away. 'He's told us all a million times about this place but no one seems to have seen him.'

'Well, think about it: most people have gone to work by the time Gerry's leaving his place and given that he's out at the pub most nights I'm guessing he doesn't come home until they've gone to bed. It just shows us that most people around here don't live the life of a semi-retired—' I break off as my phone rings, and reach into my coat pocket to answer it.

'Hi,' says a female voice at the other end of the line, 'can I speak to Matthew Beckford?'

'That's me. Who's this?'

'I'm calling from the Queen Elizabeth hospital on behalf of your friend Gerry Hammond. He's OK, but last night he had an accident on his moped and was brought to us with suspected concussion. We've had him under observation overnight; the doctors are happy enough to sign him off for release as long as he has someone with him, and you're the person he asked us to call.'

'I'll be there as soon as I can.'

It's after one o'clock by the time Odd Owen and I pull into the hospital car park in Odd Owen's ex-Ministry of Defence soft-top Land Rover Defender, bought the previous summer from eBay. It's hard not to feel like an extra from the TV series *M*A*S*H* but any such enjoyment is tempered by the fact that of all the people Gerry could have called, for some reason he has picked me. Some people might be flattered, but I can't help conclude that anyone who has to turn to me in an emergency is someone with no other option. If that's not the very definition of desperate then I don't know what is.

Directed to the fifth floor, Odd Owen and I search the ward and find Gerry sitting in a wipe-clean armchair next to a regulation hospital bed. He looks a complete mess: there are scratches and bruises across his face, his left arm is in a sling, and the left leg of his jeans has been cut right up to the thigh revealing yet more bandage. He looks old, worn out, and a little bit scared. While I'm sure that with time and sleep he'll be physically back to normal, on the inside I suspect something might have changed for good.

'You OK?'

'I just want to get out of here.'

'No problem, we'll have you home in no time.'

I help Gerry to his feet, while Odd Owen grabs his coat and the crash helmet that had no doubt saved his life, and the three of us make our way down to the car park.

'Back to your pad then, Gerry?' yells Odd Owen, starting up the Land Rover as I help Gerry fasten his seat belt. The noise of the engine is deafening, like the sound of twenty tractors all spluttering to life at once, and I can't hear Gerry's response so I bellow at Odd Owen to switch off for a minute.

'Sorry, mate. What did you say?'

'Head to Edgbaston,' says Gerry.

'Is that where that young thing you're seeing lives?' grins Odd Owen.

Gerry shakes his head.

'So what's there?' I'm intrigued.

He looks out of the car window. 'My wife and kids.'

46

While it's unlikely that even the coolest of TV producers would think that the Birmingham home of the former lead singer of The Pinfolds might make a suitable choice for a revival of the classic TV panel show *Through The Keyhole*, even if they had I doubt whether any of the panellists would have guessed that the house we were currently gazing at from the relative discomfort of Odd Owen's Land Rover belonged to Gerry Hammond. Not that there was anything technically wrong with it. It was a nice enough modern house with a neatly kept front garden and roses growing up the trellis near the front window that any family with 2.4 children, a dog and a Volvo would happily have called home, but Gerry Hammond? It just didn't make sense. How could the man once voted the third 'Coolest Man on Planet Earth' by *Melody Maker* live in a place like this?

Odd Owen grins. 'Do you know what, he nearly had me then! I was thinking Gerry can't live in a place like this.' He turns and looks at Gerry. 'Joke's over. Now where do you really want us to take you?'

Ignoring Odd Owen, Gerry begins struggling with his seat belt.

'You're not saying you really live here? No offence, Gerry, it's just that this place is so . . . it's so . . .' I throw a look in Odd Owen's direction, begging him not to finish the sentence, while Gerry opens the door.

'Thanks for the lift,' he says flatly.

'No problem.'

I tell Odd Owen to stay in the car and follow Gerry.

'Listen mate,' I say, helping him up the front step, 'just ignore Owen. You know what he's like.'

'He's one hundred per cent right though, isn't he? Why would the one and only Gerry Hammond be living in a place like this? I mean, just look at it! Do I look like I belong here?'

'So the swish pad in Moseley? You made all that up?'

Before he can offer a reply the front door opens and a woman dressed in a dark grey trouser suit and heels steps out. She's pretty, with olive skin and shoulder-length dark hair. She looks Spanish or possibly Italian and at a push, I'd say she was in her late forties.

'Are you OK?' There's a slight accent to her voice. 'I was worried sick.'

'It looks worse than it is,' says Gerry calmly. 'The kids get off to school all right?'

The woman nods. 'They asked after you, but I just told them you were up early.'

'You working from home today?'

She shakes her head. 'When I saw you weren't home I called in sick. I just haven't got round to getting changed yet. Are you sure you're OK?'

'I'm fine.'

The woman puts her arms round Gerry and I sense that although she loves him there's a tension between them that neither seems willing to address. Maybe she knows about his girlfriends. Perhaps he thought he'd been getting away with it when she's been aware of everything since day one. 'How many times have I told you to give up that stupid moped? Now it's nearly killed you! Well, I hope it's smashed to pieces! If you even think about getting another one don't bother coming home because I will just pack my bags, take the kids and go.'

Realising that she isn't alone with her husband the woman glares at me like I'm an eavesdropper. 'Alanza, this is my friend Matt,' says Gerry. 'Matt, this is my wife, Alanza.'

She doesn't smile. She is no more pleased to see me than to see her husband in his current mangled condition and I wonder if this is why Gerry called me to get him rather than her. She looks like she's got a fierce temper and I could well imagine wanting to do all I can to keep it from being unleashed.

'I should go.'

'No,' says Gerry, and he turns to Alanza. 'Can you just give me a minute?'

Alanza glares at him, clearly affronted, but returns inside the house, leaving the two of us alone.

'Look, I'm sorry, mate.'

'No need for apologies. I'm guessing you've got your reasons for keeping all this private.'

'I have, and maybe I'll tell you about it all one day, but in the meantime I need you to do me a massive favour: would you run the shop for a while until I'm better? It should only be a day or two, but you'd be getting me out of a hole.'

'I'd love to mate but . . .'

'But what?'

'But nothing,' I reply and the look of relief on his face makes me feel like I've done the right thing, 'just get me the keys and I'll do it.'

Determined to do the best job I can, I spend what remains of the afternoon back at the shop on my own, checking emails, working on rotas, contacting volunteers to let them know that we will definitely be open tomorrow and generally making sure that everything is ready and in order for my first day at the helm. It feels good to have a purpose again, to have my brain up and working on something, but even better to be doing it for a cause other than earning myself yet another big slice of commission. I'm not just helping Gerry out, I'm helping people around the world who I will never meet: people without shelter, without food, without clean water, and if that isn't a good reason to get out of bed in the morning, I don't know what is.

Returning to the house just after seven I put the key in the front door as quietly as I can, hoping to sneak up to my room, but I hear someone call out from the kitchen: 'It's the new guy!' and the next thing I know four faces are looking down the hallway at me.

Much as I want to ignore them as I'd planned, the pressure of social convention proves too much and I reluctantly make my way to the kitchen where the four housemates are seated around the table eating spaghetti Bolognese.

'Hi,' says a cute blond girl with an Irish accent, 'are you hungry? We've got plenty left over.'

I'd dropped into the chip shop on my way home so that I wouldn't have to go anywhere near the kitchen but this girl seems so friendly it feels needlessly rude to say no.

Over the course of the meal I learn that the Irish girl is called Aisling and is a newly qualified teacher. Then from her left I'm introduced to Reena, a history MA student; Alexi, a former drama student from south London who now works in the box office at the MAC; and Clive, a Glaswegian political sciences graduate currently making ends meet by temping in the offices of a local building society.

My new housemates seem like nice enough people and while they are nonplussed at how someone who once had a career could end up living in a dump with them ('You actually own a house but you're choosing to live *here*?'), they are polite enough not to ask too many probing questions although they do look horrified when I finally confess that I'm a week away from turning forty.

'Never,' exclaims Aisling, 'I had you down at thirty-two tops!'

'Mate,' says Clive, 'you don't seem that old.'

'I dunno,' says Reena, who is a little too forthright with her opinions, 'no offence, like, but if you look around his eyes you can definitely tell he's at least late thirties.'

Aisling reprimands Reena straight away. 'You can't say that!'

'It's fine,' I say, holding up my hands, 'I am nearly forty and I look like I'm nearly forty.'

'I can't imagine what it must be like,' says Alexi. 'Does it feel weird?'

'What? Being forty?'

Alexi nods, clearly embarrassed. 'It just seems so old.'

'I remember being like you guys,' I reply. "In fact it only feels like yesterday that I was sitting around a kitchen table just like this drinking cheap beer and moaning about work.'

'You must wonder where the time's gone,' says Alexi. 'I do it now and I'm only twenty-four.'

'I ask that question every single day.'

Sensing that things are bordering on the melancholy Aisling fetches two bottles of wine from the fridge and shares them out between us. After a few glasses I learn that Reena can put both feet behind her head; Alexi can do spot on impressions of several Hollywood films stars; Aisling can hold her breath for one minute and twenty-two seconds and Clive is an unabashed *Dr Who* nut, determined to name his daughter Leela, should he ever have one.

'So is that everyone?' I ask as the last of the wine is poured. 'I thought this was a six-bedroom house?'

'It is,' replies Aisling, and right on cue there's the sound of keys in the front door and in walks Rosa. For a few moments

I'm confused but following her comes the boy with the trilby hat and suddenly everything makes a horrible kind of sense. Rosa is as mortified to see me as I am her, but once the others call her through there's very little she can do other than come and be introduced to her recently dumped boyfriend.

'Matt,' says Aisling, 'this is Jonny, the longest serving resident of one-two-eight Whitehouse Lane. Jonny, this is Matt, the newest.'

Jonny shakes my hand and I can tell from his face that despite throwing daggers in my direction half the night at that party he doesn't even vaguely recognise me. 'Welcome to one-two-eight,' he replies, 'good to have you on board.' He turns to Rosa. 'This is my friend Rosa,' he says to me.

I say hello and then conversation breaks out amongst the rest of the housemates. I can't leave without making it obvious something is wrong. Finally, after fifteen minutes or so, I announce that I'm heading upstairs because I've got tons of work to catch up on and make my escape. I've barely reached the stairs when Rosa calls after me.

'It's not what you think,' she says. 'He called me tonight, I was feeling down, he asked me out for a drink – there's nothing in it – we're just friends.'

I think about Ginny and me and all the wasted years we've spent pretending that there was some kind of third way between sex and friendship. 'There is no "just" about it, Rosa, either you're friends or you're not and the sooner you learn that the better for everyone involved.'

47

Much like the 'Gerry's got a wife and kids' situation I choose to ignore the 'Rosa's back with her ex five minutes after splitting up with me' scenario because I know that if I don't I will be in grave danger of grinding to a halt, giving up on everything and going to bed for weeks on end like I did when I quit my job. The important thing is to keep moving and not let Gerry, Rosa, Lauren, Ginny or even my looming birthday take up any head space; to this end I make managing the shop the focus of all my energies.

The following morning I'm up and out of the house for eight o'clock and by the time the first of the volunteers arrive I've already answered all the emails from head office, double-checked the previous week's figures for Gerry to look over, and readied for sorting at least three bags of donations that had been unceremoniously dumped in front of the shop.

'So you're in charge now are you?' asks Anne frostily, as I open the door to let her and Odd Owen in.

'Not exactly, I'm just helping Gerry out.'

'Time was if he needed helping out he would've come to me.'

'And I'm sure he will again. I doubt I'll still be here this time next month.'

'Going back to London?'

'At the first opportunity,' I reply.

My first day in charge has its highs and lows. The highs include managing to sell an out-of-print edition of a book of Helmut Newton's photographs for a hundred and twenty pounds; receiving a call from a retired barrister wishing to get rid of all his law books (the last time we had a similar donation we made over two thousand pounds from a law firm that bought the lot); and signing up two extra volunteers willing to work two days a week each. As for the lows, where to begin? Despite my best efforts to cajole her into a better mood Anne doesn't stop moaning about being overlooked as Gerry's replacement; I have to eject a group of girls attempting to pinch DVDs; and in the afternoon the credit card reader goes down twice in the space of an hour. All in all however, when I lock the door at the end of the day and draw the shutters over the window, I reflect that today has been a good day.

Returning to the house having stopped off at Sainsbury's to pick up supplies I make my way to the kitchen and am relieved to find it empty. Although last night had been enjoyable (my interaction with Rosa and her 'friend' aside) it was probably a one-off; most nights in the house wouldn't be so convivial. No, the sooner I got into a rhythm of cooking alone, eating alone, and heading up to my bedroom alone the better it would be in the long run.

Unloading the shopping into my allotted cupboard still marked 'Dave's' I set about making myself something to eat but without cooking for Rosa, making anything even remotely complicated seems utterly pointless. I make beans on toast and at the last moment I augment it with cheese because of a half-recalled fact that after the age of forty your body needs more calcium.

'You're quite the chef, aren't you?' says a voice behind me as I begin to tuck in.

It's Aisling. 'I didn't realise anyone else was in.'

'I was upstairs talking to the folks back home – never a conversation that takes less than an hour. How's your day been?'

'Good. Yours?'

'Long, long, long. The kids were extra mental today, the parents more needy than usual, and a departmental meeting that was meant to take an hour ended up taking two. It was like *The Perfect Storm*, only in an inner-city school and with me in the Russell Crowe role.'

She heads to the fridge, pours herself an orange juice and sits down across from me at the table. 'Me and the guys were wondering if you'd be up for letting us take you to the pub the night before your big birthday.'

I stare down at my plate. Rosa had been in charge of organising my birthday celebrations and now that I didn't have her, other than the meal at my parents' house I had no plans at all. Drinking myself senseless alone in my room had a certain downbeat glamour about it, but on the other hand perhaps a casual drink with the people I'd be living with for the next few months would help ward off my inevitable descent into despair.

'How does eight o'clock in Pat Kav's sound?'

'I love that place!' says Aisling eagerly, 'Friday, eight o'clock in Pat Kav's it is.'

I want the next few days to take an eternity so that I can cling on to the last vestiges of my thirties for as long as possible, but of course time is on fast-forward. Every day I wake up thinking about the problems ahead and five minutes later I'm heading to bed reflecting on how the day had simply run away from me. In between I run the shop, speak to a gloomy Gerry from time to time when I need advice; check my emails for messages of hope from Lauren (there are none: the house resolutely refuses to be sold); take calls from Mum ('Yes, I will be there on time for my birthday lunch, no, Rosa won't be coming with me,') and generally try and keep it all together; but one morning I wake up following a dreamless sleep, and it dawns on me that today is the last day of my thirties.

'So I'm assuming you won't be in tomorrow?' asks Anne when she arrives at the shop that morning.

'No, but I did get a text from Gerry saying he'd definitely be back in so it shouldn't be a problem.'

Anne shrugs, unimpressed. 'I think you should know that as of Monday next I shall be taking my skills which are so desperately undervalued here to the Cancer Research shop on Kings Heath high street. I'm sorry that I can't give you more notice, but it's indicative of my strength of feeling over the way that certain issues have been dealt with.'

My heart sinks; it hadn't occurred to me that Anne might have wanted the management position and had simply been biding her time until Gerry moved on but now it seems obvious.

'You're not undervalued, Anne. This place would fall apart if it weren't for you.'

'I have said everything I have to say on the matter,' she says with a sniff.

The day gets worse after Anne's 'resignation'. I have to throw out a homeless guy who comes in shouting about squirrels; a teenager starts an argument with me over what he claims is a faulty computer game even though it works fine on the office PC; the credit card reader goes down three times and then breaks completely; and when we cash up the till is down by thirty-five pounds. From start to finish the whole day is horrible, so when I get a text from Aisling sometime after six asking if my pre-birthday bash could start earlier than advertised, I text her straight back: *I'll be there in 5. Mine's a pint of Stella.*

48

It's late (or it could be early, I have no idea because I have drunk an awful lot of beer and can't focus on my watch), and I am sitting in the rear bar of Kav's, nursing my umpteenth pint, gently ribbing and being ribbed by Aisling, Reena, Clive and Alexi.

'And another thing,' I slur, 'what is it with your generation and the need to say "Yeah?" after everything like you're in such desperate need of affirmation that you can't go a second without checking that someone's listening?'

'Never mind all that, yeah,' says Reena, oblivious to the irony, 'what's with your generation always harping on about the past? If you're not getting emotional about going to see some rubbish band doing a twentieth anniversary tour you're clogging up our festivals with the same rubbish bands! I barely want to see The Libertines get back together and they were my generation! Why would I want to see a bunch of grey-bearded old blokes being wheeled on stage in order to bang on about how their lives were changed when they discovered Acid House and dropped their first ecstasy tab!'

The whole table erupts in raucous laughter.

'Do you know what? If anyone had told me a year ago that I'd be spending the night before I turned forty surrounded by a bunch of zygotes who hadn't even been born when I was seventeen I wouldn't have believed them.' I raise my glass in the air, 'I'm drunk, tired and more than a bit emotional but do you know what? You guys are all right!'

I get resounding applause for my speech and in return offer to get a round in. I head to the bar, then register that my bladder is full to bursting and so make for the toilet instead. All the urinals are taken so I have no option but to hide away in the stall and close the door behind me.

Struggling with my zip, I eventually manage to get it down and as I relax my bladder I reflect on how far I've come in a year: yes, my marriage is over; yes, I quit the best paid job I've ever had; yes, I moved back to Birmingham; yes, I fell in love with an ex and ended up losing a best friend in the process; yes, I fell in love with another girl and managed to screw that up too; but put all that aside for a moment and look at me now: I'm out in the pub, on the last day of my thirties, hanging out with a bunch of young people who might in fact turn out to be good mates. I'd been knocked down but not knocked out. I'd been bruised but was still alive and kicking. Everything that life could throw at me has come my way and I'm still here. And tomorrow I will turn forty, and though I won't have a job, house, wife or even my beloved shed, I will have my dignity.

I zip up my jeans and am about to flush when I hear Clive's unmistakable Glaswegian brogue and Alexi's south-

London-geezer tones. Clear as day Alexi says to Clive: 'If I'm living in a dump like one-two-eight and think that working in a charity shop, flirting with girls half my age and trying to play the cool dude with a bunch of twentysomethings is a good idea for a grown man the night before I turn forty, promise you'll kill me, yeah, because honestly mate, if I actually think that's a life then I will need putting out of my misery.'

They erupt into raucous laughter and I'm not sure what to do but then I take a deep breath and step out just as they're both zipping up their trousers. The look of horror on their faces says it all.

'I thought you were at the bar,' says Clive fearfully as Alexi looks on. 'We were just shooting our mouths off. We didn't mean anything by it.'

I don't say a word. I leave the pub and take the money that I was going to spend on a round to the off-licence down the road and buy a small bottle of bourbon. After tearing off the wrapper with my teeth I take a sip and then another sip, then finish off the entire bottle and once I'm well and truly on my way to not knowing which way is up, I switch on my internal autopilot and head in the direction of Ginny's house.

As my finger hovers over Ginny's front doorbell, I have no idea why I'm here. I have no idea what to say to Ginny, how I'm going to respond if Gershwin answers the door or even what to do if they're both out. All I know is that I have officially had enough. I haven't just reached my breaking point, I have gone way beyond it and snapped in two. I'm not just in danger of losing it, I have lost it completely and have no idea how to get it back.

I ring the doorbell and my head starts spinning so much that I have to lean against the door. This is a really bad idea, I know it, and yet there's nothing I can do to stop it.

I stare at the bell. Why haven't they answered yet? Did they not hear? Maybe I'm so drunk I didn't ring it properly. I reach out to press the bell again then I see Ginny's face at the window. Moments later she opens the door.

'Matt, what are you doing here?'

'Why haven't you been in touch?'

'What do you mean?'

'I mean why haven't you been in touch? I was there for you! I was there for you when you needed me so why weren't you there for me?'

'Have you been drinking?'

I'm bewildered by the stupidity of her question. 'Of course I've been drinking! Do you think I've turned up on your doorstep the night before my birthday by accident? My life has turned to arse, Ginny, pure arse. It's falling apart around my ears, and you're the only one who can save me.'

'Matt,' says Ginny desperately, 'you can't be here! Gershwin's upstairs, he'll be down any minute. Please go and I promise I'll see you tomorrow and we can sort this whole thing out! But you can't be here right now!' She snatches a look over her shoulder. 'I'm sorry, Matt, I'm really sorry.' Then she slams the door shut in my face.

I don't move a muscle, not quite able to believe that Ginny, my Ginny, the woman who I'd walk a mile over broken glass to see has slammed her front door in my face. It doesn't compute. It refuses to penetrate my skull. And then the message reaches home: Ginny's just slammed the door in my face; she's turned away from me in my time of need. A response is called for: I determine to ring her doorbell until it falls off the wall. Focusing every last drop of energy I have into the index finger of my right hand I jab it right into the centre of that doorbell like an Olympic archer hitting a bull's-eye and keep it there with a determination that would have made the little Dutch boy proud. I'm not moving it for anyone, not until I get someone to come and answer this door.

I have no idea how long it takes for the door to open again (time in my current state of mind has lost all meaning) but when I see Gershwin it's as if I can no longer contain the rage that I have been desperately holding back since the day Lauren told me she no longer loved me. With my finger still fixed to the doorbell I yell at the top of my voice: 'I shagged Ginny a week after I came home to Birmingham and the week before last we met up and I took her to a funeral!'

The confusion on Gershwin's face as he looks from me to Ginny's horrified expression would have been amusing had his fist not been drawing back at the same time. He launches it, fully primed, in the direction of my face with such speed that I watch in awe as it closes in on me. Reaching maximum velocity it completely fills my vision and then makes contact with my nose sending me spinning like a rag doll into the air.

For a moment, I feel nothing, and wonder whether I am dead, but then a small pinprick at the centre of my face gradually mushrooms into a nuclear explosion's worth of pain. I am alive, as the taste of blood oozing from my nose down into my mouth attests, but only just. As I lie on the floor, I open my eyes and see my watch right next to me. It is a quarter to one in the morning and almost down to the exact minute forty years ago today in a hospital a few miles from here I came kicking and screaming into the world.

Ginny kneels down next to me; she's crying and shouting at Gershwin to go and get some towels.

'Are you all right? Is anything broken?'

'I'm forty.' My voice barely registers above a whisper.

'You're what?'

'I'm forty,' I tell her and then I pass out.

Days left until I turn forty: 0

49

It's an odd feeling to open your eyes and not be in the place you hope you might be (lying in bed next to Rosa) or in the place you ought to be (my hideously uncomfortable bed in the hideous room in the hideous house that I share with the hideous housemates who despise me) but are somewhere you don't recognise at all. I'm in fact in a double bed in a tastefully neutral bedroom. I turn my head slightly and my throbbing nose hurts so much I feel my head is about to fall off. Out of the corner of my eye I see my former best mate's ex-wife sitting next to the bed watching me closely.

'So you're awake now are you?' says Zoe.

'Now I'm really confused. Why am I at your house?'

'You're not, you're at Ginny's.'

I look around the room. Yes, I am indeed in Ginny's guest bedroom.

'What are you doing here then?'

'Gershwin woke me in the middle of the night worried that he'd killed you. He called me over to take a look even though I haven't worked on an emergency unit in a decade.'

'So am I OK?'

345

'You might be mildly concussed. If I was you I'd go to hospital. It wasn't like we didn't try to take you last night but you made such a commotion I thought it would be better to keep you here.'

'So, you've been watching me all night?'

Zoe laughs. 'You know I love you, Matt, but not that much. I took it in turns with Ginny. In fact you've just missed her. I can go and get her if you like.'

I try to sit up and my head does the throbbing thing again.

'I can't believe this is what forty feels like.'

'Gershwin got you good and proper,' she says, handing me a couple of painkillers and a glass of water. 'The way I hear it you're lucky a bloody nose is all you got.'

'Oh, so it's all my fault is it?' I lift my head to swallow the pills and drink all the water in an effort to speed them through my system more quickly.

'Of course it's not just your fault. It takes two to tango and with Gershwin in the mix this was always going to be a mess. But when it comes to you getting a slap on the night before your birthday of all nights, you know as well as I do that you only have yourself to blame. What were you thinking, telling him about you and Ginny? How did you think he'd react? He knows that you and Ginny have always had a bond and all you've done is confirm his worst fears.'

With an enormous effort I sit up and look her in the eye.

'What's happened?'

'He's gone. Sent Ginny a text this morning to say he slept in his car and that he's going to stay with friends while he sorts his head out.'

'Why doesn't he just go back to his house?'

'Because it's rented out. Has been since they moved in together.'

'So how was Ginny about him leaving like that?'

'How do you expect? For all her faults she does really love Gershwin and I haven't seen him nearly as happy as he has been with her since we split up.'

'So you're taking his side now?'

Zoe sighs. 'What's going on here? Do you think you're still seventeen and can get away with all the larks you and Gershwin were always reminiscing about whenever you got together? No one needs to takes sides, Matt, like you're having a spat in the sixth-form common room! Yes, it's tough when a marriage fails, and no, it's not exactly great when you wake up and decide that you hate your job but you're a grown man and the sooner you start acting that way instead of like a hormonal overgrown schoolboy the better.'

Zoe may have a point but I've long since stopped listening to her as something twice as pressing and three times as scary dawns on me. I look at my watch.

'What's wrong?'

'I'm about to be late for my own birthday party.' I grit my teeth through the pain and launch myself trouserless out of bed. 'My mum is literally going to kill me.'

'Where have you got to get to?' Zoe makes a show of averting her eyes.

'Worcester.'

'When should you be there?'

'Ten minutes ago.'

Zoe picks up her handbag and takes out her car keys. 'Take these.' She dangles them in the air. 'It's the silver Toyota parked out front. I know this is seventeen types of madness but, well, consider it a birthday present. If you damage it, you pay for it, job or no job, right?'

I take Zoe in my arms and give her a huge peck on the cheek and a good old-fashioned bear hug. 'You're a lifesaver, you know? Any time you need anything at all, you come to me and I'll sort you out. I owe you big time.'

'All I need right now is for you to put your trousers on!'

This isn't an unreasonable request and so as she turns away I pull on my jeans and take a five-second glance in the mirror above the chest of drawers. My face is bruised and battered and my shirt splattered with blood, and though there isn't a great deal I can do about the former a quick rummage through the chest of drawers where I find a black T-shirt belonging to Gershwin sorts out the latter. I tell myself that I'll have plenty of time to clean up my face on the journey to Worcester but in the meantime I need to get going and I'm halfway out of the door when Zoe stops me in my tracks.

'What about Ginny?'

'What about her?'

'What do you want me to tell her when she wakes up?'

It's a good question, given that last night I turned up on her doorstep wrecked out of my head and detonated six tons of plastic explosive underneath her relationship.

'Tell her I'm sorry.'

'And that's it?' asks Zoe.

'I've got to go.' I feel her disappointment radiating in my direction.

'I'll talk to you later.'

Picking up the huge bunch of flowers that I'd bought on the way over from Birmingham, I climb out of the car and go over in my head the likely progress of the day: Mum will be in a mood until we've eaten; Dad will be in a mood because Mum being in a mood always makes his day worse; my sister will start telling me how worried Mum has been all morning and then have to stop mid-sentence to attend to the kids; my brother-in-law, sensing tension, won't say much; and my nephews will pile on top of me the moment I cross the threshold and beg me to play anything with them so long as it's dangerous.

The first sign that things might not go as anticipated comes as the door opens to reveal my brother Ed, who I had no idea was coming up from Reading; the second is when a small child appears whom I recognise as my brother Tony's eldest and the final sign comes when Ed makes way for my mum and she has the biggest grin on her face. She holds out her arms and calls: 'Where's that baby of mine?' I look around, thinking that one of Yvonne's kids must have escaped, only to realise as she puts her arms round me that she's actually talking about me.

'What happened to your face?'

'I got into a fight with Gershwin. It's a long and miserable story that can probably wait for another time if that's OK? I just want to enjoy today, Mum, with you and Dad and whoever else you've got stashed away in there. What's going on?'

'What do you think's going on, bro?' says Ed, shaking my hand. 'It's a gathering of the clan just for you, you big idiot.' He steps back to reveal Yvonne and all her family, Tony and all his, and Ed's wife Sheena with their two kids. As they gather round the weirdest thing happens: I feel myself on the verge of tears. I want to ask forgiveness for the state I'm in. But there's no need: this is family.

'I don't know what to say. This . . . well, this really . . . means . . . you know what I'm saying.'

'No worries, bro,' says Tony. 'We'd heard you'd been through the mill a bit and so we thought we'd all make the effort to be here. That said, if we'd known it would've reduced you to tears like a big girl we would have done it a lot sooner!'

I try to twist Tony's hand behind his back but then Ed jumps on me and in a few moments we're roughhousing like the old days and laughing like idiots because we're out of shape and scared of doing any permanent damage to ourselves in the pursuit of fun.

'Will you boys ever grow up?' yells Mum.

'No,' says Tony, trying to get me in a headlock. 'I can pretty much guarantee that's never going to happen.'

At Dad's request we break up the play fighting and head straight to my parents' little dining room that looks out across open fields. After a lifetime in the urban sprawl they really have fallen on their feet finding a place like this and I'm happy for them. They deserve it.

Three generations of Beckfords sitting round the table united in the effort to make a dent in the feast that Mum has spent days preparing is a magnificent sight to see. We eat, drink and are indeed merry and as birthdays go it's looking like this one might not be anywhere near as awful as I'd imagined.

50

The dying embers of the sun are filling the sky with a last blast of colour as Mum, Dad and I stand in front of the bungalow and wave off Ed, the last of the family to leave.

'That's the most fun I've had in years,' says Dad. 'What do you think to doing it again at Christmas?'

'Count me in.' I look over at Mum and see that she's a bit tearful. 'It's always tough saying goodbye,' I put my arm round her, 'but they'll be back soon.'

'I just miss you all,' says Mum. 'I know you've got to live your lives but what I wouldn't give to see you all every day.'

Dad and I exchange wary glances. While we both understand the sentiment, I don't think either of us would be all that keen on being surrounded by family twenty-four seven.

'It's getting a bit chilly,' says Dad, changing the subject. 'Who fancies a brew?'

We head back inside and as Dad makes the tea I allow Mum to give me the guided tour of the bungalow she's been threatening me with all afternoon. It's nice that they've put their mark on what was essentially a collection of magnolia boxes and I can tell from the way they move around the rooms that to them this is already home.

'So what are your plans now your birthday's behind you?' asks Mum as we stand in the kitchen sipping tea. 'Carry on as you are until you get some good news about the house?'

'I haven't got a clue.' I look out of the window at a blue tit pecking at the bird feeder. 'Carrying on like I have been doesn't exactly make me feel great but then again the idea of going back to the IT world . . . well, you know how I feel about my old job.'

'But you've got to do something, haven't you?'

'Which is why I might just have to suck it up and go back to contracting in London. The bills aren't going to pay themselves.'

'You know there's always a place for you here,' says Mum. 'I know we don't always see eye to eye but this is, and will always be, your home, and don't you dare forget that.'

I thank Mum and go and search out my dad, finding him sitting on the sofa in front of the TV.

'I've just come to say goodbye, Pop.'

He stands up. 'You don't have to go, you know. Why don't you stay the night?'

'I'd love to but without going into a lot of stuff that you won't want to hear I made a pretty big mess last night and I need to clear it up.'

'It wouldn't be related to those bruises on your face?'

'Just a bit. I've got a lot of apologising to do but it's nothing I can't handle. Or at least I hope so.'

My dad holds out his hand and I shake it firmly. 'It's been good having you around, son. Don't be a stranger will you?'

Gathering together my birthday presents (a jumper from my parents; a digital camera from Yvonne; a remote-controlled Dalek from Ed; and a George Foreman grill from Tony) and what little remains of my birthday cake, I say one last goodbye to my folks and head out to the car.

The image of my parents waving from their porch reminds me of something Ginny said after I told her about my parents' plans: 'Maybe they want to make some new memories.' She was right; that's exactly what they'd done here today. And not just new memories for me or my siblings but for my nieces and nephews and for themselves. They'd got it right, my parents, now all I need to do is follow suit and we'll all be happy.

It's after seven as I arrive at Ginny's on foot, having dropped off Zoe's car along with the most expensive chocolates I could find at the local Shell garage. It feels almost criminal to even think about ringing her doorbell for a second time in twenty-four hours given the havoc I caused last time around.

A short, sharp, shrill burst of noise and the act is done. Now all I have to do is wait and take what's coming my way, whatever that might be. Another punch in the face? A bucket of water? A threat to call the police? It's impossible to calculate what a woman might be capable of when you've single-handedly destroyed her relationship and her dreams.

Ginny opens the door and her face falls.

'What do you want?'

'I want to make things right.'

'Don't you think you've done enough?'

'I'm sorry, Gin, really I am.'

'So sorry that you sneaked away this morning without saying a word?'

Hoping to lighten the mood by a few degrees I hold my hands in the air as if in surrender. 'Guilty as charged.'

'Do you think this is some kind of joke?' she spits. 'Do you think anything about this situation is even remotely amusing? I'm so angry with you right now, Matt! Why do you always come back home when things get tough? Why did you have to spring back into my life and ruin everything? I was fine before you came back from London and now look! Are you happy now that we're all as miserable as you were when you arrived? Well, you've done your job, so why don't you just go back to London and stay there for good!'

For the second time in twenty-four hours Ginny slams her front door in my face but whereas last time I felt indignant, this time I know she's in the right. She's right about me always running back home. She's right about me spreading misery left, right and centre and she's right about the disaster I leave in my wake. I don't need Ginny to love me. I'm not sure I even need her to like me, but I can't stand having her hate me.

I ring the doorbell again. Just once but long enough to get her attention. She opens the door, but rather than launching another verbal attack she simply heads down the hallway to the living room without saying a word and sits down on the sofa. Reasoning it wise to keep my distance, I take a seat in the chair opposite and watch as her cat takes up residence in his mistress's lap and purrs loudly for attention.

'How's your face?' she asks eventually. She seems less angry now, not exactly at peace but less like she is about to hit me.

'A bit sore, but nothing I can't live with.'

'I can't believe he thumped you like that.'

'If I'd been in his shoes I'm sure I would have done the same.'

'Zoe said the only reason he didn't do any permanent damage was because you were so drunk that your body didn't resist the punch. What were you thinking, coming round here in that state?'

'I wasn't thinking at all.' Alarmingly this is the absolute truth. 'A lot of stuff that had been brewing for a while came to a head last night and I just needed someone to talk to.'

'And I turned you away.' For the first time I feel like Ginny's really listening to me. 'You said it last night, and you were right: you've always been there for me in the past but last night I wasn't there for you was I?'

'It was a difficult situation.'

'And one I helped to create, but that doesn't mean I didn't let you down.'

'And it doesn't mean that I had to go shouting my head off like an idiot either. Just let me know where Gershwin is and I'll go and see him and tell him it was all lies.'

'But it isn't though, is it? I did sleep with you; you did come with me to my gran's funeral, and if this whole mess proves anything it's that trying not to hurt people by keeping the truth from them never works.'

'So what do you want me to do?'

'I don't think there is anything you can do. I called Gershwin this morning but he barely said a word.'

'Well at least let me try.'

'I don't think that's a good idea. Where would you even begin?'

'With the truth. That seems as good a place to start as any.'

The address Ginny gives is a decent taxi ride away from Kings Heath, so I walk up to the high street in search of a cab and eventually pick one up outside the Hare and Hounds. The driver and I get talking and it turns out that his cousin who's about my age went to Kings Heath Comprehensive. When he tells me the kid's name is Paul Granger, it rings a faint bell but not loudly enough for me to picture his face or recall anything about him. Nonetheless, I feel a connection has been made, we have succeeded in making the world just that little bit smaller and as we reach our destination I realise that in spite of my initial reticence to see people from my past, having these connections has been one of the best things about being home. Once I'm back in London I won't be bumping into people I know in the supermarket, or making conversation with cabbies whose cousins were in the year below me at school or catching up with schoolmates whose lives have changed beyond all recognition. It'll be business as usual and I'll return to being one of the herd on the Tube reading a book, newspaper or playing Angry Birds on my phone surrounded by a community of travellers with whom I'll never exchange a word.

The cab pulls up at a nice little terrace on a tree-lined road a stone's throw from Bearwood high street. I ring the bell and a grey-haired guy answers the door and I tell him I'm looking for Gershwin. The man welcomes me inside and as he makes his way along the hallway he calls out: 'You've got a visitor!' As we arrive in the living room a confused-looking Gershwin stands up and stares at me.

'What are you doing here?'

'I've come to talk.'

Gershwin's friend looks concerned. 'Everything all right, mate?'

'Everything's fine,' he replies steadily, not taking his eyes off me.

His friend hesitates before addressing Gershwin. 'Emma's upstairs putting Jake to bed. I'll be in the kitchen if you need me.'

'Cheers,' replies Gershwin. 'This shouldn't take too long.'

I enter the room and close the door behind me. The only noise in the room comes from the TV.

'I haven't come to make trouble.'

'So why are you here?'

'To tell you the whole truth.'

'Isn't that what you did last night?'

'If it was maybe I wouldn't be standing here right now.'

A flicker of suspicion crosses Gershwin's face. 'Are you saying you were lying?'

I shake my head. 'Everything I said was true but it's not the full picture. The bit I missed out last night is that Ginny loves you.'

Gershwin looks at me blankly.

'Listen,' I continue, 'I know there's a lot of stuff I could go on about but seriously, what would be the point? All that matters is that Ginny chose you. She wants to be with you.' I hold out my hand. 'I know with everything that's gone on we're not going to be friends but for old times' sake let's at least try not to be enemies.'

For a moment Gershwin simply stares at me and I wonder whether he's about to finish off what he started last night but then, albeit reluctantly, he shakes my hand.

'Before all this kicked off Ginny and I were talking about moving . . .'

'She told me you were looking at Bournville or maybe Kings Norton. They're both really nice areas. You should have no problem finding a nice place around there.'

'Thing is, it turns out we're moving a bit further than that. I got told last week that my job's relocating to Bristol . . . and with her being pregnant, it feels like we're getting a fresh start.'

'Ginny's pregnant?'

Gershwin nods. 'We found out last week.'

It's a real shock. Ginny and Gershwin, they're going to be a family. They're moving on. They're making the life they want to lead instead of waiting for it to happen. 'Congratulations, mate. I really mean it. I wish you two nothing but the best.'

Gershwin walks me to the front door. I feel like we both have a lot to say but aren't sure how to say it. I get the feeling though that the second I've said goodbye he'll be on his way back to Ginny. Why wouldn't he? He's got everything to look forward to.

We shake hands one last time.

'Look after yourself, mate, OK?'

'You too.' I walk away but at the front gate Gershwin calls out after me. I stop and turn. 'Don't be a stranger,' he says, and for a moment I see in his eyes a glimpse of the cheeky schoolboy who used to be my best friend in all the world.

51

Looking up at 128 Whitehouse Lane silhouetted against the night sky as I climb out of a minicab my thoughts turn to ponder the sort of reception I'm in for from my housemates. I haven't had so much as a text from any of them all day. As I walk up the path however I'm surprised by how calm I feel. It's as if last night's antics burned up the last residue of my lifetime's supply of angst and now all that's left is me. Truth is, I've indulged myself for too long, over too little. Stuff happens, that's life, but the point of it all is not to let it sink you.

I open the front door to see Aisling, Reena, Clive, Dan and Alexi sitting frozen around the kitchen table, waiting to see what I'll do next. Part of me wants to give the two idiots I overheard the night before a piece of my mind, another wants to head upstairs and forget they even exist, and a third part of me wants to turn round and never come back. With so many possibilities, each with its merits, I don't know what to do for the best but as I find myself leaning towards the delivery of a few home truths I get a text from Gerry: *Mate, am in the Cocks on my own and will be here all night. PS.*

Have a birthday pint with your name on it so come down if you can!

I glance up at my housemates still frozen in time and then back at the screen. A night out with my favourite fallen idol versus a night in spent metaphorically knocking heads together. No competition.

'The birthday boy himself!' cries Gerry, leaning over and throwing his good arm round me, like the last week hasn't happened. I give him a moment to spot the bruising on my face. 'What happened to you? You didn't have a road/body interface while coming off a Lambretta did you?'

'Sadly not,' I reply. 'Forty is what happened to me.' I clamber up on to the stool next to him, take a sip of the drink that he's thrust into my hands and, starting with Anne's defection to Cancer Research, I relay the entire story of yesterday up to and including my loss of consciousness.

'I always knew this birthday was going to be monumental,' says Gerry, chuckling, 'but I never imagined it would be this wild: extreme boozing, ex-friend baiting, a fist fight resulting in a knockout – stop please, you're making me nostalgic for The Pinfolds' first tour of the States!'

'I know, it's too juvenile for words and I'm thoroughly disappointed with myself.'

'Really? Not a little bit proud? Yeah, the night might have ended with you unconscious on the floor but it beats my fortieth hands down.'

'I could have split up Ginny and Gershwin for good and for what?'

'I thought that's what you wanted?'

'Who knows what I want? I thought I wanted Lauren until she moved on; I thought I wanted Ginny until she made it clear that she didn't want me; I was beginning to be convinced about Rosa but then I threw it all away. I don't know what I want, Gerry, not in love, not in life. It's like the only thing I want is the thing I can't have because once I get it I haven't got the faintest clue how to keep hold of it.'

Gerry raises his glass in the air and I automatically raise mine too. 'Welcome to my world! I'd love to say that it gets easier the older you get but you know as well as anyone that I'd be lying. Speaking of which . . .' He looks at me sheepishly. 'I'm guessing I sort of owe you an apology.'

'Honestly, mate, you don't owe me anything.'

'I think I do.'

He tells me everything. The woman Odd Owen and I met is indeed his wife, but not his first. His first was Beth, whom he had known since his teens. They fell in and out of love throughout their early twenties and unbeknown to anyone outside the band they got married in New York two weeks before 'Newhall Lovers' came out. Things were good for a few years but then Beth got pregnant and Gerry became distant and things came to a head when he found out that Pete McCulloch had been sleeping with Beth behind his back. That's when the band imploded. Pete and Beth stayed together for a while but when they inevitably split up Beth started divorce proceedings and the settlement wiped out virtually all of the money Gerry had made. Determined to keep living 'the dream' Gerry had moved to Amsterdam to stay with friends and then Spain, which is where he met Alanza, a lawyer, and fell in love with her. When she got pregnant they made the decision to move to the UK to raise their family. With Gerry all but unemployable by then it made sense that he would look after the kids while she went out to work, but as the kids grew older and needed him less he started hanging out with his old crowd and not long after his forty-ninth birthday, Gerry Mark Two was born.

'I guess I just wanted another shot at being young again,' he says, by way of conclusion. 'A last blast before I gave up the ghost like everyone else around me.'

'And now?'

Gerry shrugs. 'Lying in that hospital bed, thinking how different it all could have been had there been a car behind me when I came off the scooter, it just made me think about what was important, and how if I carried on down this road I was going to mess things up for good. So I'm done with it all: the girls, the going out all the time, everything. I don't know whether I'll be any good at this being a husband and father lark, but I'm going to give it a proper shot.'

Looking self-conscious, Gerry mutters something about that being enough girl talk for the night and offers me another drink. Feeling in the mood for a change now I'm forty I ask for a Guinness and as he waves to the barmaid I get a text, the contents of which completely stop me in my tracks.

'What's up?' asks Gerry. 'You look ill?'

I'm barely able to get the words out. 'It's from Lauren . . . apparently we've just sold the house.'

Gerry's roar of congratulations is loud enough to make everyone in the pub stare at us but I'm barely aware of it. After all this time and all this heartache the house is finally sold.

'I have to speak to Lauren.' I head outside and dial her number. She replies so quickly that she must have had the phone in her hand.

'Lauren, it's me. Is it true? Is the house really sold?'

'To a couple called the Masons.' she says. 'The estate agent showed them round for a second viewing earlier in the week and they made the first offer yesterday. I would've called you but with your birthday and everything I didn't want to until I had something concrete to say.'

'So did we get anywhere near what we wanted?' If anything was going to mess up my plans for the future, not getting enough for the house would be it. I couldn't afford to have any more debt hanging over me than I already had.

'They drove a really hard bargain . . . but yes . . . it's amazing, Matt, we've got enough to pay off the mortgage, for you to take out the proceeds from the sale of your apartment in Oz, and a little bonus each for the two of us!'

'And how long until it all goes through?'

'This is the best bit! I made it clear that the only way we'd knock money off was if they could complete quickly and they agreed to four weeks! Can you believe it? Four weeks and this whole thing is done.'

I feel weird. It doesn't quite feel right to be so happy about something that will take Lauren and me a step closer to leading separate lives. 'Listen,' I say quickly, 'I'd better go but thanks for sorting everything out with the house. I know I've been less than useless these past few weeks but I do really appreciate everything you've done.'

I tuck my phone into my jacket pocket and go back to the bar to bring Gerry up to date.

'Why do I feel annoyed that Lauren's so happy that the house is being sold?'

'You're happy aren't you? Or was that someone else I saw a minute ago with a big grin on his face?'

'Don't get me wrong. I am happy. It's just . . . I don't see what it is Lauren's got to be happy about. I'm happy because in just under a month I'll be able to move out of the hovel I'm in and back to London. But what's in it for her other than not having to be quite so involved with me?'

Gerry laughs. 'It's starting to make sense now: you living with her for so long even after you'd separated; you getting all weird about her online dating even though you'd been off with Ginny; and now you're sad because once the house is sold you won't be part of her life? Mate, if you still love her you need to tell her before it's too late.'

London

52

Home.

As the black cab that brought me here pulls away from the edge of the pavement I scan the house for signs of change, that things have moved on. The most obvious difference is the sale board at the front of the house with a red 'sold' now emblazoned across it. The last time there had been a For Sale sign up Lauren and I were doing the purchasing. The day we moved in I remember taking down the board and feeling ten feet tall as I did so. *This house is no longer on the market*, I'd told myself as I ripped it down. *This is our home.*

I pick up my bags and make my way up the steps to the front door then pull out my keys, fumbling my way through the bunch until I find the right ones. Collecting the post from the floor I step inside the hallway, punch the four-digit code into the burglar alarm keypad on the wall (the date of our wedding anniversary – Lauren's little joke so that if I ever forgot I wouldn't be able to get into the house) bring in my stuff and close the door behind me.

The house is deathly quiet. I wonder if Lauren will call or text at some point during the day but then on the kitchen counter I spot a message written on a sheet of A4 obviously snatched out of the printer in the downstairs study.

Hi Matt. There's food in the fridge, help yourself and I'll see you tonight so that we can talk. L x.

I open the fridge. Sure enough it is absolutely packed: apples, oranges, cheese and a whole stack of ready meals. I pour myself a fruit juice and take a sharp knife to a block of Cheddar and then search the cupboards for crisps or a stray packet of dry-roasted peanuts. But there's nothing remotely crisp-like apart from a half-eaten pack of rice cakes that might as well be made from cardboard for all the taste they have.

Searching around in the kitchen drawers I find the keys to the back door and head out into the garden. As I'd expected, Lauren hasn't ventured out here for a while. The grass is long overdue a cut, and it's the same story for pretty much everywhere else: the privet hedge on the left-hand side is in desperate need of a trim, the flower beds could do with a tidy and one of the fence panels at the end of the garden has come loose. There's so much work to do that I'm half tempted to spend what remains of the day sorting it out. The appeal of getting some last-minute use out of my shed is strong but then just as I'm trying to recall where I might have left an old pair of trainers my phone rings.

'Hi, am I speaking to Mr Beckford?'

'Yes.'

'It's Claire Barrow here from Millward and Lewis, we're looking after the sale of your property. I've just had a call from your buyers Mr and Mrs Mason and they know it's an inconvenience but Mr Mason's mother has come to stay and they're desperate to show her the house. I've left a message with Mrs Beckford but she hasn't got back to me yet and I can't really do it without your or her permission, so I was just wondering if it would be OK?'

'It's fine,' I reply, 'I'm more than happy to show them round if you like.'

'Really? Mrs Beckford seemed to indicate you were resident in the Midlands.'

'I was,' I reply, 'but I'm back. Send them round and I'll give them the full guided tour.'

The Masons turn up just after three, by which time I've showered. Shaved and had a tidy-up. Mrs Mason junior is short, pretty and heavily pregnant, while Mrs Mason senior (much like Mr Mason himself) is tall, thin and incredibly well spoken. I ask them if there's anything in particular they'd like to know and after a few minutes of polite refusal I'm bombarded with queries about the central heating, and how old the roof is, and what the neighbours are like and have we ever been burgled and while I'm happy to answer all their questions I can't help feeling they've neglected the only question that matters: 'Were you happy here?'

'So what were they like?'

I'm standing over a bubbling pot of chilli and Lauren is sitting a few feet away with a glass of red. There was a little bit of awkwardness to begin with (how could there not have been at the prospect of having once again to share the space that she'd become used to thinking of as her own?) but we soon got past that by opening a bottle of wine. Now on our second glass, and talking about someone other than ourselves, it almost feels like life before it all fell apart.

'They seemed nice enough.'

Lauren laughs. 'What does that even mean? You've always been terrible at this kind of thing. Were they tall, short, fat, thin, head to tail in designer outfits, what? I need details!'

'She was pretty and pregnant; he was tall and studious-looking; and the mum seemed a bit batty: she kept asking daft questions like: "What time does the post tend to arrive?" and "Will you be taking your wheelie bin with you?" They didn't offend me but I wouldn't go so far as to say that I actually liked them.'

Lauren's eyes glint knowingly. 'You didn't like them because they were posh.'

'No, I didn't like them because they didn't seem to appreciate how special this place is. They didn't comment on the fireplace that we scoured reclamation yards for months to find; or ask about those curtains that you had specially made; or remark on the coving we spent a bloody fortune having restored. And when I left them alone for a while upstairs I overheard Mrs Mason junior commenting to Mrs Mason senior how "the bathroom suite will be the first thing to go", like she's some sort of bloody interior decorating expert!'

Lauren laughs. 'I think she is. The estate agent emailed me some forms last week and with a first name like "Fernella" the temptation to Google her proved too much. She runs a design studio over in Fulham so chances are this time next year the whole place will be unrecognisable.'

'And that doesn't bother you?'

She reaches a hand to tuck a stray strand of hair behind her ear, a gesture I've seen a million times and yet now seems absurdly alluring. 'I try not to think about it and if you want my advice neither should you.'

We stop talking about the Masons and concentrate on sharing news about mutual friends and acquaintances and it is surprising how much has changed in such a relatively short space of time: some couples we know are pregnant with their first children; others are quitting jobs to go travelling and a few putting their own houses on the market to join the great exodus out of London.

'It suddenly feels like everyone's beginning to execute the plans they've been working on their whole lives,' says Lauren, as I serve up the food. 'As if everyone has decided that it's time to stop playing at life and start living it.'

During the meal she compliments my cooking, telling me that tonight's chilli is my best ever. Considering how often I've made it during our time together this is no mean feat. I'm not sure how truthful she is being because I couldn't get hold of half the fresh ingredients I'd needed but still, it was a nice thing to hear and as we go outside to sit on the patio with a fresh glass of wine we seem to be getting on better than I'd dared hope.

'So,' says Lauren, 'are you going to tell me what happened to your face or do I have to guess?'

'Trust me, you don't want to know.'

'I think you're probably right. Am I allowed to ask how your birthday was or is that part and parcel of the face story?'

'It was fine. It came and went and I survived.'

'So the world didn't fall apart like you expected?' Lauren laughs. 'It's Y2K all over again!' She looks down at the floor. 'I really wanted to call, you know, and wish you happy birthday, but it didn't feel right. I felt like I should keep my distance.'

'This is ridiculous.' I put my hand on hers. 'How did we get to the stage where we can't even wish each other well?'

For a moment she looks at me in a way she hasn't done for the longest time. It's a look suffused with longing and desire but above all, love. I lean across and gently kiss her lips and for a moment she closes her eyes and then slowly pulls away, shaking her head.

'I sent off the D8 this morning,' she says, not looking at me. 'My solicitor says that as long as you don't contest it, it shouldn't be anything more than a formality.'

'What are you citing?'

'Unreasonable behaviour.'

'Sounds about right,' I say, and then I get up and go back inside.

53

Lauren's gone by the time I wake and when I go downstairs in search of breakfast I find another note on the kitchen counter:

Thanks for dinner last night. It was gorgeous! I won't be home tonight. I think we both need a little space right now and so I'm going to be staying with a friend. Feel free to stay as long as you need. Text me if you want anything.
Lauren x

I fill a bowl with cornflakes and milk and as I spoon it into my mouth I do a lot of thinking about Lauren's 'friend' but none of it is particularly constructive. Is this a real friend or did one of her internet dates go better than she'd hoped? And would it be wrong of me to check the history on her browser in order to find out? I finish my cereal, slurping the last of the milk from the bowl but I resist the temptation to check her browser history. Lauren doesn't love me any more, at least not in the way that matters and if I care at all for her then the least I can do is wish her well and keep my nose out of her business.

I make myself a couple of slices of toast, brew up some coffee and continue breakfast in the living room in front of the TV. It'll be easy to kill a couple of hours here as Lauren hasn't bothered changing my selections on Sky+. There are about a million episodes of *Top Gear* to work through and an entire series of *Horizon*, and *Mythbusters* too. As a distraction from the fact that there are now legal documents out in the world officially proclaiming my failure as a husband it's a pretty good one and by the time I switch off the TV I feel moderately less like the guy no one ever invites to parties.

I take a shower and shave and once I'm fully dressed (jeans, T-shirt and the jumper Mum bought for my birthday) I try to work out how I'm going to fill the day ahead. I think about putting together my CV and circulating it amongst various recruitment agencies; I consider nipping out to the local Thomas Cook and seeing if I could get my hands on a cheap last-minute holiday paid for from the large amount of cash that will soon be sitting in my bank account; I even contemplate staying in bed all day and doing absolutely nothing. But what I actually end up doing is logging on to Rightmove and start looking for somewhere to rent.

I type my search requirements into the website (I'd like a one- or two-bedroom flat within a three-mile radius of the house) and within milliseconds there are enough properties to keep me busy flat-hunting for weeks. I put in a call to Choice Estates, who are looking after the first flat on the list that I like.

'Choice Estates, Ray Collins speaking, how can I help you?'

'I'm interested in renting one of the flats on your books: a two-bed Victorian conversion on Selsey Road.'

'I know the one,' he says, 'Flat one, two-two-seven Selsey Road? Lovely property.' He takes down my details and then completely throws me with his next question: 'Is there any chance that you're free right now, Mr Beckford? I've just had a viewing cancellation and I've got half an hour free before the next one. If you'd like to take a look right away I'd be more than happy to squeeze you in.'

Did I really want to look at a property now especially given that there were four weeks left until I needed to move? Wouldn't finding a place now make things more real than they strictly needed to be? I'd only rung for something to do later in the week and now here I was being asked if I wanted to see the place that day.

I open my mouth ready to decline but stop myself. What if all I'm doing is stalling because I'm not ready to move on? What if I'm playing for time like I did when Lauren and I were still living together? I'm forty now. There's nowhere to hide. I've done the hard part; now all I have to do is push on through.

'Meet you there in five minutes,' I say, and then I grab my coat, and a piece of fruit and leave the house.

The letting agent and I both arrive at the property at the same time. He holds out his hand for me to shake but embarrassingly my hands are still sticky from the orange I've just eaten so I end up wiping them on my jeans, which seems even worse. He's a professional though; he doesn't flinch, he just flashes me that rictus grin all letting agents have when you're nothing to them but walking commission and ushers me into the flat.

'As you can appreciate, this apartment has been finished to a very high standard having recently been renovated by the current owner. You could literally move in tomorrow and all you'd need to do is unpack your things.'

He's not wrong. The entire flat: living spaces, kitchen, bedrooms and even the garden, all have had everything done that I could want. What's more I can even imagine the kind of furniture that I'd have in here and where I'd put my TV. The whole flat has a good feel about it and as he waits for me in the kitchen and I give the place a second tour alone I can really picture myself living here: the designer kitchen where I'll cook meals for some beautiful and intelligent woman I'll meet through work; the living room where we'll relax with a glass of wine afterwards and in which, sound-tracked no doubt by an Adele album, I'll open up about my chequered relationship history; and finally the bedroom where as my new love and I enter I will make the joke: '. . . and this is where the magic happens.' As potential futures go it's not at all bad-looking which is why no one is more surprised than me when I find myself responding to the letting agent's question: 'So what do you think?' with the words, 'It's great but not for me.'

'So what kind of thing are you looking for exactly? Larger? Smaller? More modern?'

I shrug. 'Over the last ten to fifteen years I've done a lot of moving. I suppose what I'm looking for is something that feels a bit more like a home. Does that make sense?'

'Absolutely,' he says earnestly but I can tell from the glassy look he's giving me that he doesn't get it. 'I'll have another look through our books this afternoon and if anything leaps out at me I'll be sure to bring it to your attention.'

We don't shake hands as we part (he's not going to be caught out twice), and although I'm in the mood for a walk in the park followed by a read of the paper I force myself to return to the house and continue my property search, because now that I know what I don't want (which apparently is the perfect flat in the perfect area) maybe it's going to be a lot easier to work out what I *do* want.

At home I start the search all over again and print out a new list of potentials: a sleek modern two-bed with views of the park and close proximity to the Tube; a two-bed mews house a bit further out than I would have liked but which does have a garden; and: a huge one-bed mansion flat with massive windows, loads of original features and parquet flooring throughout.

I like the mansion flat most of all. It looks grand from the outside but worn and comfortable on the inside as though after years of trying too hard it has come to the conclusion it has nothing to prove any more. I call Robinson's, the letting agent, but the call goes straight to voicemail and as I prepare to leave a message I realise that my heart's already not in this flat. It's pricier than I want it to be and further away from the Tube too, but the thing that really unseals the deal is the fact that it's got one bedroom: buying it would be like saying to the world out loud: I've given up hope. This is as good as it gets.

Returning to the web I try changing the parameters of my search: different areas, price ranges and numbers of bedrooms but the more choice I get the less interested I am. None of these places looks right; none of them feels like they could be home.

After a while I really start to throw out the rule book. In a couple of weeks I'll be a man with a lot of cash sitting in his bank account. I won't have to live in London, I won't even need to live in the UK if I don't want to. The world is my oyster. On a whim I take a look at a couple of letting websites based in France, then Australia, the Netherlands, the USA and even some in the West Indies but as tantalising as some of these places are (especially the beachfront property overlooking Womans Bay in Barbados) they just don't feel right. They're not what I'm looking for to see me through the next chapter of my life.

And so I return to the UK. I try Brighton (because it's by the sea); Manchester (because these days it's where everything seems to be happening); Bath (because I quite fancy living in one of those white Georgian terraces) and even Edinburgh (because Lauren and I once went to a wedding there and loved it). But none of them does it for me, none of them has that spark, that special something I'm looking for.

Finally I do one last search. It's a massive long shot and completely off the wall given that I've changed the search requirements from 'rent' to 'buy' but as I press return I think to myself, Well, what harm can it do?' The results come back in an instant and at the top of the list is an entry that pulls me up short. I stare at the screen for a good five minutes, shaking my head and laughing to myself. It's perfect. Absolutely 100 per cent perfect. It's got everything I want and even though it's quite clearly been messed about with (the front and back rooms have been knocked through, hardwood flooring has been laid in every room and the kitchen's been extended), at its heart it still remains the same. And best of all, clearly visible in a number of shots of the garden is a shed. And not just any old shed but a vintage eight-foot by six-foot overlap softwood apex shed that I know for a fact has been lovingly maintained for its entire existence. Once I've composed myself I pick up my phone and dial the estate agent's number.

'Direct Move, Kings Heath, Karen Samson speaking,' says a female voice with a delightfully chirpy Birmingham accent. 'How can I help you?'

'Hi, my name's Mr Beckford. I'm enquiring about one of your properties: eighty-eight Hampton Street, Kings Heath.'

'The recently developed three-bed semi?'

'That's the one.'

'Oh, that's a lovely property. It's only been on the market about a week. I took a couple there to see it only yesterday, it's got such a wonderful finish on it. I was really impressed. One family owned it for the best part of forty years until they part-exchanged it with a developer earlier this year. It's been completely modernised from top to bottom. When would you like an appointment to see it? All our slots are booked up today and Tuesday but I might be able to fit you in on Wednesday.'

'I don't want to make an appointment to see it. I want to buy it.'

The woman from Direct Move can't quite believe her ears. 'You want to buy it? I'm sorry, have I got the wrong end of the stick? Have you already had a viewing?'

'Not in so many words.'

'But you want to purchase the property without viewing it? Excuse me for asking,' she says cautiously, 'but is this some kind of a wind-up?'

It was a good question, especially given that some people would see it as a major step backwards to return to my home town. Even worse to cash in my pension, scrape together every last bit of money I'd made from the house sale and buy outright the home where I grew up. Not to mention doing so at the age of forty, without a partner in tow or a clue about how I was going to make a living for the next thirty-odd years. And yet I'm going to do it anyway.

'I couldn't be more serious,' I tell the woman from Direct Move as I offer the full asking price and the name of my solicitor so she can confirm the details.

'I don't know what to say, Mr Beckford. In all my time in this business I've never had a buyer purchase one of our properties without at least one viewing in person. Are you sure you can't be persuaded?'

'No need, I'm already sold.'

'Well, if you don't mind me saying it certainly does seem to have made a lasting impression on you!'

'What can I say? Some places just look like home.'

Epilogue

So after nearly five months of craziness that saw me fall in love with Ginny, move in with my parents, fall out of love with Ginny, become best mates with my all-time teen hero, fall in love with Rosa, move in with a bunch of students, get punched in the face by Gershwin, purchase my childhood home and have my wife begin divorce proceedings, what wisdom can I impart to those about to turn forty? Well, here it goes:

1. Waking up in bed alone on your fortieth birthday is far from the worst thing that can happen to you . . .
2. . . . but being punched in the face by your best mate is pretty near the top of the list.
3. Once you're forty you no longer have to care what people think about you but it's never a good idea to give them too much ammunition.
4. No matter what happens you should never, ever move back in with your parents. You both deserve better.
5. At forty you realise you've spent half your life trying to leave home and the other half trying to find somewhere

to belong. Wanting to belong is good but it can bring out the crazy.

6. It turns out it's true that forty's not the end of the road, it really is just the beginning.

7. Self-imposed deadlines . . . who needs them?

Days left until I turn 50: 3627

TURNING THIRTY
The hilarious forerunner to TURNING FORTY

Unlike most people, Matt Beckford is actually looking forward to turning thirty. After struggling through most of his twenties he thinks his career, finances and love life are finally sorted. But when he splits up with his girlfriend, he realises that life has different plans for him. Unable to cope with his future falling apart Matt temporarily moves back in with his parents.

During his enforced exodus only his old school mates can keep him sane. Friends he hasn't seen since he was nineteen. But things will never be the same for any of them because when you're turning thirty nothing's as simple as it used to be . . .

'Not just readable, fresh and witty but sophisticated in execution . . . funny but also poignant.' *Independent on Sunday*

'A warm, funny romantic comedy.' *Daily Mail*

'Mike Gayle has carved a whole new literary niche out of the male confessional novel. He's a publishing phenomenon.' *Evening Standard*

'Delightfully observant nostalgia . . . will strike a chord with both sexes.' *She*

'Mike Gayle manages to weave everything together with such a warm-the-cockles-of-your-heart manner that once you've finished reading TURNING THIRTY you want to turn right back to the beginning and start all over again. It's real life - but better than we know it.' *B Magazine*

'Funny and endearing . . . chuckle-on-the-bus readable.' *Heat*

HODDER